# The Red Bus

## A Postcard to an Assassin

Enjoy!
Carol
Tonnesen

Carol Tonnesen

i

To Karl
Who is my dream come true!

Other titles by the same author:

The Fishing Bridge: A Postcard to a Traitor

The Highlands: A Postcard to Deception

Rumrunner's Reef: A Postcard to a Smuggler

The Zephyr: A Postcard to a Thief

The Golden Isles: A Postcard to Fear

To enjoy more postcard mysteries visit:

www.postcardmysteries.com

Or find them at Amazon.com

This book is a work of fiction.  The characters and murder plot in this book are fictional.  Any resemblance to actual events, people, or places is coincidental.  This story is suggested by a very special postcard and the historical events that took place in 1934.

Many thanks to:

Kelly Keller Remarcier:  Editor

Kelley Hensing:  The Red Bus Cover Art

# 2004

# Chapter 1

## Kate

The bright red double-decker bus caused the otherwise pale pastel-tinted postcard of Piccadilly Circus to stand out on the cluttered shelf. Until Kate's eyes fixed on the red bus, her mind had been wandering as she drifted aimlessly through the antique shop. The sign next to the stack of postcards read *Old European postcards 30 pence.*

"There you go again, Grandma, checking out the old postcards! How many times have I seen you sorting through stacks of them at antique stores?"

Though this was said gently, Kate felt compelled to defend her actions.

"I'm looking for one special one," responded Kate to her granddaughter, Aylee.

She gazed wistfully at the postcard of the red bus, tears pricking at the corners of her eyes. Silly really, thought Kate, it's just an old postcard from a long time ago. A very special postcard, she reminded herself. Catching a glimpse of herself in a mirror, Kate took a moment to straighten her vibrant purple hat. She decided to pull the small veil down a bit lower on her face to cover her tears. Daubing at her eyes with her handkerchief, Kate quickly transacted her purchase and left the shop. She would study the postcard with the red bus more closely at home later.

"Why do you collect old postcards?" Aylee asked, her gaze showing both amusement and tolerance.

"You don't think a woman of my advanced years should engage in such frivolous endeavors?" asked Kate with an impish smile. Advanced years, indeed. She may be in her nineties, thought Kate, but her mind and her self-image were as sharp as ever.

"It's not like that one's even a very interesting postcard. It's just some old red bus."

"Someday, if you're ever curious enough, I'll tell you why this postcard is important," responded Kate a little sharply. She clutched the small bag in her hand protectively. The postcard seemed to be calling to her, reminding her of past events, a dangerous but surprisingly happy time.

Later that day, Kate was pleased when her granddaughter appeared at the door of her sitting room with two cups of tea and a plate of biscuits.

"The day's turned rather rainy and dreary. It's a good time for tea and storytelling. Why don't you tell me about your postcard?"

Kate studied her granddaughter's precious face, wondering if the young woman was serious about her request. Would she believe the story Kate had to tell? Or would her granddaughter react more like her entirely too practical mother who, years ago, responded to Kate's postcard story with an exaggerated eye roll?

"Are you sure you're really interested in the story behind a seventy year old postcard?" Kate asked.

"Why not?" Aylee said flippantly. Then she added softly, "Why did you cry when you found it?"

Kate regarded her granddaughter again, marveling at the similarities between them. Perhaps it was the right time in her life to tell her.

"Never mind my tears," she said, taking a sip of tea. "The story begins when I was about your age. Like you, I was waiting for something to

4

happen in my life. At the time, I felt as if a chapter of my life was closing and another about to begin."

"How could you possibly know something like that? Mom always said you were a bit illogical."

"Whenever your ever-so-sensible mother tells me that I am behaving illogically, I remember one of my favorite quotes from Blaise Pascal—'*Le Coeur a ses raisons que la raison ne connait point.*' The heart has its reasons that reason does not know. My dear, sometimes in your life, you feel things for no apparent reason. When that happens, you've got to learn to trust your instincts. Sometimes it is best not to force a change. Instead you've got to wait and listen."

"Is that what you were doing then? Waiting and listening?"

Kate fingered the postcard in her lap before answering and continuing with her story.

"My friends and I gathered up our courage and had our tarot cards read. For me, it was the first and only time. Among the usual platitudes about health and wealth, the reader said that soon an older man would give my life new direction. An older man! Imagine how my girlfriends laughed at that! At twenty-four, what I needed was a young man!" Kate laughed at the memory. She could tell by the look on her granddaughter's face that Aylee was having a hard time imagining her grandmother as a young woman. "It had been a while since I had engaged in anything more than a casual friendship with a man. None of the men I met seemed right for me. My girlfriends thought I put too much hope in my mother's saying that behind the moon, beyond the wind, I would find someone to cherish. I just ignored my friends teasing and continued to look for the man who would cherish me too."

Kate shook her head in amazement. All those years ago, she had received a postcard that had set her life in motion. Was it the same one she found today? Finding a magnifying glass in the drawer near where she sat, she examined the front of the postcard more closely. Her granddaughter looked over her shoulder. Suddenly, Kate laughed.

"Wouldn't it be fun to be like Mary Poppins?" Kate asked. "Do you remember the scene from your favorite movie?"

"The one when Mary Poppins, Burt, Michael, and Jane jump into the sidewalk chalk picture? I always thought it would be exciting to go to the county fair with them," her granddaughter said a bit longingly.

"What if you could leap into this postcard? What would it be like to meet that man there, the one in the grey suit with the black Homburg standing with his back to the viewer, his hands clasped behind his back, looking neither left nor right?" asked Kate rather wistfully as she pointed to a man in the lower left hand corner of the card.

"I know we used to play this imagination game when I was a kid, but Mary Poppins is a movie, Grandma. People don't jump into postcards."

"Don't they?" Kate asked cryptically. "Humor an old woman. Let's play our little imagination game."

"All right," agreed Aylee slowly. "If it's that important to you."

"Let's start with this man here, the one in the grey suit and black Homburg. Who is he? How did he happen to get captured in a 1930s photograph postcard of Piccadilly Circus?"

Kate pointed at the man in the grey suit and black Homburg who stood with his back to the viewer, his hands clasped behind his back, looking neither left nor right.

"He's just some guy waiting for a red bus."

"Perhaps," answered Kate with an inscrutable smile.

Kate ran her fingers lightly over the front of the card, remembering. The light from the fire caught the emerald ring on her hand causing the deep green stone to flash as if lit from within.  Cautiously, hopefully, she turned the postcard over.  In strong, clear handwriting, it read:

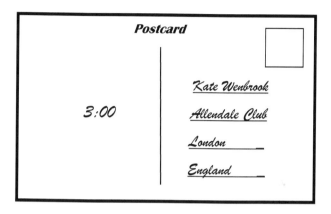

"Hey, isn't Wenbrook your maiden name?"

"Yes it is," Kate answered simply as she studied the postmark.  June 12, 1934.  She couldn't help the little frisson that ran down her spine.

"This postcard was sent to you?  You found a postcard today that was sent to you seventy years ago?  I can't believe it!  Seventy years ago, someone wrote your name on a postcard and sent it to you!  And now you've found it again.  Amazing."

"I lost it a long time ago, probably during one of our moves.  I never thought I would see it again."  Kate felt the tears prick behind her eyes again.  "Be a darling and get that old box of books I had your father bring down from the attic yesterday."

"Sure, but aren't you going to tell me about the postcard?"

"In due time, my dear," answered Kate.  "Right now, get the box.  You'll understand why in a moment."

When the box appeared, Kate rummaged around in it until she found a 1934 London guidebook.  She grasped it like a lifeline when she uncovered it. Holding the postcard in one hand, she turned the pages of the guidebook in her lap with the other.

"Here it is, the entry for Piccadilly Circus." Kate handed the guidebook to her granddaughter.

*"The name Piccadilly is said to derive its name from the pickadils, or ruffs, worn in the early Stuart period. This famous spot has been to a great extent transformed during recent years, very striking modern buildings having replaced the more humble shops. Great as the change is above ground, the reconstruction below the Circus has been even more remarkable, although in the new Tube station serving the Piccadilly and Bakerloo lines there is little hint of the extraordinary engineering feats entailed by its construction. Piccadilly Circus is a very important traffic "hub" both above and below ground, main thoroughfares and "tube" railways radiating hence to north, south, east, and west. Piccadilly Circus Station is used by more than 25,000,000 passengers yearly. Upwards of 45,000 road vehicles alone pass through the Circus in the course of the day; the "roundabout" system is in use here. Sir Alfred Gilbert's graceful statue of Eros, dedicated to the 7th Earl of Shaftesbury, makes a welcome reappearance after an absence of several years,"* read her grand-daughter in a clear voice.

"Imagine dear," said Kate. "25,000,000 passengers yearly. 45,000 road vehicles each day. One of which was a red double-decker bus. Imagine meeting a man wearing a grey suit and black Homburg at three o'clock, on a day in 1934 just because he sent you a postcard. What would he be like?" Kate pointed to the man in the postcard.

"Meet him? What would he be like?" said Aylee, her practical side taking over. "You couldn't possibly meet him. You know as well as I do that the man in the postcard wasn't the same man who sent the card. Logistically, it's impossible to be both in a postcard and sending it at the same time."

"Of course, you're right." Kate couldn't help but smile at herself and the absurdity of what she had been thinking. "But without believing that, there is no story, is there?"

"What are you saying?"

"Open the guidebook again to the front page," Kate said by way of an answer.

A name, written in the same strong script as the postcard, graced the page: Henry Littleton.

Picking up the magnifying glass, her granddaughter studied the postcard again. Kate could tell that now every feature of the postcard piqued her curiosity.

"The handwriting isn't just similar, it's identical! Look at the capital "H" in Henry and House, the "L" in Littleton and London, even the "on" in Littleton and London, they're exactly alike. How extraordinary, the postcard and the guidebook belonged to the same man—imagine finding that postcard after so much time has passed. But—I don't understand—"

Kate just smiled her enigmatic smile.

"The building in the background of the postcard is the London Pavilion," said Kate. "If I remember correctly, it was originally a music hall, though in early 1934, the structure was altered significantly and converted into a theatre."

"There it is again, Grandma, that magic number 1934. What's going on here? Curiouser and curiouser. You're beginning to sound just like Alice in Wonderland."

Kate felt a sense of wonder as she sat there holding the postcard and the guidebook.

"My postcard of a red bus. My own personal rabbit hole."

Her granddaughter looked carefully at Kate's expression. There were secrets there that she wanted to know.

"All right, we'll play the imagination game and make up stories about the people in the postcard. Anything to get at the truth. Let's start with the man standing near the lamppost across from that roadster."

"Why don't you tell me about him?" prompted Kate.

"Well, he appears harmless enough, with his hands behind his back. Do you think his body is a bit tense? Maybe it's the angle of the picture. I don't know about the other two men in the postcard, though. They don't seem quite as nonchalant."

"Why not?"

"One is wearing a long grey coat and leaning against the fountain. He's actually staring straight at the guy by the lamppost. I think the grey overcoat is strange."

"Why?"

"Because the postcard appears to have been taken on a fine day, that's why. No one else has on an overcoat. One of the cars even had its convertible top down."

"There you have it. Surely the man must be up to no good, why else would he be wearing an overcoat? I wonder what he could be hiding," laughed Kate. She always enjoyed playing this game of imagination with her granddaughter. They both had quite active imaginations and it encouraged them both to be observant of their surroundings. "Tell me about the other man."

"The camera shutter caught the third man as he ducked behind a lamppost. Definitely very suspicious behavior."

"Without a doubt, they must be up to no good."

"Grandma, check out this woman in the crowd waiting to cross the street. She could be you. Okay, it might be stretching things a bit to say that, but the woman in the postcard has on a deep plum skirt with a matching jacket similar to the one you have on right now."

"I've always liked the color purple."

"We're being silly, making up stories," Aylee laughed out loud.

"Well, then, on a more serious note, let me tell you about 1934," said Kate as she searched her memory for information. "All most people learn in school about the year 1934 was that the world was in the midst of the Great Depression. Very few people realize it was quite a year for gangsters in the United States. Bonnie and Clyde, Pretty Boy Floyd, John Dillinger, and Baby Face Nelson all met their end in 1934. Elsewhere in the world, there was unrest in the Sudan, countries defaulting on their World War I debts to the United States, Hitler was rising to power, and many nations began the rearmament process."

Returning to the London guidebook, Kate gently leafed through the pages as if hoping to find something after all these years. Her heart skipped a beat when a marriage announcement cut from a newspaper, yellowed with age floated out of the pages. Holding the fragile piece of paper in her hands, Kate stared out into space remembering. Her granddaughter gently took it from her and read the printed words out loud.

> Littleton—Wenbrook London, June 12, 1934, St. Paul's Cathedral, West Chapel. The Honorable Henry Littleton and Miss Katherine Wenbrook, both of London, were joined in holy matrimony by the Rev. R. Wright at 8 o'clock Tuesday evening. They begin their bridal tour in Paris before taking the Orient Express to the Near East.

"Henry and Kate," whispered Kate.

Kate picked up the guidebook again. Clasping it between her palms, she could sense a bulge in the middle, as if someone, a long time ago, had pressed an object between the pages. She held the book in her hands and allowed it to fall open. The faint fragrance of the faded rose drifted up to her nose. The memories came flooding back.

"A rose, a guidebook, and a postcard?" Her granddaughter's voice cut through Kate's musings.

"Not just any postcard, my dear," said Kate as she stroked the postcard lovingly. She paused for a moment, a smile playing on her face. "Seventy years ago, I received a postcard that changed my life. This postcard. What an adventure that red bus took me on!

# 1934

# Chapter 2

## Henry

*W*ould she receive his postcard in time?

If she received the postcard in time, would she understand its message?

Ever since Henry had sent the postcard of the red bus, these two questions had buzzed around in his brain. His superiors had said that to get together with his contact, he should send a postcard to Kate Wenbrook of Allendale Club. The front of the postcard should be of the place he wanted to meet. On its back should be a simple message stating the time of their *rendezvous*. Both agents would know that the meeting would take place two days from the post-marked date. He had been careful to have the postcard hand stamped to ensure the postmark was legible. All he had had to do was wait the allotted two days. It sounded simple enough in theory. Henry only hoped that it would work in practice.

Henry had chosen the postcard of Piccadilly Circus because of the man standing with his back facing the viewer, his hands clasped behind him, looking neither left of right. When he purchased the postcard with the red bus on it, he had smiled to himself. The man caught his imagination because he looked a bit like Henry himself. Henry had a medium grey suit and a black Homburg. He would wear them to the meeting. He might even stand in the same place. This was the sort of thing that appealed to Henry's sense of fun. He had been so excited about his assignment that, at the time, choosing the postcard had been a lark. Now that the meeting approached, Henry felt his sense of humor might be out of place. The seriousness of the job he was about to undertake was sinking in.

At 26, Henry had been working for the Secret Intelligence Service (SIS) since graduating from Oxford. Though he'd never meant to take up espionage as a profession, one thing had lead to another and here he was four years later. At first, he had a short stint in Section VIII, monitoring radio communications from the section's agents and operatives in the field. Since Henry had a solid working knowledge of German, French and Italian, his superiors assumed he would be a natural. Unfortunately, Morse code did not come to him as easily as languages.

He moved on to Section VII. There, his responsibilities included travelling around Britain gathering information about various manufacturing industries. He took his job seriously and discovered he was good at it. His superiors noticed his ability to gather key information, find discrepancies, and ferret out the truth. In several instances, he had been able to right wrongs and bring miscreants to justice. To Henry, what he did wasn't magical or special. He observed, formed hypotheses, verified that his observations confirmed his hypotheses, and acted. Fortunately for his career, others around him thought he had potential.

Eventually his work had progressed to a position in Section V. During the past year, he had become quite well-versed in the political activities of nations around the world. Only recently had he had any interaction with the counter-espionage branch of his section. Henry had always felt a bit awkward around his more glamorous peers. They acted so sure of themselves, so suave and calm under pressure. He wanted to be like them, part of their fraternity. He wanted to be seen as a young man of determination and imagination. Sometimes he thought his job did not allow him to give proper scope to his talents. He wanted, just once, to do a great deed. Until this assignment, he assumed that it might be just a dream of his. Now, here he was, sending a postcard to someone he didn't know in hopes that she would help him in his quest.

Henry wondered what his contact would think when they first met. He knew he was pleasant enough looking. Six feet tall and trim from rowing, his even features rarely drew anyone's attention. Pleasant, yes, he could be considered pleasant looking. He hoped that would be enough to convince her to join him on this job. He considered what her response would be to the postcard. Would she recognize the irony of sending a postcard with a man in it that might be him? He hoped she had a sense of humor. Espionage may be serious stuff, but, he always been a firm believer that a little humor went a long way to lighten an otherwise disturbing situation. His acquaintances, though they admired his intelligence, thought him a bit different, too high-spirited and full of mirth. Would she? What kind of woman entered the spy business anyway? What would she be like?

On his way to Piccadilly Circus on the afternoon of June 14, Henry had purchased a London 1934 guidebook. He figured the guidebook would allow him to loiter away the time posing as a tourist. Loitering wasn't as easy as he thought it would be. Henry paced around the fountain nervously. He stared with dismay at all the people. Again, he asked himself: how would she ever find him? Henry could laugh out loud at his foolishness. A man of his intelligence relying on the commonly held belief in the saying that a person who stays long enough at Piccadilly Circus will eventually bump into everyone they know. He had overlooked the 'everyone they know' part. He and this Wenbrook woman had never even met. What had he been thinking, he asked himself for the hundredth time. In this mass of people how would they find each other? He didn't have time for eventually linking up with her. Henry needed to meet with her today, at 3 o'clock. Time was of the essence. Worse yet, it was running out. Apprehensively, Henry read a few excerpts from the guide book. However, he could not concentrate. The words swam in front of his eyes.

Now that he stood in Piccadilly Circus, Henry couldn't help but wonder what had he been thinking. Why had he chosen Piccadilly Circus? He had seen the recent statistics: 25 million people a year; 45,000 vehicles a day. Yes, he had wanted anonymity, but this was ridiculous. How would she ever find him in this sea of humanity? How would she know it was him anyway? They had no photographs or descriptions of their contact agents, only code recognition phrases. He hoped it would help her locate him because he posed as the man in the postcard. After all, he dressed the part in his grey suit and black Homburg. He might as well see if she recognized him. It was the only thing he could think of to do. He drifted over to the lamppost, placed his hands behind his back, and stood there trying to look natural.

He studied the cars going by slowly. The red bus vied for the road with several other vehicles. A sleek black sedan with a camel-colored convertible top followed closely behind the bus. Further away, a boxy blue and black car blocked a cream-colored convertible as it tried to pull away from the curve. His father had liked cars. Henry could remember standing on street corners as a boy while his father entertained him by telling him about each of the cars that passed by. Based on what he had learned back then, Henry was able to tentatively identify the black sedan as a Bentley. The boxy black and blue car could be a Standard 10. He thought the cream convertible might be a MG NA Magnette four-seat touring car.

It didn't take long for Henry to feel ridiculous standing there next to the lamppost. How he could possibly have thought that she would be able to pick up on the one clue the postcard provided, he did not know. He hoped fervently that she would know to search for the man in the grey suit and Homburg standing with his back to the viewer, his hands clasped behind him, looking neither left nor right.

As 3 o'clock approached, Henry's worries increased exponentially. She would never find him in this crowd.

# Chapter 3

## Kate

Kate looked again at the postcard she had received. It was rather unremarkable and showed a red bus driving in Piccadilly Circus. Her eye was drawn immediately to the man in the lower left-hand corner. Oh, she thought, don't tell me this is the 'older man' the tarot reader had told her about. The fates must be joking, a man in a postcard. Or worse, the man who sent the postcard could be in his dotage. Just what could the fates possibly have in mind?

Kate knew that a man named Henry Littleton had sent the postcard. Her superiors at SIS had told her to expect one. She didn't know much about Henry, her contact with the SIS. Just yesterday, she had finally plucked up her courage and investigated her mystery man through SIS channels. She did so reluctantly at first. After all, her active imagination had begun to form an image of him in her own mind. She didn't want to find out that he had a dark, secret past or that he was old enough to be her father. Information was scarce, but, if she had found the right Henry, apparently he was quite active in the Secret Intelligence Bureau.

During her investigation, Kate had found out a lot more than she had previously known about the British secret service known as the Secret Intelligence Service. She discovered that it had been founded in 1909 to serve both the Admiralty and the War office. From its inception, its primary focus was to control secret intelligence operations in both Great Britain and overseas. From the mid-1920s onward, SIS had several sections. She imagined being in Section V and involved in tracking counter-espionage reports and activities from overseas. That certainly sounded interesting. Section N caught her attention too. People in that department were responsible for exploiting the contents of foreign diplomatic pouches. She could not see herself fitting into Section D. Kate decided she would not feel comfortable conducting political covert actions during time of war. Section VIII did not sound appropriate for her either. While she would not have minded monitoring radio communications with operatives and agents overseas, they probably wanted someone familiar with Morse code. Which one did Henry work in?

Kate wondered if Henry was part of the Directorate of Military Intelligence Section 6, the infamous MI6. Would he be a charismatic, enigma of a man? Probably not. It would be just her luck that her mystery man turned out to be a file clerk in Section VII. She imagined Henry, day after day, slaving away generating and filing long economic reports about the state of trade, industry, and contraband. Not terribly exciting. For some reason, she wanted Henry to be all that is good, brave, and true. How much more interesting he would be if his job involved counter-espionage, agents, and the contents of foreign diplomatic pouches.

Based on what she knew about the current state of world affairs, the department's work centered primarily on the activities of Hitler and the German government. Hitler, leader of the Nazi Party since July 1921, had been elected President in 1932. Following the death of Hindenburg, on January 30, 1933, Hitler had declared himself both President and Chancellor of Germany. On March 23rd of that year, he had declared himself dictator of Germany. On the first of January, the new year got off to an inauspicious start when Nazi Germany activated the 1933 Law for the Prevention of Hereditarily Diseased Offspring. This law required the compulsory sterilization of any citizen who, in the opinion of a Genetic Health Court, suffered from a list of alleged genetic disorders. The ramifications of this broad law placed anyone in the general population at risk. At the end of the month of January, the Reichstag, the body that represented the German states in the national government, had been abolished. This essentially eliminated the multi-party political system in

Germany and resulted in the loss of many of the key civil liberties of German citizens. Despite the signing of a ten-year German-Polish Non-Aggression Pact and other similar diplomatic ventures, the world watched Germany with growing concerns.

For a few moments, thoughts of espionage and intrigue worried Kate. True, she wanted more excitement in her life; otherwise she would not have left her job as a file clerk at a department store. Just by chance, a month ago, she had answered an advertisement in the *Times* only to discover that the government job she was applying for involved working within SIS. Following a series of interviews, to her surprise and pleasure, she had been hired. During the week leading up to today's meeting, Kate alternated between excitement over her new job and trepidation that it would turn out to be more than she could handle. Today, dread stalked her. She needed to muster her courage in order to face Henry at Piccadilly Circus.

Though it was early for her appointment with Henry, Kate felt stiff after having spent so much time spent sitting and reading files. She needed to get some air and a walk would clear her head of Henry and their meeting. Well, maybe not entirely, she smiled secretively to herself as she tucked the postcard into her purse.

She dressed carefully for their meeting in her favorite plum suit with its matching hat. She paused for a moment to admire her reflection in the mirror. Her conservative suit and sensible shoes sent the message that she was a young woman who wished to be taken seriously. Then she caught a glimpse of her hat. The vivid purple feather rose from the brim like a flag—definitely not the hat of a levelheaded person. Oh well, Kate thought, she liked her hat. She checked the set of her hat one last time in the mirror and marched out the door.

Upon leaving her flat, Kate walked toward Regent Street. For a while she strolled aimlessly, looking in shop windows, enjoying the fine spring day. She took the time to consider her current circumstances and reflected on her reasons for taking this job. They were many and varied, but it all came down to her need to inject some excitement into her life. Wondering whether a job with SIS might mean too much excitement, for a time, she even contemplated turning back. But deep inside, Kate knew where she would finally end up. Piccadilly Circus.

When Kate finally neared Piccadilly Circus, she was more perplexed than ever. Here she was, standing in her postcard trying to decide whether or not she really wanted to meet Henry. Red double-decker buses passed in front of her. Kate checked her watch. It was still too early to arrive for her appointment with Henry. Glancing around, she saw that on her right was the Regent Palace Hotel. A cup of tea would be very nice right now, she thought. Kate entered hotel and made her way to the Rotunda Court.

Kate had always loved the Rotunda Court restaurant. The crisp white linens, liveried servers, potted palms, and high rotunda windows that allowed in the June sunshine never failed to cheer her. She chose a comfy corner chair next to a small table and ordered tea, scones, and fresh strawberries. Kate settled in for a bit of people watching. It was a game she used to play as a child. She would watch the people around her, study their faces, and tell herself stories about their lives. And such interesting lives they led too. Kate had quite an imagination. That's what was going on with this postcard; she was imagining a life for Henry and a job for herself.

The clatter of dishes brought Kate wide awake with a start. She hadn't realized how tired she had been. Asleep! How could she have fallen asleep! Drifting off on her first day on the job just wouldn't do, Kate scolded herself. Such disgraceful behavior on her part could only be partly excused by the comfortable chair. Kate took herself off to the ladies lounge to splash water on her face to revive her. There she applied fresh lipstick and combed her hair. She took her time adjusting her hat. Enough dawdling, she told herself sternly. It was time for her to be on her way. Kate heard a clock strike quarter to three.

On June 14th, 1934, Kate stepped out the hotel and into the postcard—her very own personal rabbit hole.

# Chapter 4

## Henry

*A* red bus pulled up to the curb where Henry was standing. Would she be on it? Probably not. One of the reasons he had chosen Piccadilly was because of its proximity to her flat. She could easily walk from one to the other. He watched the people getting off. Several men in business suits appeared, then a woman with a small boy in tow. Next, two elderly women deep in conversation emerged, but no one exited who could be Kate. His eyes rested for a moment on a man in a long grey overcoat on top of his suit. Henry frowned, thinking it odd that the man wore an overcoat on such a lovely spring day. Strange, too, how the man resembled one of the figures in the postcard. Henry's eyes drifted away from the man and toward the fountain. He could not get his mind off the man's heavy outerwear. Henry returned his attention to the man and studied him more closely. As if sensing Henry's eyes upon him, the man stared directly at Henry. Now it was Henry's turn to feel uncomfortable. He shifted his eyes back to the fountain and fumbled with his guidebook. His behavior hardly resembled that of a tourist, Henry thought angrily to himself. Here he was, drawing as much attention to himself as the man in the grey overcoat.

Henry glanced around again at the people flowing past him. How would he recognize her in this crowd? Why hadn't he thought of all these complications before sending that blasted postcard? They never told him to be wary of complications in spy school. When questioned, they just said to rely on your training and your good sense. Improvise. That's what they said to do, improvise. Well, he was improvising right now and it wasn't helping. Henry scanned the crowd of people about to cross the street.  In the distance, he heard church bells ringing the hour.  Three o'clock.  Their meeting time.  Where was she?

Henry thought back to the conversation he had had with his superior the previous week.

"Henry, my dear fellow," the man had said with hearty good cheer.  "The home office thanks you for your excellent work on the industrial dye case."

"Thank you, sir, for the chance to work in such an interesting field," Henry had responded politely.

"Based on your performance, we feel it's time for you to join our counter-espionage branch," he continued.

The announcement, so calmly made, took Henry by surprise.

"You have been appointed to lead a mission to Belgrade next week."

"I could hardly hope for such an opportunity," Henry stammered in amazement.  "After all, my work so far has focused on analyzing reports.  My field experience is limited.  Surely this is beyond my scope."

"Nonsense," the man responded.  "Just get the job done right, that's all we ask."

All they ask indeed, thought Henry as he suppressed an urge to pace.  Again, he scanned the people near him.  No one remotely resembled a woman searching for someone.  As a matter of fact, they all seemed rather purposeful as they strode by.

Henry gave up the pretense of reading the guidebook and turned to study the cars on the street.  The black Bentley still cruised slowly behind the red bus.  As he watched, it stopped abruptly and a man in a black suit disembarked.  The man hesitated a moment as if surveying the scene.  Next, he stepped briskly up onto the curb, his manner purposeful yet wary.

Henry gave the black-suited man from the black Bentley little thought and returned his focus to the MG NA Magnette four-seat convertible touring car parked at the curb in front of him. Sharp car, he thought, staring at it admiringly. He wouldn't mind owning one of those. He could see himself motoring around the countryside with a lovely woman at his side.

Nearby, a car horn honked bringing Henry's thoughts back to the present with a jolt. Heavens, what had he been doing? It was three o'clock; he should be focused on locating Miss Wenbrook instead of daydreaming about racy cars and lovely women! He'd be better off back in his office filing reports for all the good he was doing here. He certainly hadn't gotten off to a proper start on his first real job. He couldn't even keep his mind on the job.

Henry studied the faces of the women walking by him. Intent on their own lives, they paid no attention to him. No one of interest came into his view. He could hardly imagine that Miss Wenbrook would be the woman pushing a pram or one walking a small dog. Henry shifted his gaze to the people waiting to cross the street. At that moment, the crowd parted and he saw her standing across the busy street. He did a double-take. Henry could hardly have failed to notice her. Her large plum hat with its jaunty feather would draw anyone's attention. Despair coursed through his being. Oh no. That couldn't be her, not this person wearing a ridiculous purple hat sporting a huge feather waving like a flag. This was his first assignment in the world of espionage. He needed someone practical and reliable to help him. No sensible person in her right mind would wear such an outrageous hat. Henry looked again, his eyes following her as she crossed the street. As she drew closer, he could tell she was searching for someone. When she hesitated for an instant, he began to hope he was mistaken, that it wasn't her.

His hopes didn't last long. She looked directly at him, as if she recognized him, as if she expected him to be standing next to the lamppost wearing a grey suit and a black Homburg. Henry met her gaze and he knew. Every fiber of his being knew. The woman in the ridiculous feathered hat was the person he had been searching for.

25

# Chapter 5

## Kate

*A*nxious, nervous, a little frightened, that's how she felt as she walked toward Piccadilly Circus. Ordinary people didn't engage in these sorts of activities. When she had applied for a job with SIS, Kate had not wanted to be ordinary anymore. She had read a quote from Coco Chanel *"If you were born without wings, do nothing to prevent their growing."* At the time, Kate thought she needed to grow some wings of her own. Now, reality had set in. Her courage deserted her. A persistent voice in her head told Kate to forget growing wings and go home to her grounded life. Once there, she should stay home and avoid complicating her quiet existence. As she stood there waiting to cross the street, Kate took a deep breath and considered her situation. All she would have to do is turn around. No one would ever know. Kate could send a letter of resignation to SIS and that would be that. They would just have to find someone else. If she was quick, maybe she could get her old job back as a clerk. However mundane the repetitious tasks were for her lively mind, it was a good job that paid well. Kate began to turn slowly away from the curb.

Mid-turn, Kate hesitated. Her sense of adventure drew her to Piccadilly Circus. What would await her there? The postcard, the red bus, and Henry, it was all their fault! Yes, Henry. It didn't matter that she hadn't met him, he was the one who got her into this mess so he better just well get her out of it. Kate heard a clock in the distance sound the hour. Three o'clock. Henry had better be there. Otherwise—otherwise what? Run back to her normal world and hide? Was that the answer? Kate straightened her hat and took a firm and deliberate step into the street toward Piccadilly Circus.

And there he was, waiting for her with a perplexed look on his face. Henry, the man in the grey suit and Homburg standing with his hands clasped behind him, next to the lamppost. Right where he should be.

Kate quickened her stride to reach him. Why wasn't he stepping forward to meet her? As she grew nearer, she began to get angry—angry because she was so scared. Was this the right man? Surely it must be him. Who else would be standing next to the lamppost? It dawned on her that she had read a lot into one postcard. What if it wasn't Henry? The man she approached with such determination could turn out to be some poor fellow waiting for a red bus. In either case, Kate wasn't sure what she should say to begin. What were those identification phrases she had been taught? Try as she might, Kate couldn't remember them at all. Her mind and emotions were in turmoil. What should she say? "Hello. I'm Kate. Are you Henry? Are you the man who sent me my postcard?" Perhaps, "Hello Henry" would suffice.

# Chapter 6

## Henry and Kate

"*I*s it you?"

# Chapter 7

## Henry

*C*aptivating. Beneath that preposterous hat, that's what she was, captivating. Those large emerald green eyes gazing apprehensively at him made Henry want to stare into them forever. Green eyes, pert nose, auburn hair, in short, a very attractive package. And there was something else, something indefinable, an aura of vitality in her that matched the hat. If only she wasn't wearing such an extraordinary hat. As she continued to look steadily at him as if seeking a lifeline, Henry found himself at a loss for words. Now that she was here, this woman he sent the postcard to, where did he begin?

Before Henry could tear his eyes away from hers and summon his thoughts in order to give the coded recognition phrases, he noticed a man in a black suit loitering only a few steps away. Henry recognized him as the same man who had, just moments before, stepped out of the black Bentley. The man's body seemed to cant in their direction, as if he was very interested in what would happen next. The man's closeness gave Henry a pang of disquiet. This would never do. He and Miss Wenbrook must not be overheard exchanging the stilted recognition phrases. At the very least, they would draw questioning stares. At the worst, the odd sentences would alert enemy agents to their presence. His superiors had warned him that there were individuals who would try to prevent him from completing his assignment. Henry could not be sure if the man was an enemy agent or even had any interest in them, but he definitely wasn't going to take chances. He had better act as if this were the most natural of meetings, two friends meeting in Piccadilly Circus for a bit of sightseeing.

"Hello," Henry said, his voice sounding overly loud and hearty to his own ears. "How lovely to see you again!"

Affixing a smile to his face, Henry grasped the woman firmly by the arm and guided her over to the fountain graced with the statue of Eros. Her tug against him told him of her reluctance to be led anywhere. Even the feather in her ridiculous purple hat quivered with indignation. She probably thought he was a madman. Her next words confirmed his suspicions.

"Who are you and what are you doing?" she hissed under her breath.

If anything, by his actions, Henry was attracting more attention to them. Anyone seeing the mixture of anger and fear on her face would think he planned to do her harm.

"Why don't I read to you the history of this statue?" Henry said keeping a strained smile on his face.

The man in the black suit stalked nearby. It seemed to Henry that the man was taking an unwarranted interest in two people admiring a statue. Obviously, this wasn't the time for code words and introductions. So Henry continued to smile broadly and opened his guidebook. With one hand keeping a tight grip on her elbow, he began reading.

*"Sir Alfred Gilbert's graceful statue of Eros makes a welcome reappearance after an absence of several years."*

"Actually, it's not Eros," she interrupted abruptly. "It's his twin brother Anteros."

Her statement caught him off-guard, not only because he actually thought it was a statue of Eros, but also because the ridiculous purple feather vibrated and bounced above her auburn shoulder-length curls. Henry decided he would have to do something about that feather. It drew entirely too much attention to its wearer.

"We know Eros in popular culture as Cupid," she continued. "However, Cupid would be a totally inappropriate subject for the Shaftesbury Memorial Fountain. After all, the 7th Earl of Shaftesbury, a man noted for his philanthropic works, would hardly be well-represented by Eros, the god of romantic love, don't you think?"

Henry merely gaped at her, nonplussed at her behavior. Was she a fellow spy or an innocent tourist? Did he have the wrong woman? If she wasn't his contact, why wasn't she struggling to get away from him? Noting his lack of response, the woman answered her own question.

"Sir Alfred placed Anteros, the god of selfless love, on top of the fountain. He felt Anteros would reflect well on the Earl's generosity. You might also find it interesting to know that Anteros is the first statue in the world to be cast in aluminum."

Reflexively, they both looked up at the statue. Henry's attention returned to the man in the black suit who had moved to stand even closer to them. The man could not be more than five feet away now. Henry noticed she followed his eyes without moving her head. Her green eyes widened slightly when she saw the man in the black suit. Perhaps she finally understood what or who was disturbing him. She bumped against him as she moved closer to Henry and away from the man. To steady them, Henry put his arm around her. She did not pull away as he glanced quickly around, seeking a safe haven. He made his decision and cleared his throat.

"Had enough sightseeing for today, darling? Yes? Good. Care to see a film?"

# Chapter 8

## Kate

"*D*arling? A film? Would you mind telling me who you are and what on earth you are doing?" Kate whispered a bit crossly as the man in the grey suit tightened his grip on her.

Before he could answer her questions, Kate noticed a man dressed in a long grey overcoat despite the warm June day. He reminded her of the man dressed similarly in the postcard. How peculiar, she thought. The man was staring at them. A gust of wind tugged at his coat revealing a holstered gun. Alarmed, she forced herself to keep calm as she allowed Henry to guide her through the crowd. Was this man really Henry? She had yet to exchange the recognition code with the man grasping her arm so tightly. For all she knew, this man with the guidebook was some kind of fanatic who preyed on young women who visited Piccadilly Circus. Should she point out the man with the gun or was that man Henry? The man in the long grey overcoat may have allowed her to see his gun as a signal to her that she was with the wrong man. Kate wondered how she could subtly point out the man with the gun to the man who stood next to her. She wanted to gage his reaction. She also wanted to know why he was concerned about the man in the black suit. Kate had a hard time hiding her shock when she saw the man in the black suit ducking behind a lamppost. Actually, she had a strong desire to get away from all three men. This was all too confusing. She felt distinctly uncomfortable and more than a little frightened. Her heart hammered in her chest.

Kate heard a *phffft* sound and water from the fountain splashed up at them. Out of the corner of her eye, she saw sun glinting off the barrel of a gun held by the man in the black suit. He had shot at them, thought Kate numbly. She seemed frozen to the spot, unable to breath. Not Henry, he grabbed her arm and pushed them into a large group of people about to cross Shaftesbury Avenue. Did everyone in this little scene have a gun except her? Were there more than just the three of them? Which one was Henry? What had she walked into when she crossed the street? Panic began to rise in her throat. Definitely time to get out of here, Kate thought as her survival instincts kicked in. Quickly she looked at the three faces of the men around her. Without a doubt the face of the man with the guidebook appeared to be the lesser of many evils. Kate allowed herself to be pulled along after him hoping that by mingling with the crowd they could throw off their pursuers. Kate wondered why the people nearby had not panicked at the muffled sound of the shot. Given the background noise of the traffic, they probably equated it with the sound of a car's backfiring. She did not think Henry realized that there were actually two pursuers to elude. In the rush to get away, she had not gotten a chance to point out the man in the grey overcoat.

As Henry pulled her into the lobby of the London Pavilion, Kate had time to notice that the theatre advertised *The Orient Express* starring Heather Angel, Norman Foster, and Ralph Morgan. From reading a review in the paper earlier in the week, she knew the movie was based on Graham Greene's 1932 novella *Stamboul Train* and took place on the Simplon Orient Express. Funny, Kate thought, the things that flow through your mind in a crisis.

Inside the theatre, it was cool and dark. In the muted lighting conditions Kate couldn't tell if they had been followed by anyone. Hopefully not. She certainly did not want to get involved with either of the two men from Piccadilly Circus. With their hard faces and cold eyes, they could have stepped right out of a spy novel, which was why Kate had decided to go with the man wearing the grey suit and black Homburg. At least his face looked friendly. She tried to control her breathing and think.

As they neared their seats, Kate looked back to see if the men had pursued them. Neither was in sight. Grateful for small favors, she turned her attention to Henry. If this was Henry, she cautioned herself. He was so close that he was practically standing on her toes. Despite the dim lighting, she could definitely see Henry. He was what her grandmother would have called an eyeful. Yes, Kate thought, taking in his tall, lean frame, even features, and strong chin, he certainly did appear easy on the eye. Tall and broad shouldered, the fit of his clothes revealed the shape of his muscles under his suit. He had thick dark brown hair, an open, honest face, and his deep blue eyes sparkled humorously even in the dim light. A smile played on his lips as he looked at her.

Gazing up at him, Kate found herself getting angry again. What did he find about this situation even remotely worth smiling about? Granted, he didn't know this was her first adventure in the world of espionage, but still, he had to be aware that they were being pursued or rather, he was being pursued. Surely they were not after her. She just got here. Those men must have been watching Henry. Why didn't he appear to be the least bit nervous? Kate personally knew she was in the first stages of an all-out panic attack. In the big scheme of things, it was still all his fault, no matter how good-looking he happened to be. Just wait until she told him about the man with a gun in the grey overcoat. Let's see if he smiled then.

# Chapter 9

## Henry

*A*s Henry propelled Kate toward the theatre his mind whirled with questions. How had he been spotted? Was this Kate? Or was she an innocent bystander? Or was the lovely young woman he held tightly by the elbow really a counter-agent who somehow pointed him out to the shooter? Had she seen the gun before the shot rang out? She must have, there had been panic in her face. Had she seen someone suspicious moments earlier? What other reason could he give for her touristy comments about the Shaftesbury Memorial Fountain? Who or what had she seen?

Henry did not think it had been the man in the black suit that had fired the gun. He could tell by the way her eyes widened that she had not seen him earlier. Henry thought back. He had seen Kate glance over his shoulder just before making her little speech about Eros and Anteros. Was there something about her voice that seemed nervous? How would he know? He had just met the girl.

Henry all but groaned aloud as they made their way down to aisle to their seats. He'd blown it right from the start. He hadn't even asked if she was Kate. She had no way of knowing he was Henry. *Exchange introductions in code before proceeding further.* Even the average man on the street knew that in the world of espionage you exchange recognition phrases first. But no, not Henry. First, he had stood there like a tongue-tied youngster. Of course, he had taken a lot on faith. After all, Henry had not even troubled to ask her if she was Kate. All he had said when they first met was: "Is it you?" Come to think of it, she had asked the same question at the same instant. He remembered how their voices came out as one as they gazed into each other's eyes. For a moment, it felt as if the world had stopped turning on its axis. Had she felt the same thing? Henry wondered what would have happened if he hadn't seen the man in the black suit. Disturbed by the man, they hadn't even answered that question before proceeding to the fountain. There they had exchanged inane information about the Shaftesbury Memorial Fountain. Instead of acting like a professional, Henry had scurried across the street like a frightened rabbit trying to get lost in a crowd, dragging a woman he hadn't been properly introduced to into the theatre. What was he thinking?

He was thinking that, unluckily, he hadn't lost his pursuer. Over the heads of the people, he thought he recognized him as they entered the theatre. Well, no time for a film today. They needed to get out of here. Too bad, he wanted to see *Stamboul Train*, if for no other reason than to see the legendary train on film. The Orient Express. Henry had always wanted to ride on the Orient Express, all the way to Istanbul. There he went again, losing focus. He would have no chance of riding that train if he didn't get them out of this situation without getting shot. Once away from the men menacing them, Henry needed to find a safe place so he could tell Miss Wenbrook, if that was indeed who she was, about their assignment.

Henry smiled at the recollection and looked down into her scowling face. What he saw there made him return his attention to the situation at hand.

After they seated themselves toward the front of the theatre, Henry could not help but notice that she was inspecting him from head to foot. He proceeded to do the same to her. His eyes confirmed his first impression. Five feet four inches of tawny beauty topped off by a ridiculous bright purple hat with an enormous feather. He could not imagine her being an enemy spy, she looked too innocent, too frightened. Besides, that feather acted like an arrow proclaiming her presence. No one could miss seeing that feather regardless of the distance, including their pursuers. He couldn't imagine an enemy agent willingly drawing that much attention to herself. For a moment, she looked so vulnerable, Henry wanted nothing

36

more than to take her into his arms and comfort her. As he instinctively moved to do so, over her shoulder, he saw the man in the black suit. The man sat much too close for comfort.

"Perhaps it's time we exchange recognition codes despite all that has happened," Kate whispered to Henry.

He leaned closer to her and caught the scent of her subtle perfume. Light, gentle, refreshing. He wondered if the same words could be used to describe the woman next to him. Then the brim of her hat bumped him, reminding him that she was a stranger in a strange hat. With an effort he pulled himself together.

"This whole thing got off badly, didn't it? We've made one mistake after another. But, I suppose we should exchange codes," he said quietly but with more confidence. "Better late than never."

"I prefer to take the red bus to Piccadilly," Kate murmured, wondering if this was the best SIS could do.

"Wouldn't a black taxi be better?" he answered, obviously thinking the same thing.

"Good, well...that's done."

"Have you seen the man to our right?" Henry asked in a low voice. "The one in the black suit?"

"Yes, he's the man who shot at us," she answered in a quaking voice. "Have you seen the man in the long grey overcoat sitting in front of us slightly to the left? He carries a gun too."

Two of them, Henry realized, shocked. After watching the man in the long grey overcoat get off the bus, Henry had ignored him. His superiors had not warned him that there might be two of them and yet Henry had failed to remain alert to the possibility. Quickly he reviewed his options. The two men effectively blocked exiting the way they had come in. The arriving patrons made passage up the aisle to their left difficult. If they waited until the film began, they might become hemmed in by people in their row. Just then, the two men changed seats to move closer to where Henry and Kate sat. Never had a theatre seemed so small to Henry.

"We have got to get out of here," he said, stating the obvious. Henry flushed under Kate's withering glare.

"Really? Whatever for?" she mocked him with feigned disbelief in her voice. "Don't you want to see the film?"

Improvise, improvise, shouted Henry to himself. But how? That was the question. They had few choices in the crowded theatre. Henry's eyes scanned his surroundings frantically. Again, the men moved closer to their seats. Cornered, they were cornered. His choice of escape route had placed them firmly in a trap. For a moment, panic caused his heart to pound and his brain to cease functioning. Henry chided himself, he needed to calm down and think clearly. Taking a deep breath, he reconsidered their situation with deliberation. The seats besides them remained open and the aisle had begun to clear of late arrivals. Their best route of escape lay to their left. If he could just figure out the swiftest and most secure way out. Nervously he racked his brain for a plan. Henry did not relish the thought of ending his assignment before it began. As he watched the men, Henry couldn't dispel this feeling of impending doom.

# Chapter 10

## Kate

While they watched the opening credits roll, Kate looked at her watch. Disbelieving the time, she placed it near her ear. It ticked softly and steadily. In the brief span of ten minutes, she had met a man in a grey suit wearing a black Homburg, exchanged trivial information about a fountain, been shot at, dragged across the street, and run to ground in a theatre. To say the least, she had an uncomfortable feeling about all this. The whole thing was so far out of her realm of experience, that Kate didn't know how to cope with the situation she found herself in. Ruefully, Kate chided herself for wanting a more interesting life. Intent on her goal, she had taken steps to make it happen. Now here she was frightened out of her wits and wondering what she had gotten herself into. Suddenly, she longed to return to her quiet life. Answering the postcard had turned her world upside-down. Its arrival had already steered her life onto a new, unexpected, and dangerous course. Kate was beginning to realize that it wasn't such a great idea to get entangled with a mystery man in the middle of his mystery. Events unfolded so quickly that she had not had time to fully consider the behavior of the man sitting next to her. Fortunately, so far, he had made only protective gestures toward her. Given the aggression of the other men, he seemed to be her safest option. She sat stiffly in the dark, poised to run.

Quit crying over spilt milk, she told herself firmly. Right now, she needed to concentrate on getting out of this theatre and away from the men pursuing them. Options, escape, hidden doors, what opportunities presented themselves?  Only the theatre's dimness provided Kate with any hope of escape.

Kate risked a quick glance at Henry's face.  It clearly betrayed his anxious feelings.  Kate would have felt sorry for him except that she blamed him for her current circumstances.  This was the man the SIS had chosen to accompany her on a mission?  Fat lot of help he was turning out to be.  He ought to be taking charge of the situation.  She wanted to shout at him to do something about getting them away from here.  Instead, she refrained from making a caustic remark.

Kate didn't believe for one minute that the crowds in the theatre provided her any protection.  She had read enough spy novels to know there were many ways to do away with someone without causing alarm.  Kate definitely did not want her short and previously uneventful life to end here.  She remembered what her grandmother had said about being in trouble.  The only one you can count on to rescue you is you.  Knowing she would have to rely on her own initiative, Kate concentrated her attention on the practical matter of escaping.  Authors of mystery novels always thoughtfully included a way out of a bad situation.  Kate hoped the same was true in real life.  With feigned casualness, she surveyed the walls searching for a carefully concealed exit.  She breathed a sigh of relief when she spotted it.  The door, nearly hidden by the decorative curtains that covered the wall opposite of where they sat, would do nicely.

Kate subtly nudged Henry.  She tilted her hat and pointed with the feather toward the wall.

"Look.  Do you see it?  The door behind those curtains?"

"Where?"

"Slightly behind us and to the left."  Again, she tilted her feather toward the hidden door.

"How did you know there was a door there?"

"There's always a door."

"There's always a door?"

"Otherwise the heroine can't escape."

"Can't escape?" Henry's voice mirrored his perplexed expression.

"Do you have a better idea?" Kate asked sarcastically. She could tell she had piqued his ego.

"What if we get blocked into our row? What if it's locked?"

"Do you ever think positively?" asked Kate, wondering at his lack of enthusiasm. "If we're lucky, late-comers will select seats that obstruct the passage to the aisle for both of our pursuers."

"That's a tall order."

"All we can do is wait and see."

As the opening credits began to roll, to their own left, the row remained empty. Just as the music swelled for the opening scene, Henry grabbed her hand and pulled Kate out of her seat and down their row to the door. Kate held her hat firmly to her head with her free hand as she followed him across the theatre toward the door. She glanced over her shoulder to see both men struggling to reach them by climbing over the other patrons in their rows. She could hear the film-goers saying "down in front." The train on the screen emitted a high pitched whistle that covered the sound of gunfire. As she and Henry slipped through the door, the woodwork near their heads splintered when a bullet struck it. As they fled, they could hear the loud cries of surprise and shock coming from the audience.

# Chapter 11

## Henry

*H*enry pulled Kate down the narrow corridor they had entered. At the end, another unlocked door led out into the alley. Running toward Piccadilly Circus, he tried to think quickly. Stumbling over the seated patrons at the theatre would hold up the men's progress for only a few minutes. He and Kate had to go someplace safe, someplace where they could talk without arousing suspicion, someplace private. That it had to be nearby and that they couldn't be followed went without saying. Improvising, he swiftly considered his options.

"We could mingle with the people on the sidewalk and lose them in the crowd," Henry said, thinking out loud.

"We could board one of the red buses," said Kate as they scanned the roadway which was oddly devoid of red buses.

"Naturally, one can never count on one being available when you need it. We certainly can't stand around and wait for a bus."

"How about a cab?"

"Cabs and buses are notoriously easy to follow," stated Henry firmly.

"Maybe we should duck into one of the nearby buildings?"

"Once inside, there might not be a place to hide. We could hardly feign having business in one of the offices. Better to get as far away from Piccadilly as possible."

"All right, if you don't like any of my ideas," said Kate. "Where should we go?"

Henry's eyes fastened on the sign for the underground station and he knew what to do. The tube station at Piccadilly Circus would be perfect. There the Bakerloo and Piccadilly lines intersected.

"This way! We can lose ourselves in the maze of tunnels of the underground. We can see which trains are arriving the soonest and pick a destination from there. That should give us a number of choices." Henry pulled Kate down the entrance stairs. "If we go east on the Piccadilly line, we could exit at Covent Garden."

"No, that won't do," said Kate. "Covent Garden market buzzes with activity on Tuesday mornings, but it'll be quiet now on a late Thursday afternoon."

Breathless from running, Kate turned to look behind them. Henry glared at her bright purple feather bobbing in the air like a beacon. It would have to go.

"Better yet, why don't we travel further on? We could get off at King's Cross/Saint Pancreas. The people there will provide cover...if I could just think of a quiet place nearby where we could talk."

"Nothing comes quickly to mind so that stop won't do either. How about west on the Piccadilly line?"

"I can't think of anything. How about the Bakerloo line?"

"Where could we go on the Bakerloo line?"

"To the north, all I can think of is Oxford Circus or Regent's Park. Neither of those is busy enough to be suitable. We'll be too exposed at either location." Henry continued to think as they raced through the underground station. "Wait a minute! What about going south on the Bakerloo line. That will take us to the Embankment. I remember seeing an advertisement for pleasure boat tours in the front of the guidebook. If we could board one of those without being seen, we would have at least two hours of uninterrupted time to talk."

Henry steered Kate through the crowd, at times roughly pushing ahead of people. Quickly he covered the ground to the ticket booth where he impatiently paid a shilling each for two passes. The passes would allow them to travel easily throughout the underground system. Expensive, but in case their pursuers necessitated a quick change of plans, he wouldn't be slowed down by ticket sellers. The signboard announced that a train would be departing south on the Bakerloo line in one minute. Perfect. If they could make this train, they might just get away. Once at the Embankment, they could pick from one of the many holiday day-tripper boats that cruised the Thames.

As he pulled Kate down the tunnel with him, Henry glanced around to see if they had been followed. He noted Kate doing the same thing. She shook her head no and followed him as he quickly led the way down the stairs to the south Bakerloo line. Unlike most other underground line platforms, the Bakerloo line north and south platforms were laid out back-to-back. A single crossover tunnel at the north end allows passengers to see both platforms at once, an unpleasant thought given that the men pursuing them had guns.

As Kate and Henry reached the southbound platform, they simultaneously looked back at the crossover tunnel. There they were. Two men, guns ready as they raced to cover the distance to the platform. Shots rang out. People scattered and dove for cover. As he thrust Kate unceremoniously onto the awaiting train, Henry heard Kate's quiet plea.

"Please let the doors close on time."

Fortunately, the doors hissed shut and the train pulled away from the station leaving their pursuers standing frustrated on the platform. Henry took a few deep breaths and waited for his heart to cease thumping madly in his chest. Having heard the desperation in her voice, Henry took time to really consider the woman standing next to him. Only her face, which was ghostly pale, gave any indication of their exertions of the past few minutes. He had to admire Kate. On the surface she looked cool and unruffled, yet, he could feel the faint tremor emanating from her body.

She had pluck; he would say that for her.  She kept up with him and played along even though she surely didn't have a clue what was going on.  She'd even found the concealed door at the theatre.  Despite her strange choice of head gear, she was stronger than she looked.  Several times, he had seen her fear and anxiety clearly written on her face, yet she had not protested, screamed, or complained.  Actually, she hadn't even asked any questions.  Not really.  That's curious.  Wouldn't anyone ask questions if they found themselves in this situation?

# Chapter 12

## Kate

*T*his was all too much. Kate had been pushed, pulled, jostled, and shoved enough for one day and she had only known this man for 20 minutes. She asked herself for the umpteenth time: was this even Henry? Kate wondered if all SIS assignments started with a bang or a gunshot like this one had. Surely the adventures they'd just had were not normal. Why was she allowing this to happen to her? Kate wished she had never received that silly postcard. None of this would have ever happened. She caught her reflection in the window glass. Kate blinked because she hardly recognized herself. Her reflection showed a calm and collected woman. Unbelievable. She had been shot at, chased across Piccadilly Circus, followed into a theatre, shot at again, dragged down into an underground station, and shoved onto a train. The woman reflected back at her had hardly a hair out of place. Even her hat was firmly in place. Apparently Kate possessed acting skills she wasn't aware of. With quaking hands, she adjusted her hat on her head slightly. Performing such a normal action soothed her shattered nerves. Kate drew in a deep, calming breath. To quiet her senses further, she pulled her lipstick out of her purse and touched up her lips. There. Now she was ready for anything. If only she could stop her hands from shaking.

"We have to do something about this!" said Henry firmly as he reached over and snapped the feather in her hat neatly in half.

"Oh, no!" Kate wailed. "My hat!" Her dismay over the limp feather dangling over her right ear pushed other thoughts out of her mind. "How dare you do that!"

"It's drawing attention to us!"

Kate glared at him for a moment with anger, unable to forget that this was really all his fault.

"Drawing attention to us? They're after you, not me. I liked my hat! Especially the purple feather!" she said in an aggrieved tone.

"After what we've just been through and all you care about is whether or not I've ruined your hat?" Henry said incredulously. "You liked it? With that crazy purple feather?"

"You men never can understand the importance of being properly dressed," Kate sniffed as she turned her back on him.

To Kate, clothes were like armor, protecting her from what the world had to offer. Given all they had been through, armor would not have been a bad idea. She straightened the lapels of her suit.

"I can't believe you are primping in the reflection of the window," Henry snorted.

"If you must know, I am trying to act natural," she answered coolly. That seemed to shut him up, she thought with satisfaction. Kate watched a red blush creep up Henry's neck as he looked away from her.

Out of the corner of her eye, Kate studied the profile of the man next to her. While he looked a bit flustered, he had an open, honest face, a face a person could trust. In it she could see a patient watchfulness that spoke of courage and resilience. She had not really expected that. If he was Henry Littleton, the spy, shouldn't he have a face shrouded in mystery? Didn't all spies look alike with their hard faces and sharp, cold eyes?

"How did you know to stay with me? Did you know it was me? I don't remember telling you my name," Henry said as he returned her appraising stare.

"You were the only one who looked like the man in the postcard, the one standing next to the lamppost," Kate said without hesitation.

"You figured that out? I wondered if you would," laughed Henry, looking inordinately pleased that his plan had worked.

"It wasn't that hard—a simple leap of imagination."

For a moment, they just stood there without speaking, each taking the other's measure. Eventually, Kate broke their staring contest and picked up the conversation where they left off.

"Henry, where are we going? All this running around is all fine well and good while we were being pursued, but it is time to talk."

Smiling proudly at his hastily conceived plan, he opened the guidebook and showed her the advertisement for the Oxford and Kingston Steamers.

"How about taking a ride on a pleasure boat? I have heard it's a delightful way to spend a summer's afternoon," he said with a grin.

She could tell he was trying to act unconcerned and unaffected by all the commotion earlier. She had imagined the SIS men would surely display a calm demeanor even in the most trying situations.

"Yes, well, if you think we haven't been followed," she said, looking around.

"I think this little train ride has helped us put some distance between us and our pursuers. You'll see, this plan will work out," Henry said confidently. "On the boat we can talk. There is so much to tell you and so little time."

Before he could say more, the train came to a halt at their station. Henry gently took her by her elbow as she exited the train, holding her close to him in order to protect her. He carefully scanned the disembarking passengers. Seeing no suspicious characters, Henry guided them toward the exit. Emerging from the tube at the Embankment stop, Kate noticed

48

that Henry could not help wanting to hurry as they walked quickly toward the tour boat docks. Gratefully, she sensed he was getting in command of himself and the situation.

It proved easy to find the tour boat operators. Luckily for them a two-hour pleasure cruise was about to depart. Kate waited impatiently as Henry bought tickets.

"Relax. Try to act casual. We can't draw attention to ourselves," Henry warned.

"Are they here?" Kate asked in alarm, looking around wildly. "Do you think there are others?"

"No. I'm just being careful," said Henry as he looked at the people around them. "No one seems to be taking an interest in us. I'm sure we'll both breathe easier when the boat leaves the dock and moves upstream."

She may have appeared calm on the outside, but on the inside, Kate's mind raced along much faster than the river. The abrupt beginning to their mission unsettled her to say the least. Kate had never been trained for situations like these. Certainly she should stop right now. No one would blame her if she dropped all this espionage stuff and returned to her former life. Her first attempt at growing wings was off to a rocky start, she thought wryly. She thought about telling Henry that she had changed her mind. She would tell him she intended to drop out as of this moment.

The whistle of a boat and the shouts of the crew prevented her from speaking her piece. Instead of saying anything she found herself studying the man next to her. So this was Henry. Despite the events of the afternoon, he appeared as unruffled as the surface of the Thames. Tall and muscular, he gave off an aura of strength and capability. He struck her as the kind of man a person could rely on, a man who would rise to the occasion to do the right thing. When he turned to face her, she found herself gazing into Henry's amazingly blue eyes. They were the deep blue of cornflowers blooming on a summer day.

Kate remembered how he had gently taken her by the elbow to aid her as she stepped off the train. He had made the same gentlemanly gesture when she boarded the boat. Kate thought about how he had helped seat her at the theatre. Henry had performed these subtle actions almost automatically. All these small gestures made her feel respected and cared for. Her grandfather, whom she adored, had told her over and over that a man worth having was one who paid attention to the comfort and well-being of those around him. Her grandfather said that the truth to a man's character lay in the little deeds performed without fanfare. He had encouraged Kate to find such a true gentleman for her own. Henry, although he didn't realize it, had passed her grandfather's test with flying colors. Kate's train of thought paused for a moment. How odd that Henry would remind her of her grandfather at a time like this.

# Chapter 13

## Henry

"*W*ell, that didn't go too badly," Henry said as the boat moved out into the river. "We survived being shot at, making a mad dash across Piccadilly Circus traffic, racing in and out of a theatre, and running down into the Underground while being shot at again. Now we can sit back and enjoy two delightful hours cruising on the Thames."

"You're being rather flippant about it all. Personally, I don't feel nearly as calm as you look. Then again, I'm sure that you are far better at this espionage business than I am."

Henry pulled himself together and tried to match her expectations about his *sang-froid*. After all, he would not seem at all confident if he blurted out that this was his first mission. He cast about for a reason to abandon this particular topic.

"Why don't we find ourselves a quiet table and enjoy a bit of refreshment?" Henry said as he guided them toward one of the small tables in the shade of the boat deck awning. Once they had ordered tea, Henry mustered all the self-confidence he could and told Kate about their assignment.

"Yes, well, um. Where to begin? A bit of background information would be appropriate to start with."

Kate nodded her agreement.

"Everyone who has ever taken a history course can tell you about the events that precipitated World War I."

"What does what happened twenty years ago have to do with what happened today?" Kate asked.

"Patience. Patience. The June 28, 1914 assassination of Archduke Franz Ferdinand of Austria-Hungary in Sarajevo by a Serbian activist sadly touched off a powder-keg. On that same day, in retaliation for the deaths of the Archduke and Duchess, Austria-Hungary declared war on Serbia. Because of diplomatic treaty ties, Russia, Serbia's ally, mobilized to help Serbia. By August 1, Germany, Austria-Hungary's ally, declared war on Russia. This brought the French, Russia's ally, into the war. By August 4, Germany had declared war on France and invaded neutral Belgium. This act of aggression brought Britain into the war. And, the rest, as they say, is history."

"Thank you for the succinct history lesson, but I don't see its relevance today."

"Few people realize that a similar threat exists today. The Balkans continues to be the powder-keg of Europe. Even as we speak, King Alexander of Yugoslavia is touring Europe and meeting with the leaders of Italy, France, and others in response to Hitler's rise to power."

Henry could tell by the look on Kate's face that he had lost her, so he back-tracked to provide a description of King Alexander and his importance to world politics.

"King Alexander was born in the Principality of Montenegro on December 16, 1888 and came to be King of Yugoslavia in part due to the events in Sarajevo in 1914. He was born to King Peter I of Serbia and Princess Zorka of Montenegro."

"Zorka? Surely you're joking."

"No, I am not making this up. Her name is really Princess Zorka," Henry said as he returned her smile. "She's the daughter of King Nicolas and Queen Milena of Montenegro."

"Though only the second son, he was considered a more appropriate ruler than his elder brother," he added more seriously. "When his father, Peter I, abdicated the throne, political forces in Serbia forced his brother, Prince George, to renounce his claim to the throne. Alexander made a better choice because of his participation in the First Balkan War in 1912 and his later service in the 1913 Second Balkan War. The people knew and liked him.

Henry paused a moment while the waiter laid their table with tea and a variety of sandwiches.

"I hadn't realized how hungry I am!" exclaimed Kate as she poured the tea.

Sampling a sandwich, Henry merely nodded his agreement. For a while, they ate in silence, and then Henry picked up his train of thought.

"King Peter I handed over royal powers to Alexander on June 24, 1914. As Regent of Serbia, Alexander and his armies played a role in World War I. In recognition of this service, as part of the reorganization of the Balkans following World War I, in 1918, Serbia, Croatia, and Slovenia were joined to create the Kingdom of Serbs, Croats, and Slovenes. The 1920s were full of political intrigues and crises. In January 1929, King Alexander reorganized his kingdom and its constitution. He chose to call it the Kingdom of Yugoslavia."

"I think I remember reading about that. Where is all this leading?"

"Things have been heating up again in the Balkans. On February 9th of this year, the Turks, Greek, Romanian, and Yugoslavian governments concluded the Balkan Pact. By working together to protect the borders of the region, the pact is designed to prevent encroachment on the Balkans by other nations."

"What other nations?"

"Germany and Italy namely. King Alexander has also been working to help build alliances with a number of European nations to counter Hitler's growing power. Yugoslavia is critical to all of European nations due to its location. Yugoslavia controls one of the very few land routes from Turkey and the Near East to Western Europe. It is quite strategically placed in that regard.

"What does this have to do with Great Britain?" said Kate.

Henry could tell it all was as thick as mud to her.

"Trust me, it does. I can explain more on the way."

"On the way where?" she said.

"Belgrade."

"Belgrade?" she questioned. "Belgrade, Yugoslavia?"

"Yes, we've got to get to Belgrade quickly and prevent an attempt on the King's life. We can get there the quickest if we take the Orient Express."

# Chapter 14

## Kate

$\mathcal{T}$he Orient Express. The very name conjured up mystery, romance, and intrigue. Just like every other royal, aristocrat, or adventurer, Kate wanted to experience the journey. But did she want that experience under these circumstances? Her first assignment had not exactly gotten off to a good start. She took a careful look at the man next to her. She had to admit Henry had presence. Despite all they had been through, there was a calmness in him that put her at ease. His quiet manner, the twinkle in his eye when he looked at her, everything about him was reassuring. These qualities combined to create an individual who at once radiated both confidence and mischief. The combination intrigued Kate. No doubt about it, Henry had captured her attention. Imagine journeying on the Orient Express with a man like him.

Romance, mystery, intrigue, the Orient Express and Henry. Romance? Kate sat upright abruptly, drawing an odd look from Henry. She ignored his reaction and turned her attention to her last thought. Romance? Where on earth had that idea come from? Obviously, the events of the afternoon had disturbed her equilibrium. Kate knew that travelling with a person provides insights into the person's character that would otherwise remain hidden in most social situations. But romance? Did she feel comfortable with the possibility of romance? Kate turned that thought over in her mind. She vividly remembered the thrill that coursed through her at the sound of his voice when he had first spoken to her. Though she had never lost her head or her heart to any man, let alone one she just met, Kate could imagine succumbing to his firm, baritone voice. Kate decided she wouldn't mind a little romance with Henry.

Romance, mystery, intrigue, the Orient Express and Henry. It was a heady combination. Not that romancing Henry would be easy. Kate looked across the table at Henry, who continued to drone on about the situation in the Balkans. All wrapped up in his history lesson, Henry didn't even seem to notice her at all. She, on the other hand, could hardly follow what he was saying. His thick brown hair, his sparkling blue eyes, and deep voice all seemed to cause his words to go in one ear and out the other. Kate could tell her presence was not having the same effect on Henry. He just kept talking about kings, diplomatic efforts, and countries. She could say one thing about Henry. He sure knew his history, or perhaps more accurately, his current events.

Oh well, Kate thought, there would be time on the Orient Express to capture Henry's attention. The jolt that passed through her body when that thought drifted through her mind brought Kate back to earth with a resounding thud. She couldn't believe she had been thinking about romancing Henry. That was just it, she had not been thinking. At least, she had not been concentrating on the important issues at hand. In her mind, she had already boarded the Orient Express with Henry. She never even considered the practicalities of travelling across the continent with a man she didn't know, pursuing the potential assassin of a King she had never heard of. She needed time to clarify her own thoughts and feelings. Kate had always enjoyed mystery stories and, up until now she thought it would be great to take part in one. That was half the reason why she agreed to work for SIS. Today, however, in a short few hours, she had learned about the heart-pounding fear involved. She realized now that reading about other people's experiences was an entirely different thing compared to putting yourself through it. The other experiences simply weren't real. What she and Henry were involved in definitely was. She had completely ignored the fact that she and Henry were on an assignment for His Majesty's Government. She had conveniently forgotten the events at the fountain and the theatre. She must be out of her mind. Logically, romantic thoughts of Henry should never have overshadowed memories of being shot at and pursued. To her further discomfort, Kate remembered that mystery writer Agatha Christie got her idea for her first novel, *Murder on the Calais Coach*, from a 1929 murder on the real Orient Express when it was stuck in a snowstorm for five days just 70 miles outside of Istanbul.

Kate knew enough about herself to know that she never seemed to be able to focus on the practical side on any given situation. As she continued to drink in Henry's good looks, she found herself hoping inwardly that their voyage concentrated more on romance and less on murder. To block out her fears, Kate continued to allow her imagination run away with her. It wasn't as if it was the first time in her life she had permitted that to happen. She had always been rather impulsive, though never with a man. Kate could not begin to count the number of times she had reminded herself that she really must make a greater effort to be logical and practical. She simply must exercise some measure of self-control. She grew angry at both herself and Henry. Here they were, planning an adventure in espionage, both of them complete amateurs. For the hundredth time today, Kate asked herself: "What was she thinking?"

"Henry", she said with an edge of anger in her voice. "Just how do you expect me to travel all the way to Belgrade with just a lipstick, comb, and a pocketful of change?"

# Chapter 15

## Henry

"*H*ow can you do that, indeed?" Henry said, surprised at her question. How did that question have a bearing on what he had been saying? Better yet, where had it come from? One look at her face told him Kate was angry. Though for the life of him, he could not fathom why. Working with a woman might be more challenging than he thought. "Why do you ask?"

"It's a perfectly sensible question."

"I haven't gotten that far along planning our trip. I have yet to consider all the ramifications of the attacks on us," he responded loftily.

"It's about time we did, don't you think, Henry?"

"Yes. Of course...there are considerations to be taken into account. I'll have to give it some thought."

"Give it some thought?" she cried. "Admit it. You've been improvising since the moment you received this assignment, haven't you? You're hardly staying one step ahead of me, let alone ahead of the opposition."

Stung and taken aback by Kate's insight into his character, for a moment, Henry could not think of a thing to say. Not wanting her to become alarmed by his rather precarious grasp of the situation, Henry suggested some more tea in order to buy time to collect his thoughts. Her question had troubled him and he needed to think before he responded. He refreshed their cups with the fresh pot of tea the waiter had thoughtfully provided.

"The one thing you can rely on in Britain is the use of tea to smooth over a fraught situation," Kate said sarcastically. "Henry, we can't play this by ear. Truly, I don't feel very comfortable with the whole situation. What is going to happen next? Though I admit it is very pleasant sitting here in the shade on the afterdeck of a boat, we can't just spend the afternoon chatting aimlessly about history, drinking tea and pointing out sights on the river bank. We need to be doing something more constructive."

"You make it all sound so melodramatic," he protested. "We're perfectly safe here on the boat."

"In some ways it would be lovely to while away the remainder of the afternoon floating on the Thames," Kate said heatedly. "Somehow though, I can't keep my mind away from dark-suited, gun-toting pursuers awaiting us when we step off the boat."

Their argument was cut short as the waiter appeared to ask them if they would like a small selection of cakes for dessert. Between the tea and the interruption, Henry recovered his bearings and his sense of humor.

"Yes, well, back to your original question," Henry said once they had ordered some cakes. "Lipstick, a pocket comb, and a handful of change. It would look a bit suspicious if we traveled that lightly, wouldn't it?"

His attempt at levity had done little to allay her concerns. Kate looked like an extremely cross kitten though he would never dare to tell her that. Hiding a smile that in her current mood she would definitely misinterpret, Henry continued.

"Let's see, the guidebook says that our cruise on the River Thames should last for two hours. That means we'll be back at the embankment around 5:45. First, we'll return to Allendale Club and you can pick up a few things. Next we'll head to my flat and pack a suitcase for me."

"Henry, I may be melodramatic, but you make it sound deceptively simple!"

"We'll need clothes for the part we have to play. You know the sort of thing, suits, evening clothes, accessories for well-heeled travellers on the Orient Express. We'll be attending an embassy ball in Paris and a reception in Belgrade."

"A reception! A ball!" Kate exclaimed. "I don't own any clothes appropriate for a reception and a ball!"

"Don't worry," he assured her. "We should have time for a bit of shopping before we leave London."

"Oh, no you don't. I'm not going to an embassy ball in just any old frock! Hats! I'll need hats too. Shoes, mustn't forget shoes…they'll have to match the dress. And gloves! Tell me, will the same people be attending the ball in Belgrade? I simply couldn't show up in the same dress at both the reception and the ball. That wouldn't do at all. How can I possibly pay for this? Where are we going to get the money to pretend we're well-heeled travellers? Answer me that," Kate said in a rush, without pausing for a breath.

"Why is it that women always focus on what to wear?" Henry wondered out loud, amazed at how easily the thought of a ball had deflected Kate from her original anger. Though he should have been grateful for this abrupt change of attitude, Henry grew irritated at her abrupt about face. Kate bounced from idea to idea without a thought for the one she left behind. How would he ever be able to work with this woman? "Can't you see the bigger picture here? We've been shot at, for heaven sakes. Has the embassy ball pushed pursuers and assassinations out of your mind already? You must have a little circus going on in that brain of yours."

"A little circus? Just what do you mean by that?" Kate folded her arms across her body and frowned at him indignantly.

"Yes, a little circus," said Henry, refusing to back down.

They glared at each other in frustration.

"Just where will be get the money for the clothing we need in order to blend in?  What about train tickets and hotel rooms?"

Suddenly, the complexity of their undertaking overwhelmed Henry. When he accepted this assignment, he thought there would be plenty of time for planning and preparing.  Being chased by two men certainly put a spanner into the works.  Could he risk going back to the office for better information?  Henry had to pick up a briefcase with money and travel papers.  He hoped it would contain more information about his mission and perhaps about the assassin.  He could tell that Kate was beginning to realize just how much he was improvising.  Fortunately, before she could take him to task, the waiter arrived with their cakes.  While they ate, Henry tried another tack.

"You're right; those little details will need to be worked out.  However, let's put that aside for right now.  It's time I tell you about our mission."

"Start by telling me who is chasing you."

"Yes, well, who are they? That's a good question.  Kingdoms, republics, powers, individuals?"

Kate stared at him, her questions evident in her face.

"Actually," Henry continued.  "I didn't really know."

"Surely, you must have some idea."

"Oh, I have ideas, but no concrete evidence.  My superiors had told me to watch out for operatives who wanted to thwart my activities, but nothing specific."

"Henry, if everyone knows that an attempt might be made, why is King Alexander going on with his plans?" Kate asked.

"Naturally, that question has already been asked of the King.  His response is what you would expect.  A king has his duty to protect and guide his nation.  He can't do that by hiding.  In the meantime, extra precautions have been taken to increase the King's safety," said Henry reasonably.

"So who are we after? Do we have any ideas?" Kate queried him.

"Several different factions may want to harm King Alexander. There are those within his own country who do not agree with his regime. He is a genuine believer in Yugoslavia as a nation, but, he has had limited success unifying his country. Some people would prefer a strong central government while others would prefer regional autonomy. If the King were to die unexpectedly, the entire country would unravel along ethnic lines."

"Why is this a problem?"

"We must keep in mind that Yugoslavia represents one of the key land routes for trade between Europe and Turkey and the Near East. Its position along the Adriatic coast is of strategic importance."

"Of course, if we must, we must," Kate said a bit sarcastically.

Henry frowned at her before answering.

"Many European nations see strategic advantages in alliances with Yugoslavia," he went on, ignoring her comment. "The Germans, Turkish, and Italians all have reasons to be concerned. Take for instance the Germans. Their government is not at all pleased with King Alexander's alliance building efforts. The French and Italians, on the other hand, are concerned about the Balkan Pact and Yugoslav-German Trade Agreement. We also need to consider the difficulties between the Yugoslavian and Italian governments. Each claims a right to the land and resources of Albania. Though what the Albanians think is anybody's guess."

"This is all very confusing. Let me see if I have this straight. There are people in Germany, France, Italy, Austria, and Yugoslavia who all may have reasons for wanting King Alexander dead."

"Yes, that about covers it."

"Anyone else we need to be concerned about?" Kate asked.

"No, I think that completes the cast of characters. It makes sense that our pursuers are representatives from one or two of those factions. I don't know for certain. I also don't know how they found out about us. Right now, we need to concentrate on doing our job. We need to get to Belgrade before the 21st."

"If you want to know the truth, I'm not sure I'm the right person for this job."

After their discussion over tea, Henry wasn't sure Kate was either. Henry could tell that she had little interest in involving herself in his adventure. His talk of kings, assassinations, and diplomatic issues had done nothing to convince her of the importance of their assignment. Unfortunately, it was too late to request a new partner now. Instead of responding to Kate's comment, Henry walked over to the railing of the boat. After a few moments, Kate joined him there. For a while, they both simply leaned on the rail and watched the Thames flow by. By mutual consent, conversation between them had ceased. Their shoulders touched lightly, their bodies moving in unison with the rocking motion of the boat. Anyone observing them would have thought they had known each other a long time, such was their comfortable posture.

Henry wondered at the decision of his superiors to team him with Kate. This was his first assignment, one that was doomed to fail unless he could work together with the young woman who stood beside him. He turned to face Kate. The broken feather in her hat gave her a rakish look. Above all, she had the poise that made him think that, despite their rocky beginning, she would be an excellent partner. Or, if not an asset in the espionage sense, she would certainly be interesting in the personal sense. She was truly a lovely woman. Henry thought about his career and the future he so desperately wanted to have with SIS. If he was going to succeed, he had to convince her to join him. He decided to lay his cards on the table.

"On June 20th or 21st, an assassination attempt may be made on King Alexander of Yugoslavia in Belgrade. You and I have been assigned to prevent it," Henry announced with what he hoped was dramatic flair. "Since a man travelling alone can draw attention, you, Kate, will be my cover. We shall travel as newlyweds on honeymoon to the Orient."

Kate looked a bit taken aback at that last comment to say the least.

"Married? We're married? When did this happen?" Kate spluttered when she had found her voice. "You must be mad."

Henry cringed when her final comment came out as a flat statement, not a question. He decided it would be best to approach this situation with a sense of humor.

"Did you see the announcement in the *Times*?" Henry asked playfully. "Wait a moment. I have it right here." To himself he thought, hadn't his superiors briefed her at all? Seeing disbelief written on Kate's face, Henry carefully extracted a small clipping from his guidebook.

> Littleton—Wenbrook  London, June 12, 1934, St. Paul's Cathedral, West Chapel.  The Honorable Henry Littleton and Miss Katherine Wenbrook, both of London, were joined in holy matrimony by the Rev. R. Wright at 8 o'clock Tuesday evening.  They begin their bridal tour in Paris before taking the Orient Express to the Near East.

"We had a lovely ceremony, darling," Henry said in his most charming voice. "Don't you remember, dear? The flowers, your dress, all our friends. And Mummy and Dads were so very happy for us."

Kate stared at Henry open-mouthed in horrified disbelief. Obviously, she was not taking this well. Henry decided that perhaps he should have approached the subject more seriously.

"My parents! My friends!" she wailed. "Two days ago! We got married two days ago? What will my parents think when they see this announcement? Married to you!"

"Our superiors concluded a honeymoon including Paris and the Orient Express would provide excellent cover for my mission," Henry continued a bit uncomfortably. He certainly hadn't thought he was that bad a catch. Kate seemed repulsed by the idea of being married to him. "Didn't they tell you?"

Obviously not, he thought as he watched the anger build in her eyes. They flashed like the sunlight glinting off of her auburn hair. Henry could tell Kate was not at all pleased with this new twist to their adventure. Hoping to generate a more comradely feeling between the two of them, he reached out to touch Kate's arm. He winced as she responded unfavorably and punched him in the chest. Despite his discomfort, he realized with surprise that he wouldn't mind holding and kissing Kate at all.

"Henry, what are you doing? No! Please! Don't! Leave me alone!" Kate all but shouted as she squirmed away from him. "I can't believe this is happening to me. In the space of an hour I have been shot at, chased, dragged, pushed, and pulled through the London underground, and finally accosted by a man I don't even know." Her voice rose higher as she listed her grievances. Kate pulled away from him and tugged at her clothing to straighten them.

Well, she had a point, thought Henry morosely. Obviously his attempts to convince her to take part in this assignment had met with little success so far. He could tell the events of the afternoon had begun to sink in. Under the circumstances, anyone would be nervous. Henry certainly was. She had seemed so unruffled, so cool and collected. He remembered how only the slight tremble of her hands as she fidgeted with her hat had betrayed any nervousness on her part. Henry had thought her a pro and pictured himself as the amateur. He was the one who worried that things would never stop spinning out of control. Now, he realized that his first impression of her might have been wrong. The vulnerable young woman he had glimpsed briefly at the theatre might be closer to the truth.

"Let's put our cover story aside for a moment and return to the job at hand," Henry stammered uneasily.

Next to him, Kate seethed quietly. This was not going at all well, Henry thought. Perhaps if he was more suave and debonair like the other men in his office, Kate would gladly play the role. Given her loud protestations, obviously, she did not find him at all attractive. Taking her silence as an opening, he tried again to convince her.

"On June 20th, dignitaries from several European nations will arrive in Belgrade for a meeting with the King. Originally, their visit was scheduled to begin on Tuesday, June 19th. The participants remembered that King Alexander is very superstitious about meetings on Tuesdays. And so he should be. Three family members died on Tuesdays."

Kate merely stared at him, so Henry soldiered on.

"Following the early Wednesday morning arrival of their train, opening ceremonies will take place in the square in front of the train station. After the speeches, a parade honoring the French Foreign Secretary, Louis Barthou, and the other representatives, will wind through the streets of Belgrade. On Thursday, the delegates plan to discuss their respective countries' responses to the Yugoslav-German Trade Agreement. We think the assassin will strike on either Wednesday or Thursday."

Kate continued to glare at him, hostility evident in the expression on her face. Henry noticed she was tapping her foot in an impatient gesture. Though her attention was still focused on their sham marriage, at least she had not stopped him.  Before she could protest, Henry decided to provide more details.

"Not content with the results of his April grand tour of Europe, which was designed to improve relationships with certain European countries, King Alexander has been strengthening political ties with the Germans.  On the first of this month, the King concluded a trade agreement with Germany.  The purpose of the agreement is to expand economic ties between Yugoslavia and Germany.  Naturally, this disturbs other European nations because it may mean that the Yugoslavs are seeking stronger ties with Germany in response to the Italian-Austrian-Hungarian rapprochement.  They see Yugoslavia's agreement with Germany as a serious breach in the earlier accord."

"Of course they would," Kate said caustically as if Henry had explained everything.

Failure stared him in the face.  His first espionage assignment and Henry was hanging on by his fingernails.  To his surprise, despite her crazy hat, Kate's presence steadied him and gave him confidence.  Suddenly, he knew Kate was vital to his future.  He needed her.  Yes, he needed her and he knew it.  He didn't want to go on without her.  Definitely not.

"Do come with me," Henry said.  "Please."  Even he could hear the note of pleading in his voice.

# Chapter 16

## Kate

*C*ome with him.

Kate fumed. He had a lot of nerve to stand there, mischief twinkling in his eyes, and say, come with him. Come with him! Her mind reeled as she tried to take it all in. It had been all right when thoughts of romancing Henry had all been in her imagination, but to pretend that they were married! How could she possibly cope? Married! Married to Henry! She's just met him! As a matter of fact, she hadn't even met him at the time she was supposed to be marrying him. What would everyone think of her when they saw the announcement in the *Times*? Her parents and friends didn't even know if she was seeing someone! Marriage to Henry would certainly come as a surprise to them to say the least.

Just wait until she got her hands on the person who concocted this brilliant plan. Kate really should pack up and leave this postcard. Everything Henry talked about really didn't pertain to her. The bullets aimed at them already proved that this scheme smacked of danger. And besides, the logistics of what Henry proposed took her breath away. London. Paris. Belgrade. The Orient Express. Balls. Receptions. Assassinations. Random thoughts tumbled through her head. How had she gotten into such a confusing situation? Kate could not blame it all on Henry or on the postcard. She had been foolish to answer the advertisement. She was the one who agreed to work for the SIS. She should have thrown that postcard away the moment it arrived. She should have never left her flat.

Another thought occurred to her. Kate nearly panicked when it dawned on her that though she had told people about her new job, she hadn't said anything specific. Right now, no one knew where she was. If anything did happen to her, her loved ones may never find out the truth. This realization appalled her. How could she have been so stupid? Despair flooded her as all these thoughts raced through her head. Kate stared blindly at the river's edge as it glided by. When Kate felt Henry take her hand in his, she looked up to see him watching her with a small smile playing on his lips. His hand felt so comforting over hers. Henry looked so boyishly happy she couldn't help but smile back. Deep inside her something grew warm. Was it her heart?

"I thought this job would be all about reports and filings, not running across Europe in pursuit of an assassin with a man I just met," Kate began weakly. When he did not answer, she continued to stare at the river bank, blinking back tears. "If I agree to this farce, what would my duties be?"

"Your role is to provide me with an excuse to move from London to Belgrade. As newlyweds, people won't suspect that I am really trying to find an assassin. Once our mission is over, we'll go our separate ways. Think about it. Paris, the Orient Express, Belgrade." Softly, Henry added, "we'll have the adventure of a lifetime."

"Henry, I'm not so sure I want to be involved in all this. The assignment. The Orient Express. Married. It's just a lot to absorb. We know so little about each other," her voice trailed off at the inadequacy of that statement. They knew nothing about each other, Kate thought ruefully.

"Now, that's an understatement if I ever heard one," Henry said laughing suddenly. "I daresay we shall find out a great deal about each other if we continue with our assignment."

Henry and Kate looked at each other for a long moment as the absurdity of their conversation sunk in. Simultaneously their amusement bubbled to the surface, great bursts of cleansing laughter. Every time their eyes met, a new fit of giggles consumed them. They laughed like small children do, freely and unselfconsciously. They laughed until their sides ached and tears streamed from their eyes. Their laughter released the strain that had been building. It worked like a healing balm to soothe their frayed nerves. More importantly, it forged a link between them as strong as steel. It gave them courage to face their future, together.

Once their laughter subsided, Kate noted Henry watching her, expectant, recognizing he needed her. For a moment, Kate hesitated, as if making a decision.

"Oh Henry," Kate began softly. "It's all so overwhelming. We don't even know who is following us. We will need clothing, money, and tickets."

"Think of it Kate! What an adventure we'll have! Paris! The Orient Express! Belgrade!"

"Paris. I've always wanted to see Paris," she said, longing evident in her voice.

"Who was it that said that every wife should insist on seeing Paris?" Henry teased.

"But…" Kate's protest never really got started. She couldn't help thinking that it would be wonderful to see Paris, experience a ball and a reception, travel on the Orient Express. She had asked for excitement, here was her chance.

"Cinderella, the embassy ball awaits you," Henry said, giving a little mock bow.

"You know I'll need a new hat," Kate said laughing, unable to help herself.

"Ah, yes. A new hat. I wonder if our superiors at SIS considered that little detail in their budget plans," Henry said with a broad grin.

# Chapter 17

## Henry

𝓗enry breathed a sigh of relief. Kate had agreed to come with him. His assignment was not doomed after all. Okay, so his future rested on the abilities of a woman who wore crazy hats, but at least now he had a chance.

"Let's see, today is Thursday, June 14th. We need to be in Belgrade no later than Tuesday to give us time to study the situation." Henry began planning out loud. "If all goes according to plan, tomorrow, June 15th, we'll pick up a briefcase containing everything we need. Money, passports, and travel permits for the two of us. I am sure our superiors will also have included further instructions."

"Where do we get the briefcase?"

"At the British Museum. We'll need to be there when it opens at ten o'clock."

"And then?"

"Then we'll pop over to Paris. The boat train, the Golden Arrow, leaves from Victoria Station at eleven o'clock. Barring any unforeseen delays, we should arrive in Paris via Calais in the late afternoon. The embassy ball is on the evening of Saturday, the 16th. I'll need to spend Saturday at the embassy gathering information while you prepare for our trip. We'll have Sunday to finalize our preparations. Late in the evening on the 17th, we'll board the Orient Express for the journey to Belgrade, arriving early on the morning of the 19th. That gives us a full day in Belgrade to figure out who is planning to do what and when. Easy!" Henry's broad smile creased his face. He really was much happier dealing with these sorts of details.

"Easy? Do you think it will be easy to get ready to leave while being chased around Piccadilly Circus by person or persons unknown? Really, Henry, don't you think this is a bit dicey? Not to mention that I haven't a single ball gown in my flat," Kate said, adopting a teasing, posh tone in her voice.

"There you go again, back to clothes and hats. Kate, you need to take this seriously."

"Serious. I need to be serious? You're the one without a plan. Besides, dressing the part is serious work."

"I wasn't expecting to be followed," said Henry, wincing at her well-aimed barb.

Kate merely rolled her eyes in silent reproach. In the strained atmosphere that followed, Henry considered his situation. Now that she had agreed to join him, he wondered again if Kate would really be effective as his colleague in this espionage adventure. She didn't seem to be taking their assignment seriously. That and the fact that they were being followed and shot at disturbed him greatly. Because he did not know the players, he was not quite sure how to get control of this situation. Besides, being near such an attractive woman was distracting. There was no time to consider all this right now. The boat approached the embankment pier signaling that their two idyllic hours of safety were over.

"I hope those men have not figured out where we are," Kate said, a note of fear creeping into her voice.

"Don't worry, I feel certain that it will be safe to return to your flat," Henry said reassuringly although he didn't actually feel very certain at all. "We have a lot to do this evening in order to get ready for our trip."

"Do you think either of us will be able to get a good night sleep? Given the events of the day, those two men with guns will haunt my dreams."

"I'm sure we'll be fine."

After disembarking, Kate and Henry walked toward the Embankment tube station.

"We should be able to pick up a cab to take back to your flat," he said. "From there I will go on to my own flat."

"Look, there are no cabs," Kate said, disappointed. "Not one single one."

"That leaves us with the underground system," Henry said. Seeing the look on her face, he added, "don't worry, the chances of our being followed to the Embankment were slim. We should be able to return to Piccadilly safely."

"Surely the two men wouldn't have waited over two hours for us at Piccadilly Circus. Would they?" she asked.

"No, of course not," Henry answered with confidence. "Even though Piccadilly is a busy place, loitering around for two hours would have certainly brought the attention of the local constable."

"But returning to Piccadilly is risky; those men know we were on the South Bakerloo line. Only four stops exist below Piccadilly Circus," Kate said her concern still evident.

"We have few options. We've got to get back to our flats. We'll just have to keep a wary eye out for trouble."

Just as they entered the Embankment station, Kate saw him, the man wearing the long grey overcoat.

"Henry! On the left!"

Her excited voice caused the man to turn his attention toward them. Quickly, Henry yanked her down the nearest corridor. Thankfully, because of his foresight, they were not delayed at the ticket counter. Once there, Henry shoved Kate onto the waiting District line train going west. As the doors closed, they could see the man squeeze into the last car. Unbelievable! Henry could not believe their bad luck. The man had followed them there. He saw the panic in Kate's face. Protectively, he wrapped his arm around her shoulder and pulled her to him.

"So the chase begins again," said Henry.

"Where can we go now?"

"Fortunately, movement from car to car isn't possible so we're safe for the time being."

"But, Henry, regardless of how cautious we are, the man will see us get off the train."

"Maybe not," he responded. "The cars are crowded with workers returning to their homes. They'll help hide our actions from him."

"What about the other man, the one in the black suit?"

"I don't know, darling. I just don't know," responded Henry as he pulled her closer.

For a few moments they stood quietly. Henry stroked Kate's back reassuringly. In his mind, he formed a vague plan of exiting at Hammersmith. From there they could mingle with the early evening going-home crowd. After making sure they had not been followed, he could return Kate to Allendale Club via the Piccadilly tube that shared the Hammersmith station with the District Line. They would plan to meet tomorrow in the entry hall of the British Museum.

"Let's get off at Hammersmith."

"Why there?"

"While we could transfer to the Piccadilly line earlier in our ride westward," said Henry, voicing his plans to Kate. "It would be best to allow a few stations to pass. The man in the long grey overcoat might think we have gotten off with the crowds at an earlier stop. The crush of people provides good cover for us all."

As they alighted at Hammersmith, both he and Kate saw their pursuer close by. Dismayed, Henry pulled Kate toward the only exit. Somehow they managed to squeeze through the crowds and gain some space between them and their pursuer. As they came out above ground, Henry quickly scanned the area for a feasible escape route. He pointed to a red bus about to depart for Hampton Court. They sprinted toward it, jumping onto it just as it moved off. Looking back they could see the frustrated face of the man in the long grey overcoat.

"Oh no, not a red bus," groaned Kate.

"What's wrong with a red bus?"

"Remember the postcard? It's a red bus that got me into this mess."

"You really do have a circus up there," said Henry, smiling at her comment in spite of the situation. He gently tapped her head before turning to read the posted bus route.

"Hampton Court gardens are lovely this time of year, though the chestnut trees will have finished flowering by this time. Would you like to try the Maze?" Henry said in a light-hearted voice that hid his concern for their safety. Mindful of the curious stares of their fellow passengers, Henry forced himself to relax. Swaying to the movement of the bus, Henry nonchalantly read from the guidebook:

*"No visit to London is complete without seeing Hampton Court, the elegant and stately palace built by Cardinal Wolsey. Upon its completion, the Cardinal presented the palace to Henry VIII under duress."*

"Ah, yes, King Henry VIII," said Kate, trying to appear equally unconcerned. "Didn't he build a battlemented bridge for Anne Boleyn? And, come to think of it, doesn't one of his other wives, Catherine Howard, I think, haunt the gallery?"

How disconcerting, Henry thought. Kate certainly seemed to be able follow his lead, no matter how fragile. Her ability to adapt to the circumstances reassured him.  He couldn't help wondering how they could be acting so normally under the circumstances.  In his mind, Henry continued to consider their options as the bus speed westward.

# Chapter 18

## Kate

*D*espite the fact that they had eluded their pursuer once again, Kate's stomach constricted in a tight knot as fear ran up her spine. What had Henry done to make them so interested in him? Based on the efforts being made to catch them, someone considered Henry a serious threat even though he had yet to leave London.

"Henry, what are we going to do now?"

"No doubt about it, my dear, these people certainly are persistent," Henry answered. "Hampton Court is as good a place as any to lose ourselves for a while. Then we'll try again to go back to our flats."

"I hope we will be able to travel back into London in a taxi. Our track record with the London underground system leaves a bit to be desired. Besides, my feet are sore from all the running we've done."

"A taxi or a red bus would work well," agreed Henry.

"You know my feelings about taking another red bus."

Henry rolled his eyes. A gesture not lost on her.

Though Kate had visited Hampton Court many times before, the massive and stately gate house never ceased to impress her. The Palace, so full of treasures and history, never failed to entertain her. For a shilling each they were able to enter the gardens. The gardens stayed open until dusk, which came late this time of year. The Palace, however, admitted its last visitors at 6 p.m. It was now nearly half past. Once inside the gardens, hidden among the lovely statues and stately plantings, she and Henry could revise their plans.

Mingling with the other visitors, Henry and Kate strolled along the white stone paths. The white paths contrasted with the low herbaceous borders and yew trees making the grounds appear like a white and green checkerboard. As they passed the Great Vine, planted in 1768, they discussed the possible routes for their return to their perspective flats. The guidebook provided a drawing of the garden paths and the Maze. As they neared the Maze, Kate spotted the man in the long grey overcoat.

"Oh no", Kate wailed as she pointed him out to Henry. "Quick, follow me into the Maze."

"We'll hardly improve our chances of escape by getting lost in the Maze!" Henry asked.

"Good grief Henry! Didn't they teach you about mazes in the Boy Guides?" she asked incredulously. "We won't get lost as long as we keep our right hand touching the hedge. Surely you know that the intricacies of all mazes can be tackled by holding one's hand on the right side of the hedge when going in, and on the left side of the hedge when coming out. Some master spy you are! If we're lucky, our pursuer doesn't know that little trick either. Come on, what are you waiting for?"

Kate disappeared into the maze. Henry could either fend for himself or follow her. While she knew about the trick with finding the way through a maze, it surprised her how difficult it was to run and keep a hand on the right side of the path at the same time. It didn't take long before they were deep in the maze. They could hear the man behind them thrashing around trying to find them or at least find spots in the thick hedge where he could peer through. After a lengthy series of left and right turns, breathlessly, they emerged on the other side. The man in the grey overcoat remained behind them trapped in the intricacies of the maze. They paused for a minute, unsure of where to go next.

"Quick, we'll hide in here," Henry said as he pointed to a small gardener's shed.

"A shed?" Kate asked incredulously. "Surely he will look for us here. It's standing right out here in the open. We'll be sitting ducks."

"Not if he behaves like a normal person. He'll ignore it because he won't expect us to have chosen such an obvious spot to hide. It's called hiding in plain sight," Henry added a bit smugly.

"I hope you're right," answered Kate doubtfully, as Henry pulled her along after him.

At least here in the darkness of the gardener's shed Kate could catch her breath. The events of the afternoon came flooding back to Kate, making her feel a bit dizzy. She up-ended a bucket and sat down hard. How could this be happening to her? She willed herself to breathe slowly and deeply. She prayed the man wouldn't look for them here. If she escaped from this shed alive, Kate decided she would quit regardless of how handsome Henry was or how hard he begged. She looked at the man opposite her as he watched out a small hole in the door. Could she even trust him? The few hours Kate had known him left her woefully short of confidence about her safety. Here in the dark shed, she wanted to scream with fear and frustration. She wanted to tell him, to tell anyone who could help her, the truth about how cornered and confused she felt. How could she have known what the future would hold when she answered the SIS ad? Kate had had no idea it would be like this.

Kate recalled her excitement the day of her interview. It seemed a lifetime ago. Had she really craved more thrills and adventure? She thought back to what the men had said during her interview. Something about being just right for a particular assignment they had in mind. They had not told her then what to expect. They merely assured her that her contact would fill in the details when they met. Now she knew they had left out quite a few important details, the least of which was that she was married to the man she now shared a shed with.

"He'll be sending you a postcard with details about when and where to meet," they said.

She grimaced ruefully when she remembered how excitedly she had waited for that postcard. She wondered how she could have ever been so naïve. She should have kept her job as a clerk, uninspiring as it was.

Sitting on the overturned bucket, Kate watched Henry and willed herself to be brave.

# Chapter 19

## Henry

*H*enry put his eye to a small knot hole and kept a lookout for their pursuer. As it grew dark, people began moving toward the exit. He told Kate he thought they should wait a bit longer. As the last visitors left the gardens, they would mingle among them. In the meantime, they needed to wait. Feeling securely hidden in the shed, Henry's courage returned.

"We're safe here for the moment."

"Do you really believe that?" asked Kate in a whisper.

"Yes, of course. Just take a look outside. No suspicious characters lurking anywhere," Henry said reassuringly. "By the way, that was a rather good idea you had, that dash through the Maze. Good thing you know a thing or two about mazes."

When Kate took over watching through the knot hole, Henry took time to study her. His first impression of her loveliness held true, but now he could see the strength of character in her face. Despite the conditions they now found themselves in, her anxiety showed itself only around her eyes. From where he stood, Kate's posture presented Henry with an excellent view of her trim ankles and shapely calves. He admired her curves beneath the purple fabric of her suit. It dawned on Henry that he was alone, locked in a shed, with a very pretty girl. Impulsively, Henry reached out to put his hands on her waist.

"Now would be a good time to practice being newlyweds," he murmured in her ear.

"Henry! Please! Don't! Leave me alone!" Kate said crossly as she elbowed him in the stomach. "What do you think you're doing? This is neither the time nor the place! How can I keep watch if you bother me?"

Even though he knew she was right, her words hurt him. Probably more than they should have, thought Henry. He knew he was handsome enough that most young women wouldn't mind his advances. Henry pushed his wounded feelings aside and concentrated on the task at hand. As he looked out a different knothole, Henry saw the man in the grey overcoat walk by again, still looking for them. He put his finger to his lips to signal to Kate. She stared at him, her eyes wide and round. They both breathed a sigh of relieve when the man walked away.

"Our pursuer isn't giving up on his search very easily," Henry said grimly. "At least we managed to leave the man in the black suit back at Piccadilly Circus."

A few minutes later, the man returned.

"I've got a feeling we will have to simply out-wait the man," Henry said with a sigh.

"How long?" asked Kate.

Henry glanced around the shed.

"Well, at least this shed is fairly clean and dry. In the corner there is some burlap sacking. This shelf holds some canvas cloth and thinner sheets. I assume they are used to wrap the plants during inclement weather. Fortunately, they are new and clean."

"Why are you talking about sheets and cloths?"

"Kate, I know it's not much, but we should be fairly comfortable if we need to bed down here for the night," Henry ventured quietly.

"Here! In a shed! All night?" Kate asked incredulously.

"Shh…Do you have any other suggestions? Or would you enjoy being presented face-to-face with our friend out there," Henry said, a bit miffed that she didn't immediately see the sense in his plan.

"Do you really think we must?" asked Kate forlornly.

"It would probably be for the better. See, here are some sheets and canvas to make, if not a comfortable bed, at least a cushion."

"Oh, all right. Thank heavens we had tea earlier, otherwise I would be quite hungry right now," said Kate.

Taking turns watching at the knothole, they set about making themselves more comfortable. The approaching Summer Solstice meant that the evening light lasted quite a long time. For a while, they both worked silently, each thinking their own thoughts. As darkness descended, Kate could no longer contain her curiosity about Henry.

"Henry, this is all new to you, isn't it?" Kate asked as she moved to stand closer to him.

"My first real assignment," he said, hesitant to admit it. "Yours too?"

He hoped it wasn't.

"As a matter of fact, this is my very first week working for SIS." Glancing around the shed, she asked, "Do you think our superiors believe we will succeed?"

"We have to wonder what they were thinking," Henry agreed with annoyance. "Why are they allowing two novices to play the big time?"

"Just how did you get picked for this assignment?" Her voice held a note of suspicion.

"I think the blame for that must be squarely placed on synthetic dyes."

"Synthetic dyes? Just what do synthetic dyes have to do with espionage?" she asked.

"It appears that you, like so many other people, think that espionage occurs only in the realm of politics. Before my transfer to my present position, I managed to connect all the dots and put an end to a rather nasty business of selling industrial synthetic dye secrets to foreign companies," said Henry, his voice sounding full of self-importance.

"How?"

"While reviewing performance and financial data for a company, I noted discrepancies between their earnings and the typical earnings expected in their industry," Henry said. In the dimming light he could see Kate's puzzled look. So he continued by adding an explanation.

"Typically, a chemical manufacturer will earn five to six percent net income on sales. The company I reviewed earned twelve percent—twice the usual amount. All their financial data supported this. They weren't hiding anything. They had paid their taxes. It was just odd that they were doing so much better than others in their field. I did a bit of checking around. Well, actually, a lot of checking around. My curiosity got the best of me," Henry said shyly. "I discovered that several of their key employees were paid rather large salaries given the current economic conditions. There were also discrepancies in a few of their amounts shipped. Nothing too dramatic, but it was enough to make me wonder if the numbers had been fiddled. To make a long story short, all the information when added together proved that a group of people in the firm were selling synthetic dye information to Germany. The result? Arrests, prison sentences, and no more lucrative under-handed deals."

"Well done," Kate said. "I'm impressed. Henry, you are obviously a man of many talents.

"It wasn't really anything. I'm not particularly clever, just attuned to details that seem out of place," Henry said modestly.

Kate let her eyes roam around the gloomy little shed. She giggled.

"And this is where all your hard work got you? Shot at and about to spend the night in a garden shed."

Henry was far from pleased with his predicament.

"Well, yes. It does look a bit like my promotion has worked against me, doesn't it?"

Nearby, heavy footsteps crunched on the gravel path. They both held their breath. Henry cautiously moved to put his eye to the knot hole. "Night watchman," he mouthed to Kate as the man moved past. "It's late. You've had an exhausting day. Why don't you try to get some rest?"

As dawn broke the next morning, they struggled to tidy up both the shed and themselves. Henry put on a cheerful face. Eventually, they decided they could mingle with the few early morning visitors and make their way to the exit. The man in the grey overcoat was nowhere to be seen when they crept out of their temporary hiding place.

"Wait," Henry said. He lifted her hat gently off her head and proceeded to remove the now badly damaged feather.

"There, that's better."

"I did so love that feather," Kate said forlornly.

"At least now it won't be bobbing around signaling our position to all and sundry." Noting the bleak look on her face, Henry added, "Come with me, my dear. I know just the thing to cheer you up."

Their plan worked well until they were just outside the gatehouse. There, they found themselves alone on the street. As Henry walked past a small passageway between two buildings, a large hand reached out and grabbed him about the neck. Caught off guard, Henry managed raise his arm in time to ward off what could have been a crippling blow to his head. His tormentor's carefully aimed blows meant to incapacitate Henry—perhaps injure him permanently. As he fought the man with all the skill and fury he possessed, Henry saw Kate out of the corner of his eye. Why hadn't she run to safety or to get help? His eyes opened wide when he saw Kate pick up a round "No admittance" sign.

# Chapter 20

## Kate

$\mathcal{D}$uring the attack on Henry, a jumble of thoughts ran through Kate's mind at the same time. First and foremost, she should never, never, have agreed to work for the SIS. When she answered the advertisement, Kate assumed her work with the department would be confined to ferrying documents across London and other innocuous duties. She had never imagined anything like this! Given her creative imagination, this was saying a lot about how she felt right now. Kate had been shot at, pursued, spent the night in a shed, and now someone was attacking Henry. Her second most prominent thought was that this brute intended to seriously hurt her Henry. Her Henry? That thought spurred her to action. Impulsively, Kate grabbed the nearest weapon, a round 'No Admittance' sign on a short pole. Grasping it tightly with both hands, she swung it at the man's head with all her might. The force of the blow made her teeth rattle. The man let out an audible grunt and collapsed on the ground. Her hands stinging, she dropped the sign with a clatter.

Henry shook himself off, grinning broadly. Much to Kate's surprise, he picked her up and swung her around.

"Good show, my beauty," Henry crowed, delighted over his narrow escape. Putting Kate down gently, Henry turned his attention to the prostrate man in the grey overcoat. He pulled the man into an opening between two buildings.

Kate positively glowed with pleasure when Henry said that. She felt a bit disappointed when Henry set her down, as if he had taken away a vital source of warmth from her being. Being in his arms had been magical. She had never wanted that feeling to end. Kate hid her disappointment that the gesture had obviously not meant anything personal to Henry. He was already going through the man's pockets. She looked over his shoulder to see what he had found. Henry handed her a small satchel. She could tell by the supple leather that it was expensive. Kate unzipped the zipper that extended around three sides and discovered that it was stuffed with large packets of bank-notes from several different countries.

"Henry, there must be the equivalent of thousands of pounds in here," Kate exclaimed, breathless with wonder. She fingered the bound stacks of bills. "I've never seen so much money in one place before."

Despite the need to hurry, Kate began to count the bills as if mesmerized by their sheer number.

"If you can, try to ignore the cash right now. See if the satchel contains any information on who he is," Henry said dryly.

"I'm sorry. You are so right. We don't want anyone to see us do we?" Kate asked chastened.

"You are so right, love. That could get us into quite a lot of trouble. Remember, we have a train to catch this morning. We have to work fast; we don't want him waking up while we're still here. I'll go through his other pockets."

The satchel yielded little else useful. She found an underground pass similar to theirs, a small map of the underground system, a ticket to Hampton Court, and a few scraps of paper. She placed those in her pocket and zipped up the money in the satchel. Turning to Henry, she asked what he had found.

"Nothing. Just some loose change, a few spare bullets, and this," he told her. He showed her a pistol briefly before putting it in his pocket.

"What are you going to do with that?" Kate cried in alarm.

"Deposit it somewhere where it won't be found easily," he answered. "Let's get out of here." Henry got to his feet and dusted the worst of the dust off his clothes. He retrieved his battered Homburg and checked to see that the coast was clear. Fortunately, the Friday morning streets were quiet.

"Near the underground station, we'll find a taxi to take us back into London," Kate said.

As they neared the station, Kate noted that Henry used his handkerchief to wipe the gun clean of his fingerprints and tossed it in a construction dumpster. His swift moment went undetected by anyone nearby.

In the taxi, on their way to the British Museum, Kate found it comforting to be next to him. She looked up at Henry. He gazed confidently back at her and put his arm around her.

"Come along old girl. Like I said earlier, I know just the thing to cheer you up. We'll go round to a nice pub and have a good breakfast while we wait for the museum to open. What do you say to that?" Henry said as he directed the driver to a pub.

After they exited the cab, Henry reached over and straightened her hat. As he winked at her, Henry's seemingly endless supply of good humor lifted Kate's flagging spirits.

# Chapter 21

## Henry

*W*hile waiting for their food to arrive, Henry took a good look at his suit, inspecting the tears resulting from his earlier fight. Shaking his head, he voiced his thoughts.

"It's too bad that we weren't able to do much more than tidy up a bit in the shed and here at the restaurant. We don't look like we have slept particularly well either."

"So, here we are, a bit rumpled, getting ready to go to the British Museum." Kate sighed over the condition of her clothes and hat.

"It will hardly do to travel on the Orient Express looking like this, will it? Hopefully, Paris will be a bit calmer and allow us time to recover."

"Henry, what about the money we found?" asked Kate, her hand resting on the satchel.

"We'll turn it in when we have time," he answered.

"Given our tight schedule, that won't be for a while," Kate said. "In the meantime, I'll put it to good use to outfit us for our assignment."

"I don't know if you should do that, though, I have to admit you've earned it, saving my life like that. Amazing how you swung that sign. He never knew what hit him."

"Do you think so? It was the only thing I could think to do at the time."

Henry could not help smiling at the flushed expression on her face.

"Perhaps it wouldn't be a bad idea to use some of the money to finance your clothing needs for this trip," he said. "You can return the remainder at the end of our assignment. Besides, you're right, we haven't really got time to deal with it right now. SIS has left us a briefcase at the British Museum, which has some money, but we can't be sure how much we will have. I seriously doubt they included enough for the ball gowns, hats, shoes, and gloves you seem to feel you need."

"Henry, we've been through this before. It simply wouldn't do to travel without the right clothes. You'll just have to explain about the money later," Kate said with finality.

Giving up the clothing argument as a lost cause, Henry focused on their next moves.

"We have a little time before the doors open. Let's see what the guidebook says about the museum, shall we?" Kate said as she began reading. *"Begun in 1753 with the library and collection of Sir Hans Sloane, it had continued to add wings and treasures ever since."*

"If I remember correctly, it has an extensive Egyptian collection."

"Henry, the British Museum is enormous. The entrance hall alone is cavernous," Kate said as she studied the plan of the museum she found in the guidebook. "How will you ever find the briefcase?"

"Darling, it will be at the coat check station," he answered.

"Oh, yes, of course. Silly me," Kate stammered.

"Of course, after picking up the briefcase, I don't plan to linger. We have an eleven o'clock train to catch and the museum doesn't open until ten."

"That doesn't give us a whole lot of time to spare, does it? It's going to be horrible travelling in these clothes. Just look at us."

Later at the museum, their appearance attracted the disapproval of the ticket seller. The man noted their tired faces, Henry's unshaven jaw, and their disheveled clothing with a sniff of disdain. Henry and Kate chose to ignore him. Once they had their tickets, Henry left Kate at the visitor's information desk perusing a guide to the museum. The line at the coat check station was mercifully short so he was able to retrieve the briefcase quickly. As Henry turned to join Kate, out of the corner of his eye, he saw the man in the black suit. Henry nearly dropped the briefcase in surprise. How had the man come to be here? They hadn't seen him since the day before at Piccadilly Circus. Only bad timing had allowed the man in the grey overcoat to find them late yesterday. Had the man known that Henry and Kate were coming here? How could he have access to information Henry had been told only two days before? There was something going on here, but Henry could not take time to think it through.

Instead, Henry covered the space between the coat check station and the information desk and Kate in record time. Casually, so as not to upset her, he draped his arm around her, turning her slightly so the man in the black suit would be in her line of vision.

"Did you happen to notice an alternative exit to the building?" he asked calmly.

"Oh, no, not again! What is it with you Henry? Are you a magnet for trouble?" she whispered, her eyes wide with alarm.

"Me? A magnet for trouble? You can't honestly believe I wave a red flag in order to attract these people, do you? I'm not any happier about the circumstances than you are."

Henry stopped speaking as he noticed that Kate had gone surprisingly pale. He gripped her arm more tightly to support her. He eyed the man in the black suit who had not seen them yet.

"Off we go, my dear. You've had a few moments to study the map. Which direction do you suggest?" Henry said with feigned casualness.

"We need to go to the left, through the Roman Gallery. No Henry, not straight ahead, that's a dead-end leading to the Reading Room. We'd be trapped in the hall. Besides, we don't have a pass that allows us into the room."

Kate tugged at his sleeve.

"This way. The Roman Gallery leads to Greco-Roman rooms. From there we can turn into the Archaic room which leads to the long galleries along the outside wall. There is sure to be an exit there."

"If we're quick, we can even take a peek at the Elgin Marbles," he quipped, trying to help her regain her equilibrium. Obviously she was shocked at seeing their hunter again.

"It amazes me how you manage to keep your sense of humor in times like these," said Kate.

"And, you, my sweet, are turning out to be a more delightful companion than I ever could have ever imagined."

They walked purposefully toward the Roman Gallery. Unfortunately, their movement attracted the attention of the man in the black suit. Pushing from behind, Henry literally propelled Kate past the marvelous sculptures, considered to be among the most beautiful in the world. By the time they reached the Elgin Room with the famous Elgin Marbles that used to grace the Parthenon in Athens, Henry knew the chase was on. Kate, having studied the museum plan, swerved them toward an opening in the center of the room. From there she turned them right, away from the Mausoleum Room. That was fine by him. Henry definitely wasn't in the mood to contemplate mausoleums. As they ran down the narrow corridor, Henry caught a glimpse of the Rosetta stone in the Egyptian Galleries. At this point, Henry realized Kate was taking them in a circle. After traversing several small rooms and turning left, they were back in the Entrance Hall. This time the hall was packed with school children come to explore the wonders of the British Museum. He and Kate plunged into the throng moments before the children began to funnel through the small opening they had just exited. The sheer number of children served to block the passage of the man in the black suit. Henry whisked Kate outside and into the nearest taxi.

"Victoria Station and hurry, if you please. We've a train to catch."

Turning to Kate, Henry noticed she was shaking. She had pulled herself into the farthest corner of the cab looking warily about her. Henry felt an incredible wave of protectiveness wash over him. He knew that he would protect her with his life if necessary. In one swift movement, he gathered Kate into his arms.

"Thank you ever so much for the whirlwind tour of the finest objects the British Museum has to offer, darling," Henry said, smiling reassuringly into her eyes. He was inordinately pleased when a small laugh escaped her involuntarily. He noted, too, that she did not pull away from him. Unlike before, this time she rested lightly in his arms. Henry sensed Kate's anxiety draining away.

The taxi deposited them at the entrance to Victoria Station. The enormous building left no doubt that the station positively defined itself as the gateway to the world. As they entered through the huge doors, Henry paused.

"Wasn't it E.M. Forrester who said that '*railway stations are one's gates to the glorious and the unknown*'?" he asked. "Here we are, dear, at our own gates to the glorious and the unknown."

Kate rewarded him with a wan smile.

A bustle of activity accompanied the arrivals and departures of luxury trains. Henry watched as Kate's head seemed to turn in every direction at once as she tried in vain to take it all in. The whistling, hissing, banging, and scurrying combined to make them feel as if the station was the grandest in the world. They could smell the coal and hear the hissing of the engines. Outside the fashionably decorated and sophisticated waiting room, Henry noticed Kate looking at her own clothing with dismay. Unhappily, not much could be done to enable her to fit in with the elegantly dressed people waiting for the boat train to be called. He reached out and took her by the elbow.

"Well, my dear. At least we don't have any luggage to cope with," Henry said lightly.

The briefcase yielded up two tickets for the Golden Arrow, the boat-train to Paris. Knowing they needed to hurry, Henry guided them toward the train. He wouldn't feel safe from the man in the black suit until they were well on their way to the Channel. Boarding had already commenced. As they passed a news shop, Kate, much to Henry's displeasure, insisted on selecting a number of magazines and guidebooks before she allowed herself to be put on the train. She argued that they had to create some sort of impression of being travellers. If they couldn't change their clothes, the least they could do was read a guidebook of Paris. Henry viewed it as another example of her impulsiveness. When Kate emerged from the small shop, out of the crowd came the man in the black suit. So he knew about their planned departure too, thought Henry in dismay.

The man in the black suit grabbed Kate roughly from behind causing her to cry out in alarm. When she dropped her purchases, the resulting clatter had two effects. First, it drew the attention of everyone nearby, including an officer of the law. And, second, it distracted the man in the black suit long enough for Henry to plant a well-deserved punch on his nose. Blood spurted everywhere as the man reeled backward.

"Help, this man tried to steal my wife's purse!" Henry shouted to the constable. In the resulting confusion, Henry pulled Kate onto the departing train. He noted with approval that she had had the presence of mind to retrieve her purchases.

"Where did you learn to hit like that?" Kate exclaimed.

"Boxing, at Oxford. Though it seems like a long time ago, I am pleased I haven't lost my skill."

As they boarded their car, Henry studied the scene at the entrance to the platform and was grateful to see that the man in the black suit had been detained by the police. He would have to think more carefully about the ramifications of the man's appearance. It pointed to a leak somewhere in the SIS. A chill ran through him and Henry vowed to be careful, more careful than ever, when he met his counterparts in France.

They had barely enough time to find their seats before the train began to move. Once the train left the station, Henry felt the tension slowly leave his body. After resting a moment, he turned his attention to Kate. He noticed she was shaking despite trying to appear calm for the benefit of the other passengers. Henry tried to distract her, and appear nonchalant himself, by talking about the Orient Express.

"Did you know that the Orient Express was the brain-child of the Belgian engineer, Georges Nagelmackers?"

"Nagelmackers. Zorka. Henry, where do you get these names?"

Ignoring her comment, Henry continued.

"It was Georges, who, after admiring the pioneering work of George Pullman in the United States, developed the Wagon-Lits service to the Far East. Touted as the *Magic Carpet to the East*, the Orient Express made its first run in 1883."

"That long ago?"

"The train runs at least bi-weekly from Paris, with a connecting service on the Golden Arrow to London. During the Roaring 20s, it ran four times a week. The train reduces travel time to Istanbul from many weeks down to just three days, making it a very popular choice for travellers to and from the Near East."

"You're beginning to sound like a travel agent."

"I would think that you would be interested in our route," snapped Henry.

"All right, don't get upset. Go on."

Somewhat mollified, Henry picked up where he left off.

"There are actually three parallel lines running: the Orient Express, the Simplon Orient Express, and the Arlberg Orient Express. Each takes a slightly different route through Europe, although, due to the mountains, all eventually join and use the same route through Yugoslavia. The original Orient Express line runs through Germany, Austria, and Hungary on its way to Istanbul. It takes about 60 hours to make the 1,881 mile journey. The Simplon Orient Express is *Wagon-Lits* southern-most route to the east. Created following World War I, it is named for the Simplon tunnel linking Switzerland and Italy. There is also the Arlberg Orient Express which runs via Zurich and Innsbruck on its way to Budapest, where people can choose to go on to either Bucharest or Athens."

"Which one will we be taking?" asked Kate.

"Today, we will take this train to the English Channel. There we will board the *Canterbury*, a vessel set aside specifically for passengers of the Orient Express to make the channel crossing. Once across the channel, we will board the Golden Arrow, or as the French would say, *Le Fleche d'Or*, and proceed from Calais to Paris. We'll be in Paris until Sunday."

"And after that?"

"After that, we will take the Simplon Orient Express to Belgrade."

"Why the Simplon Orient Express?"

"The Simplon route allows passengers to travel to Istanbul without traversing Germany and Austria. We don't want to attract attention to ourselves by travelling through Germany. It wouldn't do our mission any good to be detained along our route.  Our train, which departs on Sunday evening, will probably have four sleeper cars and one luggage van."

"Is that the usual make up of an Orient Express train?"

"Since the very beginning, on a typical run, a train consists of four carriages providing over 40 beds, a dining car, bar, and other services befitting the most luxurious train of its kind.  Of course, the number of luggage cars varies depending on passenger needs.  As an interesting side note, the luggage cars are designed so that the luggage can be easily inspected by Customs officers at each frontier crossing."

As they left London far behind, Henry could hardly contain his excitement.  The Orient Express captured his imagination.  While he had a job to do, he looked forward to travelling on the most comfortable and luxurious train available.  The restaurant cars were well-known for the quality of their cuisine.

"Kate, the Orient Express caters to the well-heeled traveller.  You need to be prepared to mix with royalty, nobles, diplomats, and successful business people.

"Spies, too?"

# Chapter 22

## Kate

*R*oyalty, nobles, diplomats, business people, and spies! Honestly, Kate thought, men have no concept of the effort it takes to blend in.

"Henry, here we are, aboard one of the most luxurious trains in the world looking like we have slept in our clothes," she protested.

"Well, my dear, it's not as if we haven't," he answered back, concentrating on the contents of the open briefcase on his lap.

"It all seems like a dream, a very bad dream."

"Relax, dear, we're safe now. We mustn't attract any more attention to ourselves, especially after that little display outside the news shop," Henry cautioned.

What was Henry thinking? It was suspicious enough that they had no luggage besides his briefcase. Her small purse bulged with the bank notes they had taken off the man in the long grey overcoat. At least the few magazines and guidebooks she bought would give the impression, weak though it was, of their being tourists. They needed to work on their cover as newlyweds as well. They certainly did not act the way a recently married young couple would. They would have to change that if they were going to fool anyone. Kate grew annoyed at their limited skills in the espionage game.

"Do be a dear, Henry darling, and tell me what you think we should visit while in Paris," Kate said as she shoved a guidebook under Henry's nose.

As he scanned the pages of the guidebook, Kate pondered her own plans for Paris. After all, this was her first trip to Paris. She had always dreamed of going to Paris. Of course, she never thought she would be visiting Paris under such trying circumstances. Kate was not going to allow some evil looking characters to spoil it for her. She had to admit that the Paris of her dreams would have a hard time competing with the reality of their current situation. Kate fervently hoped there would be no more unfortunate incidents involving men with guns. She could hardly expect Henry or the men at SIS to understand her true plans for Paris. They were, after all, men. Fashion meant little to them. Kate vowed she would hold on to at least part of her Paris fantasy.

Kate listened while Henry planned a guided tour of important sights for Saturday. Statues, museums, and buildings were all fine well and good, but Kate knew what she was going to do in Paris. Chanel. Saturday she was going to make a bee-line directly for Chanel. Though she had only counted a few of the bank notes, they came to a fortune, an absolute fortune. She'd be able to outfit herself head to toe for this trip and still have a pile of French Francs left over. She wouldn't even have to touch the piles of cash in other denominations.

Kate knew from Henry's timetable that they wouldn't be arriving in Paris until this early evening. There would still be enough light for them to stroll around the city before having supper. One dined so late on the continent. Paris, the City of Lights, City of Love. With Henry. Where did he fit into her fantasy of Paris? Kate allowed her imagination to take flight, picturing them strolling arm in arm along the banks of the Seine. *Notre Dame*, the *Pont Neuf*, *L'Ile de Saint Louis*, the *Louvre*, the *Place de la Carousel*, Paris presented a lovely backdrop for romance. Kate hoped there would be a gorgeous sunset that they could watch from the *quai* behind *Notre Dame*. She pictured the majestic cathedral backlit by the sun.

Kate studied Henry. Already she found herself familiar with his face. She liked what she saw, from the strong line of his jaw to the arched curve of his cheekbones. When he smiled, his eyes crinkled pleasingly at the edges. Despite his young age, the faint laugh lines around his eyes and mouth revealed his sense of humor. Not that there had been much humorous about the past 24 hours. Poor dear, he looked so tired. And his suit—even though he had given it a good going over with a damp cloth to remove the dust that morning in the restaurant's washroom—still looked as tired as he did. Would Henry even have the energy for a romantic evening walk around Paris? Would there be men with hard faces full of menace following them there?

Henry's sneeze brought her back to the present with a thump. Honestly, she chided herself. She should not be wasting her time daydreaming about a romance with a man who hardly even noticed her except to push or pull her from one chase scene to another. With a shake of her head, she switched her focus to practical matters. Romancing in two day-old clothing didn't fit the picture her imagination had conjured up.

"What are you thinking about?" Henry asked as he studied her face.

Not wanting to divulge her thoughts, Kate focused on the cover of the *Vogue* magazine she held in her lap.

"Paris fashions," she answered. "It's a good thing the man with the long grey coat is financing my stay in Paris."

"You're not planning to drag me from couture house to couture house, are you?" he inquired, a twinge of horror in his voice.

Obviously Henry would rather be shot at than shop for women's clothing.

"No, silly. I realize that your time in Paris will be spent at the embassy gathering information," Kate reassured him. "How long will it take us to reach the Channel?"

"It takes just over an hour and a half for the train ride to the coast. The Southern Railway's Golden Arrow is one of the fastest in the world. Once we reach Dover, we'll embark on the steamer *Canterbury* for the 90 minute crossing to Calais. There, we will board the continuation of the Golden Arrow, or the *Fleche D'Or* as it is called in France, of the *Chemin de Fer Nord* for the two and a half hour ride to Paris." Henry paused to reflect a moment before continuing.

"Personally, I plan to spend my travel time thinking carefully about the events of the past 24 hours. There are a lot of questions to answer. Who had shot at us and why? Who are the players? What do they want? I need to size up the other side. I also need to keep my eyes open for unwanted companions on our trip to Paris. The train ride will give me time to organize my thoughts and prepare for what's to come and what we can expect."

As the Lord Nelson class locomotive pulled the ten British Pullman cars on their journey to the channel, Kate wondered again how they would spend their first evening in Paris. They would arrive too late to report at the embassy. Provided no one was chasing them, the evening would be theirs, probably the only quiet time for the next few days. Kate envisioned the two of them together in an out of the way bistro on the Left Bank. Based on his next words, Henry must have read her mind.

Glancing again at the *Vogue* in her lap, he said, "I suppose you would be happier window shopping than dining with me on our first night in Paris. You might be disappointed to know that unlike the model in the sand on the June cover, our journey won't include a stop at the beach."

"Would you care for a glass of champagne?" inquired the steward. His voice caused both of them to jump.

"I am sorry I have disturbed you," the man apologized.

"No, no. It's quite all right," responded Henry. "Two glasses of champagne would be very nice. Thank you."

Taking a glass and handing it to Kate, Henry raised his glass to her in a toast.

"To our adventure."

They travelled in silence for a while. Kate admired the interior of the umber and cream-colored railway car. Sitting back, sipping a glass of champagne, she finally began to relax. When the stewards appeared with the luncheon menus, she realized how hungry she was.

"May I suggest the *Brochet a L'Esurgeon*?" asked the waiter. "This appetizer combines herbs and caviar wrapped in a delicate puff pastry."

"Sounds delightful," said Kate. I think I will follow that with *Boudin a la Richeieu* and *Cerise Coiffee*."

"Yes, Madame. An excellent choice. Beef accompanied by a side dish of baked cherries."

I will have the *Potage a la Royale* and *La Poule au Pot D'Henri IV*, soup and chicken casserole," said Henry.

"Perhaps for dessert, you would enjoy the *Torte aux Poireaux*," suggested the waiter.

During lunch, Kate studied the intricate carving and *marquetry* adorning the interior of the car. Everything had been polished to perfection; the brass, the veneers of boxwood, rosewood, and walnut shone beautifully. She enjoyed being surrounded by such perfection following the events of the last two days. It made for quite a step up from a gardener's shed.

When they boarded the steamer to cross the Channel, she and Henry stayed on deck a moment. They had the deck to themselves and both of them savored the peace and quiet. The absence of human voices and potential threats gave them time to repair their tired spirits. After they could no longer see the white cliffs of Dover, they went into the salon.

Later, on the train, having passed through the complications of customs, Kate couldn't get Henry to make more than light conversation. How frustrating.

"Henry, I need to know, preferably in detail, what lies ahead."

"Why?" Henry asked, looking up from the papers he was studying.

"If a girl is going to get chased across a continent, she has to know what to wear."

Henry snorted. She could not believe her ears. He actually snorted.

"How am I supposed to take that?"

His head buried in his paper, he acted as if he had not heard her at all. Great, she thought, now he was ignoring her. All she was trying to do was to help him with his mission and he snorted at her. Fine, she would just concentrate on the fashions in her *Vogue* magazine and plan her shopping strategy for tomorrow. Unfortunately, this particular *Vogue* was for the United Kingdom market. She knew the clothes shown were selected because of their appropriate "Englishness". Kate hoped to find clothing of a much more daring sort in Paris. She would need to visit *Printemps* and *Galeries Lafayette* for the essentials. She'd need daywear and evening wear, with shoes, purses, and hats to match. Kate certainly couldn't miss the lingerie shops. The French made such lacy, frivolous lingerie; it would be such a shame not to invest in some. A nightgown, she'd need the perfect nightgown for nights spent on a train as romantic as the Orient Express. Oh, and don't forget perfume. She couldn't resist planning a visit to *Guerlain Parfumerie* on the *Champs Elysee*. Based on her calculations, the man in the long grey coat's largess would stretch to all that and beyond.

"Henry," Kate said as she tried again to draw him into conversation. "Tell me more about the Orient Express."

Apparently, she had finally chosen the right topic because Henry perked right up.

"I should familiarize you with the route and layout of the train," he began. "As I said earlier, we'll be taking the Simplon Orient Express. This more southerly route via Milan, Venice, and Trieste opened in 1919 and utilizes the Simplon Tunnel. This route is preferred by travellers wishing to avoid Germany and Austria. After our brief stay in Paris, we will board the train at 10:30 Sunday evening."

"At night?"

"Yes, we'll sleep through the night as the train will make brief stops at Dijon, Dole, and Mouchard before leaving France by crossing the border just past the village of Frasne."

"What about customs?"

"The porter will have our papers, so we won't be disturbed by the customs officials. The baggage car provides easy access to all but our hand luggage, so inspections can take place there. The inspectors board the train in Frasne, perform their duties, and depart in Vevey, Switzerland. There, they will board a westbound train and repeat the process in the opposite direction."

"Imagine spending your whole life on the job travelling from one country to another, never going farther than the first train stop," Kate said laughing. "How does the train weave its way across Switzerland?"

"Following Vevey, while in Switzerland, we will stop at Montreux, Martigny, Soin, and Brig, before passing through the Simplon Tunnel and entering Italy. Our Italian stops include Domodossola, Stresa, Milan, and Venice. While the stop in Venice is a bit longer than other stops, we'll soon be on our way to Trieste, Zagreb, and finally our destination, Belgrade."

"How long does our trip take?"

"We'll have two full nights on the train, beginning on Sunday evening. We arrive in Belgrade around 7:15 in the morning of the 19th."

"The diplomats arrive on the 20th, right?"

"Yes, that gives us just twenty-four hours to find and neutralize anyone planning to assassinate King Alexander."

"Do you think we'll find him?"

"Perhaps, I don't know. I had hoped these papers would provide more clues." Henry rustled through the papers in his lap. "The most interesting piece of information they provide is a layout of the train."

"Tell me about it."

"The layout of the train is fairly straightforward. Our train consists of four sleeping coaches, a restaurant car, and two baggage cars. Of course, we are pulled by a steam powered engine. The layout of the LX- and S-class sleeping cars is similar. I don't know which our train will have. LX-class cars are newer and much more luxurious. The most notable difference is the types of woods used and the highly carved, ornately styled furnishings. The sleeping cars have a long windowed corridor on one side of the car which provides access to the 10 wood-paneled compartments. Each compartment accommodates either one bed or two and a washbasin. Our cabin has two berths, one on top of each other."

"Our cabin?"

"We're on our honeymoon, remember?"

"I hadn't really thought about it."

"Since we are sharing a cabin, think about which berth you would prefer. During the day, the beds fold up and the compartment becomes a compact sitting room with a sofa and small table. We'll be able to enjoy the view out the window. At night, a thick curtain will keep the compartment dark. The toilets are at the end of the hall."

"Surely we won't spend all our time in our cabin," Kate said, her discomfort visible on her face.

"Activities on the train are naturally somewhat limited, however, you can expect to spend a significant amount of time in the dining car," Henry said brightly, reading a travel brochure. "Rene Lalique designed the interior decorations for the dining car on this particular train. The center of the car is an open plan with tables for groups of two or four. Expect meals as delightful as any experience in a fine restaurant. Besides the excellent food and perfect service, we will dine on white linen tablecloths, fine china, and silver. The plush atmosphere provides the perfect backdrop for sophisticated men and women in evening dress at dinner."

When Henry paused briefly, Kate looked over at him.

"I am sure you will enjoy finding just the right Parisian gown and hat to match your surroundings," Henry said laughing.

Honestly, thought Kate, Henry could be infuriating at times. He seemed to enjoy taking jabs at her love of clothing, especially hats. If she was truthful with herself, she would have to admit that she did not mind as much as she thought she would. Still, she would show him she could give as good as she got.

"Henry, you certainly seem to have an endless supply of trivial details about our journey. If only you knew that much about whom we are after."

"*Touché*, my dear. It's time to get ready. We're nearing Paris."

For Kate, the Paris she dreamed of was about to become a reality. She sighed.

"Is everything all right?" Henry asked. "Are you feeling well?"

"Oh, I'm all right. It's been peaceful on the train, that's all," she said quietly.

"I've not taken very good care of you so far, have I?"

"Well," Kate answered kindly, "you can't judge a journey of thousands of miles by its starting point."

"I remember reading somewhere a Chinese proverb that said something to the effect that a journey begins with a single step."

"We've taken our single step into the unknown, haven't we?"

# Chapter 23

## Henry

*H*enry awoke on Saturday morning with a start. His memories of the previous evening came rushing back. He had had fun—an odd unexpected turn of events given that this was an assignment of some importance. After stopping briefly at the hotel, they had decided to take a walk around Paris before dining. Henry smiled as he remembered walking along the *quais* of the Seine with Kate. On the *Pont Neuf*, they had paused to watch the boats on the Seine.

"Henry!" Kate exclaimed as she looked all around her. "Just look at the view! Did you know that the *Pont Neuf* is actually two bridges that straddle both branches of the Seine as they flow around the island? Can you believe we're standing on a bridge that was built in 1603? Did you know that King Henri IV was the first person to cross it? It's the oldest bridge in Paris and the first to be built without houses on it."

"We should put such a lovely setting to good use." Henry murmured softly in her ear. He put his arms around her and pulled her to him.

"Henry. Please! Don't! Leave me alone," Kate said as she wiggled out of his arms. Her discomfort made evident by the blush staining her cheeks.

"Duty calls, my dear," said Henry, refusing to let go. "After all, our cover is that we are newlyweds honeymooning in Paris. In the most romantic city in the world, it attracts attention when you move away whenever I put my arms around you. You shouldn't turn your head if I try to kiss you."

Henry reprimanded her in a mock serious tone. Kate looked not the least bit pleased to have to consider him in a romantic way. What was there not to like about him? Henry watched her face as Kate considered the implications of what he said. He watched frustration mingled with desire cross her face. The thought that she might find him attractive pleased him very much.

"All right," Kate said tersely. "Just give me some time to get comfortable with the idea. Why don't you tell me about the architecture of these buildings?"

Annoyed that she hadn't allowed him to kiss her, Henry decided to bore her with details.

"Baron Haussmann redesigned the Paris skyline during the reign of Napoleon III. Did you notice how the buildings all seem symmetrical at first glance? It is only when you study their grey rooflines that you realize that there is a lack of proportion that creates perfect harmony. Looking at them just now, I don't think a single roof, chimney, or fanlight, exactly resembles another," Henry said as he scanned the rooftops.

"It's too beautiful to be concerned about roof lines. If it is all the same to you, I would prefer not to talk about Baron Haussmann's redesign of Paris," she said, rethinking her request. "Wouldn't you much rather just breathe in the sights?"

Still smarting from her rejection, reluctantly, Henry discontinued his discussion of Haussmann's Paris.

They wandered aimlessly along the *Quai de l'Horloge* on their way to *Notre Dame*. The magnificent gothic cathedral rose high above them, its face glowing a warm gold in the setting sun. From there, they followed the *Rue du Cloitre Notre Dame* alongside the cathedral, a route which allowed them to see the flying buttresses and the rose windows.

"I think of *Notre Dame* as the soul of Paris. Can you imagine what this cathedral has witnessed since it was built in 1100? So many human lives, so much history, so much love, so much pain. Centuries of births, loves, marriages, deaths, soaked into its very stones," said Kate with awe in her voice.

"Another one of your fanciful imaginings?" Henry taunted.

Kate shot him a dirty look.

Once they reached the bridge connecting the *Ile de la Cite* with the *Ile de St. Louis*, they turned to admire the nave of the cathedral. Standing on the bridge, Kate and Henry marveled at the view of the cathedral. From this angle, they could see both sets of flying buttresses that held the thin walls upright. The surrounding stone buildings stood out darkly in the evening light. The Paris sky was in one of her most romantic moods. The slanting rays of the early evening sun mellowed the grey stone of the cathedral. The blue slate of the cathedral's roof matched the Wedgwood blue of the higher clouds in the sky and complemented the darkening blue of the river Seine. Other clouds glowed in variations of red, ranging from the palest of rose and to the deepest coral. Here and there, streaks of gold crossed the sky. An artist could not have captured such a perfect combination of colors and shapes.

"Did you know that the *Pont Saint Louis* was originally a wooden foot bridge built so that island residents could go to mass easily? It has been rebuilt several times, the most recent being during the time of Napoleon III," said Henry, needing for some reason to fill the silence that had sprung up between them. "Only seven blocks long, from this angle, the island resembles the prow of a ship tethered to the *Ile de la Cite* by the bridge."

"Hey, silly, take a look around," teased Kate. "Didn't I tell you it is too beautiful an evening to be talking about architecture?"

They walked along the tow path by the *Quai d'Anjou* on the *Ile de Saint Louis*. At one point, Henry found himself holding Kate's hand. What a surprise that had been. Henry couldn't remember the moment their hands had joined, only that somewhere along the walk they had come together. Looking at their intertwined hands, he couldn't tell where his hand ended and hers began. The feeling of her hand in his had warmed him to the center of his being.

"I read somewhere that this particular walk is considered one of the most romantic in all Paris," Henry said hoping to charm Kate into acting like a newlywed. He reached out to put his arm around her. She danced away, laughing.

"Oh, Henry," Kate laughed. "I would never have guessed you to have a romantic side! Given the activities of the past 24 hours, you seem to me to be more the action and adventure type of man. I bet you even fancied yourself as a modern day Musketeer! I can see you clashing swords with an evil-doer as a duchess trembles nearby with fear and joy. Perhaps you would enjoy visiting the house where Alexandre Dumas' hero, Athos, lived in the *Rue Ferou* in the shade of *Sainte-Sulpice* church."

Henry could see the mischievous glint in her eye. He struggled to maintain a straight face.

"Madame, you mock me," he said gravely. He gave a slight bow.

"Only your pride, gallant sir," she said as she curtsied to him.

A nearby building caught her eye.

"Henry!" she exclaimed. "That small brick building is just like a gate house. Look at what is carved in the stone lintel above the door. *'Concierge'*. Can't you just imagine a nosy old woman taking her post there at the window?"

"She'd be able to keep an eye out for illicit lovers, wouldn't she?" he said. "There is even a bell for her to ring for the local *gendarme*."

"She probably called the police every time she saw two people walking together holding hands." Kate blushed prettily when she realized she still was holding Henry's hand.

Henry laughed at her discomfort, but didn't let go of her hand. Instead, he pulled her to him.

"Yes, she would be quick to stop lovers from gazing too deeply into each other's eyes," Henry said, staring intently into hers.

Her blush deepened. Quickly, she turned her attention to a different building, searching for a distraction.

"It's all so very charming," she said, her free hand gesturing at the scene around them. "Paris! I can't believe I'm in Paris!"

Henry noticed with pleasure that she did not struggle too hard to release her hand from his.

"This island feels like a little village plopped down in the center of Paris," she continued. "There are marvelous ironwork grills on the wooden doors. Amazing. Don't you think the old-fashioned wooden shop fronts on these buildings are lovely? I particularly like the façade of this one with its dark green paint and gold trim. And over here is a small bakery. A very talented artist has painted such a lovely scene of a woman sowing seeds in a field. She's beautiful. And look at these paintings here on each side of the door to the *Patisserie*."

"I thought you didn't want to talk about architecture."

"My, don't those confections smell yummy. Oh, it's so tempting to spend money on the delicacies offered up for sale in their windows. With such lovely window displays, it makes me curious about what mysteries await inside. Oh, Henry, I would love to return here to explore these shops," Kate said as she spun around with her arms spread wide. "Even the restaurants allow wonderful scents to spill out onto the sidewalk to tempt your palate. It's all so indescribably lovely."

"It is you who are indescribably lovely, my dear," said Henry quietly. He wondered what possessed him to say that out loud. Henry found he couldn't take his eyes off her as she pirouetted around and around. Hearing his words, Kate turned away blushing.

"Henry, you shouldn't say such things, after all, it's only make believe," Kate said, a note of longing in her voice.

It surprised Henry how much her words stung. They reminded him that theirs was a temporary existence. Suddenly Henry realized he never wanted the evening to end. Though her back was to him, he reached out to touch her arm. As she turned toward him, Henry took Kate in his arms. He kissed her warmly, never wanting to let her go. When he set her gently away from him, there seemed to be nothing that needed to be said. Each of them was quiet as they strolled through the small park at the end of the island.

As they walked, Henry slipped his arm around her shoulder. His movement must have startled her because she jumped sideways. A low-hanging branch from a tree knocked her hat askew.

"Henry. Please. Don't. Leave me alone," she said fiercely.

Laughing at her fierceness, Henry reached over and straightened her hat. It was a protective, loving gesture he hadn't realized he was capable of. Kate scowled at him, but he could see tears in her eyes. Unable to help himself, he winked at her.

A small smile tugged at the corners of her mouth. Henry offered Kate his arm; she accepted and fell into step beside him. Henry couldn't help but notice how well they fit together. Arm in arm, they wandered happily past several small quaint shops, window shopping. Henry found he enjoyed watching Kate exclaim over the beautiful handmade sweaters, lace handkerchiefs, silk scarves, hats, and even the picture postcards. Unaware that he was watching her, Kate had stopped to gaze longingly in the window of a jewelry shop. There, the evening sun reflected off of a myriad of necklaces, pins, and earrings. In their midst, a single emerald and diamond ring sparkled. Though it was near closing time, the owner, perhaps sensing a sale, materialized at the door. He must have seen them peering at his window display. He was a true romantic at heart because, despite the late hour, he had welcomed them into his shop.

*"L'amour. Toujours L'amour. C'est bon d'etre en amour en Paris en Printemps,"* the shopkeeper said as he plucked the emerald ring from its resting place.

Yes, it was wonderful to be young and in love in Paris in the springtime, thought Henry. The reality of his thoughts jolted him. In love? He and Kate weren't in love. They couldn't possibly be. They'd just met. Henry had mistakenly allowed the magic of an evening in Paris to have an effect on him. He and Kate weren't in love, he repeated. Based on the way she kept asking him to leave her alone, Kate didn't even like him. The trying circumstances of the past two days could hardly be called a recipe for love. The enchantment Henry felt was a product of the evening, the river, the tiny streets, the light, anything but the workings of his heart, his logical self-proclaimed. SIS agent Henry Littleton would never allow his mind to run off with him in pursuit of romance. He had a job to do. He needed to focus. Henry looked over at Kate and logic flew out the window. After all, he thought to himself, he was in Paris with a beautiful, very desirable, woman.

"It's like something out of a fairy tale," laughed Kate, her face radiant with joy as she tried the ring on her right hand.

That laugh, thought Henry, how could he possibly ignore that delightful laugh? And her huge expressive eyes, how could he resist them? Henry groaned aloud at the predicament he had gotten himself into. There went his plan to select simple plain rings as part of their cover. Once again, he proved he was a novice at the espionage game. Henry had let the light of the evening sky, the beauty of Paris, and the warmth of her presence bewitch him. Knowing he should resist, Henry threw caution to the wind.

*"Nous le prenons."*

"We'll take it? Henry, you can't be serious!"

That was how he came to buy her the antique emerald ring. He hadn't meant to make such an extravagant purchase. Like holding hands, it just happened. The stone flashed and sparkled in the reflected light of the setting sun. Henry realized that he had seen the same fire in Kate's deep green eyes. He justified his purchase by reminding himself that a new wife wears a suitable ring. Certainly, Henry reasoned, he hadn't bought it just because of the joy he saw in her face.

The shopkeeper had raised his eyebrows only a little when Henry gently removed the ring from her right hand and placed it onto the ring finger of her left. For some reason, neither Henry nor Kate was surprised when the ring had fit perfectly. For a moment, they stood there unaware of anything but the beating of their hearts.

*"Vous avez faites votre femme heureuse, tres heureuse. Formidable."* The shopkeeper's words had interrupted.

You have made your wife very happy. Yes, Henry could see by the expression on her face that he had done the right thing. The very idea that he had pleased her made Henry ridiculously happy. He didn't regret his purchase even if the ring might be just a bit over the top.

As Henry paid for the ring, the shopkeeper told them of the history of the ring. It originated from an estate of a couple who had lived a long, exciting, and love-filled life with each other. He told them that the couple had found the secret of true contentment in a happy marriage. The man's parting comment to them came out as more of a blessing as he wished that they, too, would find the secrets of true contentment in a happy marriage.

Between the magic of the light of an evening in Paris and the words of the man who sold them the ring, what an unexpected and disturbing night it had been. Over dinner, they spent their time gazing into each other's eyes. Afterward, Henry couldn't even remember what they had eaten. On the way back to the hotel, Henry pulled her into his arms.

"All in the line of work, my dear," Henry had said as he kissed her. Instead of fighting him, she leaned into him and wrapped her arms around him tightly. He held her close and kissed her with all his might. Only the sound of a passing patrol man had caused them to pull apart. They were back at the hotel before Henry's heart beat returned to normal. Judging by the delicate flush on her face, Kate's heart was racing too.

Despite their lack of luggage, this being Paris, the concierge had not questioned their newlywed status. Henry could tell the concierge found it puzzling when Henry, being British and proper, had asked for adjoining rooms. The man had raised his eyebrows at Henry when he provided their keys. Seeing his expression, Henry had placed his arm around Kate and pulled her close to him. Instead of the hoped for response from her, his action earned him yet another "Henry! Please! Don't! Leave me alone." The concierge smirked at her reaction. So Henry had stood there, feeling a bit foolish, with the keys in his hand, one for each door in the corridor and a matching set of keys for the door that adjoined their two rooms.

Upstairs in the corridor outside their rooms they both had been uncomfortable. The force of his desire for Kate surprised Henry. He wanted nothing more than to take her in his arms and kiss her until her silly hat came off. Just as he had gathered up the courage to do just that, another couple appeared on the stairway. The spell broken, his awkwardness returned. Before he could take command of the situation, Kate had stepped inside and quietly closed the door to her hotel room. Tempting as it had been, that night, Henry did not make use of the key to the adjoining door.

Now, it was morning. Henry dressed in his only suit and regarded himself in the mirror. Despite his newly shaven face and combed hair, what Henry saw there didn't please him. His clothes resisted further attempts to tidy them up. Espionage agents are supposed to look dashing, weren't they? They did in books anyway. Henry didn't look or feel very dashing right now. The past two days had been rough on both him and his suit.

No wonder the concierge had cast a questioning glance at his appearance. After their rough encounters in London, Henry had the uncomfortable sensation that he was playacting in a poorly written spy novel. Improvising, he was definitely improvising. Well, he had better get started on his day.

Henry's original plan for today included going to the embassy and speaking with his counterparts in SIS. They would brief him more fully about the state of things in Yugoslavia. He would take the time to compile a report on the events of the past two days. Kate, however, had other plans for him. On the train, she had given him strict instructions concerning his hair, hat, and clothing. Kate had even prepared a shopping list for him including recommended appropriate haberdasheries compiled from her guidebook. Shirts, ties, suits, shoes, hats, handkerchiefs, socks, evening apparel, the list went on and on. Kate told him to focus on suits in blue and brown, apparently she had grown tired of his grey suit and Homburg. She definitely did not want him to purchase a black suit or a long grey overcoat! When he had protested about her focus on shopping, she silenced him by saying primly: "Oh, Henry, we simply must look our best on the Orient Express." Something in the set of her jaw made him think that it was a battle he wasn't going to win. He had better get moving. He was meeting Kate for breakfast at eight. After that, his next stop was the barber shop for a haircut.

# Chapter 24

## Kate

$S$aturday morning, Kate stretched in bed delighting in the opulent splendor surrounding her. Paris! She was in Paris! Sunlight streamed through the windows of her room. High up on the fifth floor, she could only hear muted noise from the street below. Beneath the deep blue velvet canopy and matching hangings, Kate couldn't resist patting the down pillows and comforters piled high on the four poster bed. The room, though not large, had a small windowed alcove with a writing desk and lamp. In both the entry and the main room, crystal chandeliers sparkled above her head. Generous closets gracing one entire wall of the room would have accommodated her luggage if Kate had had any. Even the bathroom was magnificent. Luxuriously soaking in the deep tub, with its wide mahogany surround, Kate finally had been able to relax the evening before. While lying in the tub, she could stare out the window at the rooftops of Paris.

Again Kate surveyed her lovely room. What a marvelous hotel! She had been quite surprised to find that Henry had booked a hotel in the *Saint Germain de Pres* on the *Rive Gauche*. Kate had expected him to choose a hotel favored by diplomats on the Right Bank. Instead Henry had chosen a hotel like no other. The entrance off *Rue des Beaux Arts* gave few hints on the luxuries waiting inside. On the ground floor, *the rez de chaussee*, two sitting rooms flanked the center hallway that led into a circular atrium. Five stories above a glass dome let in the northern light. Looking up, Kate had gasped when she realized that the entire hotel had been created in the round. A circular staircase curled its way up to the balconies encircling each floor providing access to the hotel rooms. Arched openings in the pale gold walls allowed light from the atrium to reach each hallway.  Heavy white ledges and gold medallions decorated the walls.  The design gave the hotel an atmosphere like no other.  Overall, the effect was very daring.  At the back of the building, the restaurant provided a view of the lovely interior courtyard.  This morning, though, Kate had ordered breakfast on the small balcony adjoining her room.

Kate reached for the thick bathrobe thoughtfully provided by the hotel.  What a glorious morning it was!  Kate's mind whirled with plans for the day.  She had so much to do.  She hoped Henry wouldn't mind rushing through breakfast.  First, Kate wanted to have her hair cut and styled.  Her next priority involved shopping for new clothes.  Kate definitely couldn't wait to replace her plum suit and hat.

Kate planned to start at the *Printemps* department store on Boulevard Haussmann.  She had heard about its elaborate stained glass cupola, a breathtaking work of art.  While at *Printemps*, she could select a variety of day dresses.  Since it would look suspicious in today's economy to make a large number of purchases at just one store, Kate also intended to buy several items for her wardrobe at the *Galeries Lafayette*.  Located just down the boulevard, it too boasted a stained glass and steel dome.  The Art Nouveau staircases and balconies surrounding it were not to be missed either.  After that, she hoped to squeeze in lunch at *Fauchons*.  She so wanted to sample their amazing teas and treats.

Once she had tidied up her appearance, Kate wanted to visit Chanel.  She couldn't wait to try on one of the famed little black dresses.  When the little black dress made its debut in May 1926, she had read Coco Chanel's comment in an interview that *"Thanks to me they [non-wealthy] can walk around like millionaires."*  Kate was sure that adding this simple item in her wardrobe she could mingle comfortably with the high-society ladies on the train.  Hopefully, she could find a string of *faux* pearls and a pair of high heels that would serve as the perfect accompaniment.  Properly accessorized, a little black dress would serve for a number of purposes.

Kate could hear the gentle cooing of pigeons on the small balcony accessed through the floor-to-ceiling French doors. When Henry joined her for breakfast there, they would be able to enjoy the view of the rooftops of Paris stretching out before them.

Henry. His name caused her stomach to flutter. Pressing her hand to it, Kate admired the emerald ring on her hand and thought pleasant thoughts about Henry and his kisses of the night before. Just thinking about those kisses sent her heart to racing. It was a good thing they would be spending the day apart. She needed time to recover her composure. Her plan to capture Henry's attention by playing hard to get had worked until their last kiss the night before. Something in the way he looked at her had caused her to melt inside. She wanted to reach out and touch his face, to run her fingers through his thick hair, and two feel his whiskers rough against her skin. Kate grew warm just thinking about him.

There was a knock at her door. As she moved to answer it, Kate frowned at her reflection in the mirror. She also needed better clothing to keep her plan to entice Henry moving forward. It would not do to get too attached to Henry just yet. Kate ran her hands over her plum suit, trying unsuccessfully to smooth out the wrinkles on the clothing as well as her life.

# Chapter 25

## Henry

"*G*ood morning, Kate," said Henry as he knocked gently on the adjoining door to their suites.

"Good morning to you too," Kate responded with a welcoming smile. Despite the fact that she had been wearing the same suit for three days, to Henry's mind, Kate looked remarkably fresh and appealing. He watched her walk toward the small balcony.

"I thought we would enjoy the morning sunshine and eat out here," she said, stepping aside to reveal a small bistro table set for two. "Isn't this just wonderful Henry? Isn't the view charming? It's all so romantic." Kate's words came out in a nervous flutter and a light blush crept up her cheeks.

"Without a doubt," Henry answered lightly. "However, that morning sunshine you mention may not be around very long. It could turn to showers soon." He pointed to the heavy clouds hovering on the horizon above the rooftops.

"I suppose my first stop will need to be to shop for an umbrella," Kate said in a disappointed voice. "Never mind, at least we have the sunshine right now." She sat down in the chair Henry held out for her.

"Last night, you clearly laid out my shopping requirements, but tell me, what plans have you for the day?" he inquired.

"Oh Henry," she laughed. "Have I become that bossy?"

"That's certainly not a good trait for a new wife, is it?" he added, joining in her laughter.

Following breakfast, Kate left to explore the Paris shops. Henry returned to his room and got to work. He finally had the time to study the contents of the briefcase more thoroughly in private. In it were maps of Belgrade, photographs of the parade route, and background information on passengers on the Orient Express. In it, too, was a British-made six-shot revolver. Henry was pleased to see that it was one of the newest guns available, a Webley Mk. VI. He hefted the 1.7 pound gun in his hand. Through long practice, he was adept at handling guns of all sorts. After checking that it was empty, Henry familiarized himself with its self-cocking mechanism. Satisfied, he loaded the Webley with the big .45 caliber rounds. Henry had been given specific instructions to do whatever was within his power to prevent the assassination of King Alexander. With that in mind, the pistol had been provided, along with a diplomatic letter stating his mission. He had had no trouble bringing the pistol into France because both he and Kate were travelling as diplomatic couriers. As he returned the gun to his briefcase, Henry fervently hoped he would never need to use it. Picking up the papers, he studied their contents intently. Finally satisfied that he had committed the information to memory, he got up to finish dressing.

Unexpectedly, the phone rang.

"*Allo*," Henry answered.

"If you want to live, leave Paris immediately," said a muffled voice.

"What? I don't understand," Henry blurted out.

"If you want to live, leave Paris immediately," the voice repeated before disconnecting.

Henry's hand shook as he replaced the receiver. Despite being pursued in London, he had not expected this. How had they found him here? Unsure of how to proceed, Henry sat down on the edge of the bed. After a few moments reflection, he decided to carry on with his original plans.

He would alert the embassy as soon as he determined he had not being followed from his hotel.

Trying to act as naturally as possible, Henry went directly to the barber shop from the hotel. The haircut made him feel like a new man. Leaving the barber shop, Henry glanced around as casually as he could. He could not see anyone lurking about, but the encounters in London had taught him to be extra careful. As he walked toward the embassy, he wondered if he was being too cautious. He and Kate hadn't seen anyone the night before as they strolled through Paris. On impulse, Henry stopped at a news shop and nonchalantly studied the magazines on display. He observed the passersby. No one even looked at him, let alone acted suspicious. In fact, Henry thought ruefully, *he* was the only one acting suspiciously. His erratic behavior while he walked—stopping, starting, gazing at reflections in windows, quick turns—was sure to draw attention to himself. He needed to get a grip on himself. Henry pictured Kate laughing at his antics. She was probably elbow-deep in designer dresses and strange hats by now, enjoying her time in Paris. All the shopping Kate intended to do would have pushed thoughts of trouble right out of her mind.

Henry stopped at a bistro and asked for a table outside so that he could keep an eye out for anyone who seemed out of place. The waiter gestured to several open tables. Henry selected one that allowed him to place his back to a wall. A row of small evergreen trees in a large rectangular tub provided cover to his left.

He ordered a coffee, hoping the caffeine would jump start his brain. He desperately needed to outwit his opponents. As he drank it, Henry considered his situation. Attracting attention to himself and the official aspect of his visit to Paris by going to the embassy made him uncomfortable. Though he needed to make contact and gather any additional information about their upcoming journey on the Orient Express, Henry didn't think that going to the embassy would be a good idea. There must be another option. His gaze traveled around the bistro allowing him to see that his answer was right there in front of him, the telephone. He could telephone the embassy from this bistro and set up a meeting somewhere in Paris. They could bring the information to him. Where? This time, Henry wasn't going to make the same sort of mistake he made at Piccadilly Circus. The *Place du Carrousel* would be much too large, as was the *Jardin de Tuilleries*. Finally, Henry settled on the bridge tourists love to visit for its famed decoration, the *Pont Alexandre III*. Given their current assignment, Henry liked the name of it too. He could linger on the bridge without attracting attention, just another tourist admiring the mythical marine creatures cavorting along the bridge. Pleased with his choice, Henry rose to make the telephone call.

# Chapter 26

## Kate

$K$ate left the hotel feeling as light as air. Breakfast with Henry had been the perfect way to start the day. What would it be like to sit across from his handsome face every morning? As she walked, she hummed a happy tune. Kate checked the time on her watch; the stores should be opening up right about now. She glanced at the sky. It had darkened perceptibly. Her first stop would definitely have to be for an umbrella. She could smell the scent of rain in the air. She remembered reading about the many atmospheric moods of the Paris sky. She smiled, thinking about the beauty of the sky the previous evening. Even today, with rain on the horizon, she couldn't help but be happy. With her mind preoccupied by her shopping plans for the day, she failed to notice a man hovering in the shadows by the entrance to her hotel.

She entered the nearest shop that might carry umbrellas.

"*Pardonnez moi. Est-ce-que vous avez un parapluie?*" she asked in French.

"*Non, desole, Madame. Mais il y a un petit magazin pres d'ici,*" he answered. That gave Kate hope. This man didn't have an umbrella, but according to him a nearby shop did.

"*Ou?*" Where, she asked the man.

"*Tournez a gauche, continuez tout droit. C'est a la droit, pres de la grande rue.*"

Kate repeated his instructions to herself. Turn left; go straight, it's on the right, near the main street. Smiling, she thanked the man and left his shop. Once outside, Kate paused for a moment to look in the window of a charming *Parfumerie*. Later in the day, she promised herself, she would visit one and select just the right perfume to send Henry's senses reeling.

Kate had only traveled a short way when she heard the footsteps of someone approaching quickly from behind. Instinctively, she swerved to her left. The man, caught off balance as he lunged for her, fell on the sidewalk beside her feet. She took only a moment to glance at his face and clothes before turning to run. Just as quickly, he reached up and grabbed the hem of her skirt. Fortunately, his fingers closed only on the lining. Desperately, Kate took her skirt in her hands and pulled with all her might. The two of them wrestled. Kate tried to kick the man. In return, he yanked on her skirt so hard he would have pulled her down on top of him if she had not been able to grab onto a nearby pole with one hand. Her hat came off in the scuffle and landed in the gutter. Just as Kate started to lose her grip on the pole, her skirt lining tore apart. The man rocked backward. Taking advantage of his awkward position, she kicked him hard in his solar plexus. Kate sprinted away, leaving the man clutching a scrap of purple cloth to his chest.

As she fled, Kate had the presence of mind to avoid running in a straight line down a single street. By turning left and right randomly onto side streets, she hoped to confuse him as well as put distance between the two of them. As she ran, Kate reviewed the man's features in her mind. His was a new face in this adventure. His thick black eyebrows resembled caterpillars. His fleshy lips had been curled back in a snarl as they fought, revealing crooked and broken teeth. In short it was an easily recognizable face that Kate definitely did not want to see again.

After running several blocks, Kate's lungs began to burn and she developed a stitch in her side. As she slowed her pace, still keeping an eye out for her pursuer, it began to rain. Oh, great, thought Kate. Of course, just when you think things can't get worse, they do. The rain came down harder. Aware that her appearance left a lot to be desired, Kate opened the door to the nearest store and stepped inside.

Chanel.

It would have to be Chanel. Just when you thought things couldn't get any worse…Kate repeated to herself.

She had hoped to enter the world of glamorous clothing looking just a bit more pulled together than she did at that moment. As she stood in the doorway, dripping, she could see her reflection in the mirror. No hat, her wet hair all tangled about her shoulders, her torn skirt hanging crookedly to one side, her stockings ruined beyond repair, she was a mess. Kate could understand the look of disdain on the faces of the clerks and dressers.

Going back outside into the downpour was not an option, especially not with the man searching for her. She couldn't count on getting away again. The first time she had been lucky. Fortunately, she had crossed the strap of her purse over her shoulder, so she had not lost it in the scuffle. Safely inside, Kate had plenty of banknotes to pay for new clothes. Gripping her purse firmly, Kate squared her shoulders to hide her discomfort and walked deeper into the store.

"*Je voudrais les nouvelles vetements. S'il vous plait,*" Kate said with as much bravado as she could muster.

She must have sounded like an idiot. Any fool could see that she obviously needed new clothes. Refusing to be intimidated, she pointedly opened her purse as if to find a comb. Her action revealed the banknotes that lay within. At least she would let them know that she could afford to pay for her new clothes.

"*Bien sur, Madame,*" came the polite, but stilted, response. The inflection in the woman's voice only served to emphasize the put down she intended.

*Bien sur.* But of course, mimicked Kate with an inward cringe. Only the French could make those two simple words sound like the ultimate insult.

The women regarded Kate like a drowned rat they had the misfortune to discover on their doorstep. Their haughty expressions conveyed their disgust at her appearance. Only the presence of so much money prevented them from throwing her out.

Sensing that she would not be receiving much help from the sales-women, Kate selected a few items on her own. She gently stroked the material, entranced by the feel of the fabrics. They were all so lovely. Well, why not, thought Kate. Instead of buying just one outfit as she had planned, she might as well do most of her shopping here. Surely the man wouldn't dare to search for her in a shop such as this one. Perhaps if she spent enough time in here, he would tire of his search and leave. Having reasoned this through, Kate shopped with abandon, much to the annoyance of the sales-women. She added gowns, shoes, purses, and hats to her growing pile of treasures. Despite the number of items she had amassed, Kate could tell by the sales-woman's face that she didn't consider Kate worth her time and effort. Finally, Kate turned to go into one of the lavish dressing rooms. As she did so, the bell at the door sounded softly.

A woman crossed the threshold and paused at the door surveying her surroundings. What an impressive entrance she made, thought Kate, taken aback. So commanding was her presence that everyone stopped what they were doing and turned toward her. Head held high, the woman walked into the store as if she owned it. Assistants immediately surrounded the woman as if she was royalty. Maybe she was; Kate mused. A quick glance in a mirror told Kate that in her present condition she would never convince anyone to respect her. She had never felt so woefully inadequate. Her spirits at an all-time low, Kate gathered a few last things and meekly departed for the dressing rooms.

Later, in the dressing area, Kate was surprised when the supremely confident woman approached her.

"I couldn't help but notice you, my dear," the woman said in a soft, cultured voice. "Just a word of advice from an old woman. Never let them see your discomfort."

"But, I..." faltered Kate.

"*La courage, ma cherie*. Courage," said the woman in a heartwarming tone of voice.

For a moment Kate got the impression the woman knew all about Kate's earlier encounter. Chagrined, Kate realized the woman was talking about the women in the salon. Kate's good humor returned as she remembered the first impression the women made on her. Actually, the sales-women were nearly as frightening as the man with the caterpillar eyebrows. Kate smiled shyly at the woman.

Having made her selections, Kate changed her new clothes. She replaced her plum suit with a very flattering rust-colored day dress with a matching hip-length fitted jacket. Kate re-pinned her hair into a becoming chignon. Crowning her head was one of Chanel's charming little hats. A new purse, shoes, and stockings completed her outfit.

"That's better. Now off you go," said the woman as she gave Kate a gentle push.

Kate stepped from the changing room feeling like a different person. Apparently, the sales-women thought she looked like one too because they approached her as if seeing a new customer.

"Madame, we are so sorry. We did not see you enter. How many we assist you?" the woman asked solicitously.

"You already have," answered Kate in her most regal voice. Kate pointed to the garments in the dressing room. "I will take them all. Please send them to my hotel. Now, I would like to pay. Oh, and would you mind calling me a taxi? Thank you."

A few minutes later, Kate stepped out into the fine misty rain and into a waiting taxi. Her heart skipped a beat when she saw her pursuer not ten steps away. The man merely glanced at Kate and returned his attention to the shops on the street. He hadn't recognized her either, Kate rejoiced gleefully as she sped away in the taxi.

"*Ou allez vous, Madame*?" asked the taxi driver.

Where was she going, Kate asked herself. To Henry? To shop?

"To buy an umbrella," Kate decided firmly.

"Ah, you are English," he said in heavily accented English. "A beautiful woman like you has no need to buy an umbrella. She has merely to ask for one."

"What on earth are you talking about?" Kate asked incredulously, thinking she hadn't understood him correctly.

"Just what I said," he answered knowingly. "You, beautiful lady, do not need to buy an umbrella. All you have to do is return to your hotel and ask the doorman for one. He will bring one to you. You will not even have to leave the taxi. Now, where is your hotel?"

"Oh, I hadn't considered that," Kate answered. She did not want to direct the man to her hotel for two reasons. First, she could not remember seeing an umbrella stand in the doorway of her hotel. And second, there was a chance that more pursuers waited there. Hearing the hesitation in her voice, the taxi driver studied her for a moment.

"I will take you to find an umbrella. We will go to the nearest four star hotel," he announced proudly.

"A four star hotel?" asked Kate with a note of panic in her voice.

"Yes. When we arrive and the doorman comes to help you from the cab, just tell him you forgot your umbrella. He will gladly give you his,"

"Surely, what you say is impossible!" she said with a laugh. "Would he really believe such a story?"

"*Mais oui, bien sur!* But of course," said the man with mock indignity.

"No, you must be joking," Kate giggled.

"*Non, absolument non.* Just think *ma Belle*. You will both be happy. You will have your umbrella. He will have taken care of a client."

"But I am not staying at a four star hotel!" exclaimed Kate.

"All that is important is that you are a beautiful woman," answered the man with a broad smile.

Light of heart, Kate returned his smile. His plan was positively mischievous. Kate disregarded Henry's stern warnings not to indulge in her penchant for whimsy. She could not resist this little adventure. As he steered toward the nearest hotel, laughter bubbled through Kate like champagne over the audacity of his proposal.

And so, that is what happened. No sooner than Kate had rolled down her window to explain her need for an umbrella, when the doorman presented her with a lovely deep blue silk umbrella.

"I don't believe it!" exclaimed Kate as they pulled away from the curb. In response, the driver gave a typical Gallic shrug.

"And now, beautiful lady, where do you wish to go with your umbrella?" asked the driver in mock seriousness.

"To the British Consulate, please." The taxi driver's umbrella ploy had restored Kate's sense of fun and well-being. Her confidence returned making her believe that in Paris anything was possible. Kate decided to meet with Henry and explain what had happened that morning.

Once there, Kate asked the driver to wait while she went inside. She had no luck reaching Henry since he had not yet arrived. Kate left a note for him and returned to the taxi.

"And now, if you please, I would like to do a bit of shopping. Would you like to be my driver for the day?" Kate asked as she handed the man a generous tip.

# Chapter 27

## Henry

$\mathcal{E}$nchanting. Positively enchanting. Henry couldn't believe this was the same woman he had been trapped in a gardener's shed with. When she entered, Kate filled the room with light. Henry could not take his eyes off of her as she descended into the lobby of the hotel in her evening finery. No doubt about it, Henry thought, Kate had put the man in the long grey overcoat's money to good use preparing for tonight's ball at the embassy. Her hair, cut in a flattering new style, positively glowed in the light of the evening sun that filtered through the domed sky light. Her Chanel dress, it could only have been Chanel, skimmed her body like a second skin. Kate hadn't selected a traditional black evening gown. Her gown reminded him of a summer sky. The tiny embroidered stars against a navy blue backdrop shimmered as she moved toward him. The simplicity of the gown suited her natural attractiveness. When Kate turned, Henry could see the back cut daringly low. A low whistle escaped his lips without him realizing it. Henry wondered how the slim straps with wispy cap sleeves managed to stay up.

Kate's charming hat drew attention to her face as it perched lightly on the right side of her head. Its veil seemed all out of proportion to the hat. Longer than a traditional veil, a single piece of the sheer fabric covered her face to her shoulders, while the remainder, gathered beneath the hat, trailed down her back. As she walked, the veil floated behind her. The stars that dusted the deep blue fabric gave the impression of a tail trailing a comet. Conversation in the lobby halted as the other patrons focused on her beauty. Henry felt ridiculously proud as he held out his hand to her.

At the embassy ball, Kate continued to amaze him. Her composure never seemed to fail her. Not when strangers chased her all over London and not now as she greeted and made social conversation with the elite of Paris society. If Kate experienced any discomfort, she wasn't letting it show. She gave no hint that she couldn't take whatever life threw her way all in stride.

In the crowded room, the sounds of multi-lingual conversations, music, and polite laughter reverberated off the walls. Henry, entranced as he was by Kate, hardly heard a sound. He stared at her as if to memorize her every feature. He noted the curve of her shoulders, the slimness of her waist, the way her hair shimmered in the light from the chandeliers, and her lovely face. Her wondrous green eyes, the delicate flush of pink on her cheekbones, the curve of her smile, to Henry, Kate looked strong and vulnerable at the same time.

Henry became aware of a man standing next to him.

"Take care."

The man's words and presence flustered Henry for a moment. He made no answer to the man's statement.

"Remember the Chinese superstition that if you stare too long at something beautiful, it will disappear."

Seeing Henry's discomfort, the man extended his right hand in greeting.

"Forgive me," the Frenchman said in his heavily accented English. "We have not been properly introduced. My name is Monsieur Antoine De la Roche."

"Henry Littleton."

Shaking hands, the two men eyed each other.

"What was it that you said just now?" inquired Henry.

"Beauty is fragile and fleeting. It should be glanced at so as not to destroy it," said the man in French-accented English. "Though, I must admit, I can understand why you wish to gaze at such a poised and lovely young woman."

"You will have to pardon me for gazing at my wife. We married recently and sometimes I can hardly believe she is mine."

"Yes, I understand. I feel that way about my wife, though we have been married many years. And here is my lovely wife, Juliette," said Monsieur De la Roche at the approach of an elegantly dressed woman.

Madame De la Roche gave her husband a warm smile as she took his outstretched hand.

"*Cherie*, you should introduce me to your friend."

"Henry Littleton," repeated Henry.

"Monsieur Littleton is newly married. May I congratulate you?" asked Monsieur De la Roche with a small bow.

"Allow me to add my congratulations," said his wife.

Kate's silvery laugh floated over the noise of the crowd. Henry turned toward the sound, his feelings for Kate showing plainly on his face.

"You have my sympathies," said the Frenchman, smiling with understanding of the young man's plight. He wrapped his arm around that of his wife as he bid Henry good evening.

# Chapter 28

## Kate

*F*or a moment, Kate just stood there spellbound. It was as if she had stepped into an enchanted castle. The embassy surpassed anything she could have possibly imagined. Kate had expected the reception hall to be rather formal and baroque. Instead, the simplicity of the modern design startled her. Breaking with tradition, the room had streamlined architecture whose modernity was accented by the sweeping curves of banquette seating in each corner. The light gold walls had minimal plasterwork. The designer had used the paneling and woodwork to great effect, visually enhancing the height of the ceiling without cluttering the walls. The woodwork had been bleached to match the light gold color of the walls. In each corner of the room, deep gold velvet fabric covered the comfortable banquette seating. Behind each set of curved seats, a display shelf held modern works of art. Free-standing chairs, some of light-colored wood, others like tub chairs, were upholstered in thick brocade cloth. The modern bronze wall sconces sent light up to reflect off the ceiling. The ceiling had been painted milk chocolate brown, surprising Kate with its richness. Centered in the wall at the far end of the room, a wide doorway led to a ballroom. To the right, another archway led to the dining room.

As the music from the ballroom flowed out into the reception hall, elegantly dressed women in evening gowns and men in well-cut tuxedos held champagne glasses and engaged in conversation. With its glittering chandeliers, marble floor, and beautiful decorations, the room was magical. Overwhelmed by so many sensations at one time, Kate definitely felt out of her element. Her middle-class upbringing had not included very many lessons on deportment in such a sophisticated environment. Now she was standing at the top of the stairs, her hand resting lightly on Henry's arm, about to begin the most elegant evening of her life. Kate took a deep breath and remembered the very important lesson she received today at Chanel. That morning, when she had sought sanctuary in the establishment at 31 Rue Cambon, she had immediately felt out of place. How could she not, all wet and bedraggled? It had taken quite an effort on her part to remain in the store. Only the threat of the man chasing her kept her rooted to the spot. Kate affectionately remembered the elegant, confident woman who had been so kind to her. She smiled when she thought of the woman's words of encouragement while she helped Kate briefly in the dressing room.

'*La courage, ma cherie*. Courage.'

"May I ask your name, Madame?" Kate asked respectfully. "Who are you?"

"No one important, but I will never let them know that," said the woman. "Now, go and remember to be the best you can be."

Kate wished the woman could see her now. Tonight at the embassy reception, Kate vowed she would be the best that she could be. The beautiful blue starlight dress she wore gave her a feeling of being armored against whatever the evening would offer. The fabric of the bias-cut gown had elasticity and cling in all the right places, making it ideal for dancing. The flared hemline rested above her ankle to show off her new round-toed pumps with high vamps. It pleased Kate to note that she had finally managed to capture Henry's undivided attention.

Interesting that the unknown woman had said "courage", Kate mused. She must have been clairvoyant to know just how much courage Kate needed in the shop as well as right now. Based on all that had happened to them so far, Kate knew she was going to need a lot more courage in the future. Straightening her shoulders, lifting her chin, Kate mimicked the woman's posture. Head held high, Kate walked into the room as if she owned it.

Henry covered her hand with his and gave her a reassuring squeeze. Henry had certainly cleaned up nicely, she thought approvingly. Kate marveled that he had managed to find a tuxedo that fit him so perfectly on such short notice. She had had to rush around madly all day in order to put together her travelling wardrobe. Henry must have made multiple purchases too. On top of all that, he had met with embassy officials for a briefing. For her, the day had gone by in a blur of activity. She knew she needed to tell Henry about her assailant, but they had not had time to meet and compare notes. When she got back to the hotel, she found a message from him telling her to meet him in the lobby at seven o'clock. It was only as Kate came down the stairs at the hotel and their eyes met that she felt the world stop spinning. Seeing him, touching his hand in greeting, had made everything right in her world again.

Leading her to the ballroom, Henry swept Kate into his arms for a waltz. He danced divinely. She loved a man who could dance. Two days ago, she could never have imagined Paris, waltzing, and Henry. Despite evil men, guns, and a night spent in a shed, Kate could not help feeling that everything was wonderful. Happiness flooded through her. Her dress was perfect. Henry was perfect. Waltzing, and whirling around the floor, Kate felt as if her feet never touched the floor.

# Chapter 29

## Henry

"*Y*ou are lovely, my dear," Henry whispered in Kate's ear. She smelled of violets and springtime. "Your hair is the color of firelight."

Kate smiled up at him and took his breath away. Unlike most women, Kate had shunned a fashionable short haircut. Instead, she wore her long auburn hair in an upswept French twist. Henry wondered what it would look like tumbling around her white shoulders. He pulled her closer to him. With her in his arms, it was hard for him to maintain his professionalism. How easy it was to lose focus when she was near. All it took was one look into her expressive emerald green eyes. Throwing caution to the wind, Henry gave into the moment and danced. He thought with amazement how much he wanted to get to know more about this warm, intelligent, lively woman he held in his arms.

Then Henry saw him, standing half-hidden by a potted palm, a man with bushy eyebrows staring at them intently. In his surprise, Henry nearly stumbled. Silently cursing himself for not focusing on his duties, Henry guided Kate over to the spot where he had seen the man. As he spun Kate around the floor, he caught glimpses of the man through the other dancers. There was no doubt in Henry's mind that he and Kate were the focus of the man's attention. Henry hadn't expected this. He imagined they would be safe at the reception. Only someone very bold or very desperate would follow them to the embassy. Henry considered his options. There was an outside chance that the man might actually be on their side. Or, he could be just an innocent bystander who had an interest in potted palms. Not very likely. Unsure of what to do, Henry stopped dancing and took Kate to the refreshment table. There, a colleague introduced them to a stately woman of great beauty and uncertain age.

"Princess Marcellina Lazio of Italy," the man said. "May I introduce Henry Littleton?"

Following their introduction, Henry formally introduced Kate to the Princess.

"*Buona sera Princess. Vorrei presentarla a Katherine Littleton, mi espousa,*" said Henry with a bow. "My wife, Kate." Henry couldn't help but notice that Kate's eyes opened wide with surprise over meeting a princess.

"*Piacere. Lieto di conoscerila Katherine.* How lovely to meet you, my dear," said the Princess to Kate before turning her attention back to Henry.

"Henry, the Princess has requested a dance with you," his colleague said.

"Yes. I would enjoy a dance with you, Mr. Littleton." The Princess favored Henry with a gracious smile that belied the demand in her request.

"Yes. What a pleasure. Of course, I'd be delighted," Henry stammered as he collected himself. He led the Princess to the dance floor, but kept his eyes focused on Kate.

"I notice you gazing at your wife," said the Princess.

Embarrassed, Henry, who had been doing just that, pulled his attention back to his dance partner. He found her studying his face very carefully. Henry wondered why the Princess wanted to dance with him of all people.

"I once had a young man who looked at me the way you look at Katherine, Mr. Littleton," Princess Lazio said rather regretfully. Then her voice softened further, as if she was speaking only to herself. "Once you have found that special someone..."

Henry noticed her face as her voice faltered. He saw a momentary spasm of pain cross her face.

"Never let her go," she continued in almost a whisper.

They danced without speaking and watched Kate as she moved around the edge of the dance floor.

"Once, I loved someone that deeply," Princess Lazio said, picking up where she left off.

"Your husband?" Henry asked gauchely.

The Princess's face held such infinite sadness that though he did not know her, Henry felt a great sorrow on her behalf.

"Don't be foolish like I was," she snapped sharply, visibly making an effort to pull herself together. "There is still time for you."

"I don't understand your meaning," Henry answered perplexed.

"You must be very careful," Princess Lazio whispered as they danced. "You have placed your young lady in a very difficult position."

Henry stared at the woman in surprise. The Princess didn't miss a beat in her dancing as she continued.

"Surely, you considered your actions before you involved her in your activities?" she asked. Without waiting for an answer, Princess Lazio went on to say, "There are people who will stop at nothing to prevent you from protecting the King. The young woman posing as your wife will give them a hold over you. Be very careful. They are watching you even as we speak."

Her warning to leave the future alone took Henry's breath away. His questions came out in a rush.

"How did you know about Kate? About the King? Who are you?" he asked, confused.

The Princess remained silent.

"Madame, you must be on our side if you have taken the risk to tell me this."

"I am on no one's side but my own," the elegant woman answered coldly. "Your wife is quite charming.  I would hate to see anything happen to her. Guard her well."

The final notes of the dance sounded as the Princess disappeared into the crowd.

# Chapter 30

## Kate

*J*ust wait until Kate told Henry that she had already met Princess Lazio earlier in the day. At Chanel. The Princess and the woman who offered Kate encouragement were one and the same. Kate found it odd that the Princess had not referred to their earlier meeting when they were introduced. Perhaps the woman thought it was inappropriate. Kate met Henry as he returned from dancing with the Princess. He appeared deep in thought. Now was probably not the right time to mention her earlier adventures.

"Is everything all right?" she asked.

"What? Oh, just fine. Shall we dance?"

As Kate waltzed with Henry, she enjoyed looking at the ring he had placed on her left hand. The night before, she had been about to refuse the ring. It seemed so extravagant for their sham of a marriage. Instead of refusing it outright, she had taken the time to observe Henry's face. What she had seen in it told her it seemed awfully important to Henry that she wear the ring. She couldn't bear to disappoint him. Well, Kate thought, it was a lovely reminder of their adventures together. Secretly, she was enormously pleased that Henry had placed the ring on her finger. Something told her it would become more and more difficult to say; 'Henry! Please! Don't! Leave me alone.'

Kate was having a marvelous time. Enclosed in the circle of Henry's arms, Kate felt secure and happy. She admired his strong even facial features as he danced with her. His face had character and strength. When the dance slowed, she rested her head lightly against his shoulder. She knew, with absolute certainty, that Henry was the man for her. It took all her self-control not to fling her arms around him right there in front of all these sophisticated people. She wanted to dance with him for the rest of her life.

When the orchestra took a break, Kate forced herself to remember their assignment. She had yet to tell him about her morning adventures. Certainly the dance floor was not the appropriate venue. She had no intention of spoiling the evening by allowing reality to intrude. Though Henry hadn't yet had time to tell her what he had learned at the embassy, he seemed relaxed and happy. Once while dancing, she had sensed him stiffen perceptibly, but that sensation persisted only a few seconds. Kate couldn't read anything in his eyes that caused her alarm.

"Are you happy, my dear?" asked Henry as they walked toward the refreshment table.

"Oh, Henry! I feel like Cinderella enjoying herself at the ball." Kate said.

She let her enthusiasm show by laughing delightedly and favoring him with a blinding smile. "I had such fun today. The whole day seemed like a dream, a very good dream. Imagine having enough money to buy clothes and hats just because you like them! It's every woman's fantasy." Kate glared at his skeptical expression. "Maybe if you imagined buying the car or motorcycle of your dreams you would understand." She was pleased to see Henry's face brighten with comprehension.

"Besides, I haven't noticed anyone the least bit suspicious lurking about," Kate said teasingly. Her comment earned her a reproving; the walls have ears, look from Henry.

While they stood sipping champagne, Kate noticed that something on the other side of the room caught Henry's eye, but she could not tell what it was. He kissed her lightly on the forehead and said he'd be right back. Kate stood there by the refreshment table a few minutes watching the dancers on the floor. She admired one particularly elegant French couple she had seen Henry speaking with earlier in the evening. They were quite skilled dance partners.

When Henry didn't reappear quickly, Kate decided to use this as an opportunity to freshen up. As she ascended the grand staircase, she paused on the landing to survey the room. Curious, she thought as she took refuge in the ladies powder room, the eyes of several people had followed her progress up the stairs.

When Kate emerged from the powder room, her face filled with dismay at the sight of Henry. He stood propped against a lovely medieval tapestry hanging on the wall. The muted blues and reds served as a backdrop for his bloody face. The eyes of the people in the tapestry all seemed to be staring at Henry with surprise over his appearance. Kate felt her heart ache for him.

"Oh, Henry," Kate wailed as she ran to him. Unhappily, she took in his bruised cheek and rumpled hair. "Are you all right?" Concern for him softened her voice. Kate impulsively reached up to stroke his cheek. Henry took her hand in his and kissed her palm gently. A thrill ran through her, tingling all the way to her toes. As he pushed her gently away from him, Kate saw the grazes on his knuckles.

"Careful darling," Henry said, touched by the sincerity evident in her tone. "Let's not get your lovely dress dirty."

Kate looked up and down the deserted corridor before pulling Henry into the washroom she had just left. There she cleaned his cuts as she listened to his recent exploits with the man he had followed.

"As we left the dance floor, I saw him leave the room. His earlier behavior, hiding behind posts and potted palms while he stared at us, made me curious about him. It seemed wise to follow him and see what he was up to. At first, I thought I had lost him. Then, we literally bumped into each other coming around a corner. He must have been trying to avoid me. I'm just glad no one came upon our resulting scuffle. He'll be quite a shock to someone if they find him in the closet before our security team gets to him. I will need to tell them as soon as I get cleaned up. I mustn't draw attention to myself."

When Kate had finished cleaning up his cuts and scrapes the best she could, Henry looked out the door. After checking that the coast was clear, he led her to the storage closet to check on his prisoner.

"Is he dead? Did you kill him?" Kate asked in a frightened voice as she peered at the prostrate man in the closet.

"No, I managed to stun him by smashing his head into a heavy cast iron planter. He'll just wake up with a rather bad headache. I did take the time to truss him up tightly. He will have some explaining to do when he wakes up. I think he is only a bit player in this drama. Tomorrow, my colleagues and I will question him further."

Taking a closer look at the man's face, Kate drew a sharp intake of breath.

"Henry, this is the same man who followed me this morning!" she exclaimed.

"A man followed you? Why didn't you tell me? Did he hurt you?" The questions came tumbling out.

"Henry, slow down. I am all right. It happened this morning, but I haven't had time to tell you yet. I don't know how long he had been following me. He could have seen me leaving the hotel. He grabbed me as I left a shop," she said.

"What? He grabbed you! Did he hurt you?" Henry interrupted, alarm in his voice. He glared at the unconscious man as if he would gladly murder him.

"We struggled a bit. But, I got away when he tore my clothes. Oh," she wailed. "My hat! I had to leave it lying in the gutter." Kate was just now remembering the details of the attack.

She noticed Henry gave her an incredulous look.

"I liked that hat!"

"Can't be helped, my dear. It's just a hat! The important thing is that you were attacked!" he said brusquely. Seeing her begin to renew her protest, Henry continued.

"Why didn't you tell me?" Henry asked as he shook her none to gently.

"Henry, you're hurting me," Kate said.

He released her as if he had been burned and looked chagrined.

"I left a note for you at the embassy. Didn't you get it?"

"No, I didn't go to the embassy today. My colleague and I met elsewhere," Henry answered. "Why didn't you tell me this earlier evening?"

"I told you, there hasn't been time," Kate said defensively.

"Are you positive it is the same man?" he asked. "Think carefully."

Kate looked at the man's face again and felt a sinking feeling in her stomach. This was definitely the same man. She recognized the way his eyebrows meet across the center of his brow. When she first noticed them Kate had been reminded of a giant hairy caterpillar. She could feel a giant hairy caterpillar travelling up her spine right now. Wordlessly, she turned to Henry, tears in her eyes.

"At least that explains the scrap of purple cloth I found in his pocket."

"There is something else you should know. I met Princess Lazio earlier today, at Chanel."

"Did she introduce herself?"

"No, we exchanged a few words." Kate surprised herself at wanting to keep those two words secret. Somehow she didn't want to share those words with anyone. They had been meant for her ears and hers alone.

"How odd that the Princess didn't mention it when I introduced you."

"There really wasn't time or perhaps she wasn't certain I was the same woman."

"Well, it can't be important. A coincidence at most, just two women meeting while shopping."

Kate did not know whether to laugh or cry when he said that. Instead, she adjusted his collar, straightened his tie, smoothed the lapels of his tuxedo, and, without realizing it, improved Henry's appearance as only a wife can.

Seeing her face, Henry bent down and kissed her gently on her cheek. Recklessly, he pulled her into his arms and gave her a passionate kiss. Kate gave into the urge to pull him closer. She could feel his heartbeat against hers as she clung to him. Abruptly, having kissed her breathless, he set her away from him.

"Let's go back to the ball, Cinderella. Despite our busy evening, it's not yet midnight."

# Chapter 31

## Henry

"*My*, that frock suits you well. Terribly chic yet suitable for proper Sunday activities," Henry said teasingly as Kate sat down to breakfast Sunday morning.

While Henry was certainly no fashion expert, even he could tell that the soft dove grey of Kate's jacket created a striking contrast for the Bordeaux red lining and lapels. Each sleeve had a stripe in the same color running down it from the shoulder to just below the elbow. Underneath, the scoop-necked dove grey blouse was trimmed at the neck to match the jacket. The Bordeaux-red flared skirt had a kick-pleat at the back faced in dove grey. Henry like the way the broad shoulders of the jacket and narrow waist on the skirt complimented Kate's figure. He had to admit that her bewitching red hat, with its high brim on the right flowing to a low brim on the left, framed her face perfectly. Above the crown, a single pheasant feather jauntily pointed toward the sky. Not another feather, Henry groaned silently.

"You look quite dapper yourself," Kate answered smiling. Obviously she had taken his words as a compliment and missed his inward groan. "I didn't have the opportunity last night to compliment you on your hair cut. I must say your tuxedo fit you very well last night, as does the suit you are wearing today." She clapped her hand over her mouth, eyes open wide.

"Oh, my goodness," she sputtered. "Henry, I am so sorry. I just realized something awful!"

"What?" he responded in alarm.

"Here you have bought all these handsome clothes and I didn't think to share the money with you."

"That's what you are upset about?" he asked incredulously.

"Well, yes. I don't want you to think poorly of me."

"I would never do that, darling."

"Did your superiors provide money to replace your clothes?"

"No, not really. They gave us a small amount for incidentals, but no clothing allowance for either of us. Apparently, they assumed we had closets full of expensive outfits just right for an elegant honeymoon on the Orient Express. Fortunately, thanks to a beloved uncle, I have a small annuity. Yesterday, I wired my bank for funds and did as you suggested, went shopping for clothes and made the purchases on your list, right down to the blue and brown suits."

"Very attractive, the deep navy you are wearing brings out the blue in your eyes," Kate said admiringly. Inexplicably, she blushed. She busied herself with her napkin to hide her discomfort. Henry basked happily in her compliment.

"How should we occupy our day, Henry?" she asked primly. "Are you busy with official business all day or will you have some time available after your *rendez-vous* with the unknown man in the closet?"

Smiling, Henry contemplated spending a day in Paris with Kate. Knowing her, she would have the entire day planned. She had taken to perusing the guidebook of Paris. Sometimes he wondered if she ever took her nose out of that blasted guidebook.

"The Simplon Orient Express departs from the *Gare de Lyon* this evening at half past ten this evening," Henry said. "We should plan to arrive a bit early to enjoy dinner at *Le Train Bleu*. The restaurant, even though it is in the train station, is supposed to be breathtakingly elegant. I've been told that the chef is very talented. Shall we say eight o'clock?"

"Sounds lovely."

"This morning, I have a few things loose ends to tie up at the embassy, or perhaps I should say, untie. My colleagues and I will see if our friend in the closet has anything to say. If nothing else critical arises, you and I should have the better part of the day together. Remember, today is supposed to give people the impression we are on our honeymoon. So, what does my lovely bride have in mind for her first Sunday in Paris?"

As Henry suspected, Kate did indeed have a guidebook in her purse. She opened the slim blue book to a marked page.

"Believe it or not, one of the chapters is actually entitled *Your First Sunday in Paris*," Kate said with a smile in her voice. "I am so lucky to have found this wonderful guidebook in the few minutes we had before leaving Victoria Station. It's titled *So You Are Going to Paris.* The young woman who wrote it, Clara Laughlin, describes each day as if she is personally treating you to her favorite parts of Paris. Some of her suggestions for our first Sunday in Paris include visiting the *Parc Monceau* to do a bit of people watching and seeing the *La Sainte-Chapelle* on the *Ile de la Cite*."

Kate turned a page and continued reading.

"According to her, we shouldn't miss the nearby bird-market and of course, *Notre Dame* Cathedral. For lunch she suggests the *Café Harcourt* on the *Boulevard Saint-Michel*. Since that's on the left bank, we should see some artist types out and about. After lunch, we might wish to rest a bit in *Le Jardin de Luxembourg*."

"While there, you can read to me from the guidebook all the interesting things the author has to say about this quarter of Paris," Henry sighed.

"If you would like, we can visit the Odeon Theatre and the Pantheon. They are only a short walk away. The author also suggests we take a cab ride around Paris in order to view the sights, including the Opera and the grand boulevards." She paused. "Of course, it would be lovely just to sit at a sidewalk café and watch the world go by."

"It sounds as if we have a busy day ahead of us." Henry gently took the guidebook from her hands. "But, tell me, if you didn't have the guidebook, what would you like to do, in your heart of hearts?"

"*La Tour Eiffel*," she said wistfully. "I would love to go to the top of the Eiffel Tower."

Henry's eyes roamed over Kate, taking in her lovely face, neat figure, and outrageous hat. His world shifted beneath his feet. Like a man walking out of a fog, suddenly everything was clear to him. He realized that sitting in front of him was someone very desirable, someone worth holding on to. Impulsively, he leaned toward her and touched her hand. He opened his mouth to speak. At the last moment, just when he was about to declare himself, his courage faltered. He returned to the safe topic of the day's activities.

"Then that's what we will do," he promised. "Fortunately, the Eiffel Tower is near the embassy, so I can take care of my business easily. I know, let's begin our day as the author suggests. When it is time for my appointment at the embassy, why don't I drop you first at the *Musee Jacquemart-Andre*? You can enjoy the museum while I question my captive. I will return to pick you up when my business is concluded. I am sure someone can suggest a good restaurant nearby for lunch. From there, we can go to the Eiffel Tower. Later in the afternoon we can visit *Le Jardin de Luxembourg*. We can ask the cab driver to take a scenic route, which he probably has planned for foreigners anyway."

"That sounds perfect. In place of the *Parc Monceau*, I'd rather visit *Notre Dame* first. Though I am Protestant, the notion of hearing mass at *Notre Dame* appeals to me. After services, we can go to the nearby bird market."

"All right, let's be off," Henry said jauntily. The day was planned to give the impression that they were newlyweds and Henry knew he would enjoy spending his day with Kate. At the same time, he planned to keep one eye open for trouble.

# Chapter 32

## Kate

*H*ow delightfully Sunday had begun.  Henry had noticed and admired her outfit, keeping his comments about her hat to an acceptable minimum.  Kate realized that she really cared what he thought of her.  She wanted to present her best self to him.  She wanted to be pretty for him.  These ideas surprised her.  Kate had never found it important to please a man before.  How much she had changed in the past three days.

Since only a few blocks separated their hotel from *Notre Dame*, they soon stood in front of the cathedral in all its splendor.  The building's perfect symmetry drew the eye upward to its matching square towers.  Due to lack of funds, neither tower had been capped with the traditional pointed steeples.  While this could have had the effect of making the cathedral squat and boxy, instead the perfect proportions pleased the eye.  The cathedral seemed to be connected to the ground and at the same time soaring into the heavens.  The large central door, one of three on the front of the building, was open to allow parishioners to enter.  Surrounding each of the doors, Kate could see the tympanums contained figures of kings and priests of the past.  Startled, she realized that the figures were six layers deep.  The tolling of the great bells beckoned all who could hear to worship.

Kate gasped as she entered the nave.  Glorious sunlight filtered through the famous Gothic stained glass rose windows.  A myriad of tiny splinters of deep blue and burgundy red light danced on the floor and in the air.  She knew from her guidebook that the northern rose window showed scenes from the Old Testament while the southern rose window was devoted to the heavenly host.

The music from the organ swelled to fill the vast space with soul enriching music. Kate marveled at the height of the walls and the size of the columns supporting them. Over 150 feet tall, they seemed to stretch upward forever, gallery atop of gallery. Yet, for all their enormous stone mass, the towering stained glass windows made the walls seem lighter than air. As the service progressed, the chants and hymns seemed to Kate to be at once familiar and new to her. Following the service, she left the great cathedral knowing she had an experience like no other in her life.

Leaving *Notre Dame*, Henry suggested they visit *La Sainte-Chapelle*. Constructed in 1248, by King Louis IX, it housed the holy relics—Christ's Crown of Thorns and a fragment of the True Cross. Here too, the magnificent stained glass windows capture the eye and the spirit.

"This place is ethereal," Kate said in awe.

"An architectural masterpiece," responded Henry quietly.

"The guidebook says that pilgrims in the Middle Ages considered *La Sainte-Chapelle* a gateway to heaven. There are over 1,000 biblical scenes depicted in the stained glass windows."

"Look at the windows! The columns separating them look pencil thin."

"And the ceiling! It has stars on it."

"It must be fifty feet above us."

Later, as they strolled through the nearby bird market, admiring the vast assortment of birds, cages, and accessories. Kate commented on the effect the two buildings, *Notre Dame and La Sainte-Chapelle*, had had on her imagination.

"Henry, can you imagine how people have worshiped in these buildings for hundreds and hundreds of years?" she asked with wonder in her voice. "I know it seems fanciful, but it was almost as if I could feel the presence of centuries of worshippers."

"They represent the marvels of human faith, don't they?" he answered as he checked his watch. "It's time for me to go to the embassy. Let's get a cab. I will drop you at the *Musee Jacquesmart-Andre*."

The few hours she spent at the *Musee Jacquesmart-Andre* while waiting on Henry had fascinated her. The museum presented an incredible collection of objects of great value and rare beauty. Unlike other museum collections, the *Musee Jacquesmart-Andre* displayed everything in the setting of a home. M. Edouard Andre and his wife Madame Nelie Jacquesmart-Andre bequeathed their home to the Institute of France with the proviso that it always remains a family home. Their collection of *objet d'art* rivaled that of any museum, yet the setting was warm and inviting, just as if you had stepped back in time into someone's home. Exactly the effect the couple had wanted.

When she finished her tour of the house, Kate decided to sit outside in the sun to wait for Henry. She had only been seated a few moments when he appeared. She noticed he seemed a bit preoccupied, but Henry smiled when he saw her. As they left the museum grounds, they discussed various options for lunch. On impulse, they decided to eat at a sidewalk café. Their fluency in French made it easy for them to order. Henry and Kate watched the people parading by their table, giggling occasionally at comments and observations made by the people around them. Beautifully dressed men and women greeted each other, embraced, and kissed on both cheeks. Kate enjoyed this experience even more than her games of making up stories for people around her. The tiny sidewalk tables had been so closely placed that they could not help overhearing neighboring discussions. As she sipped her demitasse of *Espresso*, it seemed to Kate that everyone seated at the café enjoyed watching the passersby and commenting about who they were.

"Whoever do you think that is getting out of that racy car? A duke?"

"Do you see those two? Where do you imagine they bought those striking suits?"

"I am sure that that is the Countess de Nemours."

"No, I am certain I overheard last night that she was in the country."

"Kate, we really shouldn't be eavesdropping on other people's conversations," reprimanded Henry.

"Surely, you've done this sort of thing before?" asked Kate with obvious surprise at his aggrieved tone.

"No, not really. It feels as though I'm spying on them," responded Henry.

"Well, isn't eavesdropping part of spying? You never know when a little practice may come in handy," said Kate, a mischievous twinkle in her eye. She could tell by his face that Henry did not agree.

It pleased Kate that despite the interrogation Henry undertook at the embassy, Henry retained his good humor. She tried to buoy his spirits even further by being particularly effervescent. She need not have worried; they seemed to be in their own delightful world. It was obvious to her that they were attracted to each other. Each accidental touch of their hands sent waves of pleasure coursing through her. During lunch, Henry had been quite charming and attentive. Men with hard faces and cold eyes receded into the background as Henry entertained her with stories of his childhood.

"I had no idea you were such an adventuresome young man! I would have never pictured you as the ring leader of the other neighborhood boys."

"If you don't believe me, you can ask my mother. She'll tell you I was always on the lookout for mischief," Henry laughed.

Kate greeted that comment with an uncomfortable silence. How nice it would be to let herself dream of a future where she did meet Henry's mother and father.

"It's time for the Eiffel Tower, isn't it?" said Henry, breaking the silence.

The Eiffel Tower.  Throughout the day Kate had caught glimpses of it through the buildings and trees.  Each time she saw it, her heart skipped a beat.  Kate had never imagined visiting this Paris landmark with anyone.  Now she was going to see the Eiffel Tower.  With Henry.  How romantic, she thought, smiling to herself.  On the brief walk to the base of the tower, Kate entertained Henry with information on the Eiffel Tower from her guidebook.

*"Finished in 1889, the Eiffel Tower, at 984 feet, is considered the tallest building in the world."*

"How can you walk with your nose in that guidebook?"

"Very carefully," Kate answered with a winning smile.  "It says here that the tower is held together by over two and a half million rivets!"

"Two and a half million rivets!" Henry exclaimed.  "Do you think they were counted by a certified accounting firm?"

"Silly man, how on earth could someone count them?"

"Watch your step here."

"Thank you," Kate said as she side-stepped a fruit vendor's cart.

"Glad to be of assistance, my dear.  Well, go on.  There must be more you can't wait to tell me."

"Yes, of course there is.  I am doing my best to entertain you today," she answered in a teasing tone.  "I think your logical mind will like the elevators the best.  Each elevator, one in each leg, runs on an angle as they move up the tower.  You'll have to explain to me how they do that."

"Are there stairs too?"

"Yes.  You should take them and count every one of the 1,652 steps to the top!"

"Will you climb with me?"

"Certainly not! I'll take the elevator and meet you at each of the three observation decks. You'll be able to catch your breath at 187 feet, at 377 feet, and at 899 feet."

Henry scowled as she teased him. Kate read further.

"Did you know that the tower almost didn't get built? Or that twenty years later, it was nearly torn down?" she asked. Kate continued without waiting for his answer.

"The construction of the tower was quite controversial. Artisans, writers, and ordinary citizens signed petitions to stop its construction. People just weren't used to the style of construction. It was built at a time of stone and elegantly proportioned buildings. Compared to traditional building methods, the ironworks seem so bare and exposed. Actually, that is what I find charming about it. It is enormous, yet so very graceful. Anyway, back to the history lesson. In 1909, when Gustave Eiffel's concession contract expired, it was nearly torn down. Only its usefulness as a huge radio antenna saved it. As a matter of fact, the radio antenna extended its height to 1,050 feet."

Despite Henry's intention to take the stairs, they rode the elevators to the highest observation deck. There, all of Paris spread out at their feet. The clear skies of the warm spring day provided them with a wonderful panoramic view. According to the guidebook, on a fine day, such as today, they could see forty miles. She and Henry took turns pointing out the various landmarks of Paris. *Notre Dame*, the *Sacre Coeur, L'Arc de Triomphe,* the *Bois de Boulogne*, the *Champs Elysee.*

There on the highest platform, the tower exerted its magic over them both. Henry slipped his arm around her waist and she did the same to him. She turned to say something unimportant. Their eyes met and suddenly, Kate was in his arms. Henry pulled her into a tight embrace and kissed her. It seemed so appropriate; she didn't even try to pull away. He felt so warm and solid against her. Despite their location high up in the air, she felt secure and safe in his arms.

"All in the line of duty," Henry murmured into her lips as he kissed her more deeply.

Wanting to dispel any thoughts of duty from his mind, Kate wrapped her arms around his neck and kissed him back. Their second kiss was like no other Kate had ever experienced. The earth spun beneath her as desire coursed through her. Heat seared through her body. The sounds from the street below seemed very far away. She wrapped her fingers in his hair and pulled him closer to her. Suddenly, she couldn't get enough of him.

The sound of a throat-clearing sternly behind them caused them to look up. Kate blushed a bright pink. She wasn't given to such demonstrative displays of affection, certainly not in public. A sour-faced policeman gave them a shake of his head before walking stiffly away. Henry smiled down at Kate, his even, white teeth showed white against his lightly tanned skin. She felt his smile warming her to the very center of her being. Suddenly Kate knew. She just knew deep in her soul that this was where she was supposed to be. Right here, right now, next to Henry, for the rest of their lives. Now, having set her cap for Henry, she would need to convince him of that.

Back again on the ground, reality intruded like a shadow over their day. They weren't really on a honeymoon. There, up on the tower, Kate had actually allowed herself to imagine she was. Like Henry had said, it was all in the line of duty. The thought of losing Henry at the end of their assignment depressed her more than she had thought possible. Seeing the look of dismay on her face, Henry urged her to sit down on a nearby bench.

"Don't go away," he said. "I'll be right back."

When he returned, Henry's smile banished her gloomy thoughts. He delighted her by presenting her with a bouquet of spring flowers.

"Here's a little something to cheer you up," Henry said encouragingly. "All in the line of duty, you know."

Kate looked up at him as she buried her nose in their scented petals. His gift coaxed a reluctant smile from her lips. How handsome he was, the strong line of his jaw accentuated by the afternoon sun. She couldn't bear to take her eyes off of him. The very sight of him filled her with joy. Kate knew would have to make the most of their every moment.

"Where shall we go now?" Henry asked.

"Let's walk over to the *Avenue des Champs Elysees*. Wouldn't you like to see the *Arc de Triomphe*?" Kate responded mustering her enthusiasm.

"Do I dare ask what you have read about the arch?" he teased.

"It was begun by Napoleon I. It was not completed until much later, in 1836, I think," she said in her best guide voice.

"Shall we go up?"

"Of course!" Kate answered.

From the top of the arch, they could see Baron Haussmann's grand plan for Paris.

"Isn't Paris lovely?" breathed Kate at the sight.

"Did you know that twelve broad boulevards all radiate from the arch?" Henry's question was obviously rhetorical because he continued. "The star pattern made by the roads give the intersection its name, *Place de Etoile*."

"Look, you can see all the way down the *Champs Elysees* to the *Obelisque* in the *Place de la Concorde* and the *Tuileries* gardens beyond."

After taking in the view of Paris from the top of the arch, they strolled down the *Champs Elysees*, marveling at the goods for sale in the shop windows of the famed street.

On one street corner, an elderly man operated an organ grinder. His equally elderly dog lay curled up in a basket on the top of the organ. The cheerful tunes filled the air. Watching the two of them together, Kate could swear that the man was playing for the dog's amusement. The sight of the old man and his dog enjoying each other's company as well as the music filled Kate with happiness. She generously contributed coins to the small dish strategically placed on top of the organ. The dog's eyes met hers as if to say thank you.

On their walk to the *Jardins des Tuileries*, Henry and Kate passed the *Grand* and *Petit Palais* with their unusual architecture. Like *Pont Alexandre* III, the glass-domed buildings were constructed for the 1900 Paris *Exposition Universelle*. They lingered for a while on the bridge, watching the grey-blue water of the Seine flow by beneath their feet. A myriad of barges, skiffs, and pleasure boats kept up a regular parade of activity.

"All these boats cruising by remind me of King Alexander's parade next week," said Henry quietly.

"Let's not talk about that now, let's just enjoy the moment," Kate pleaded.

"Why don't you tell me what your guidebook says about the bridge?" said Henry, obviously making an effort to pull his mind away from thoughts of King Alexander. "What do these mythical beasts and cherubs wrapped around the lampposts represent?"

"I thought you would never ask," Kate answered with a smile. "*Pont Alexandre* is named after Tsar Alexander III. With your love of history, you can't help but remember him. He concluded the Franco-Russian Alliance in 1892. According to the guidebook, his son Nicholas II laid the foundation stone in October 1896."

"Fascinating fun facts," Henry quipped. "I am more interested in these beauties." He touched one of the lampposts.

"The creatures on these incredible gilded lampposts reflect the fascination the Victorians had with mythical sea creatures. Do you see the massive columns at each end of the bridge?"

"How can you miss them?"

"The four gilt-bronze statues of fames watch over the bridge while providing the stabilizing counterweight for the arch. Each statue represents the Fames restraining Pegasus. On the right bank, the statues are *Renommée des Sciences* and the *Renommée des Arts*. That means the fames of the Sciences and Arts. On the Left Bank, the *Renommée du Commerce* and the *Renommée de l'Industrie*—"

"Let me guess. The fames of Commerce and Industry," Henry said, cutting her off.

"You're terrible," she said. "I shouldn't tell you anything at all."

"The bridge certainly is well situated. In one direction, the road leads to *Les Invalides*, to the other, the *Grand* and *Petit Palais*," said Henry, looking around.

"And downstream, is the Eiffel Tower."

"And upstream is the *Louvre* and *Notre Dame*," he finished for her.

"Would you like to walk a bit along the river down on the *quai*?"

"A most delightful idea. Shall we take these steps here?"

They walked along the cobble-stoned *quai* taking pleasure in the warm June day. Kate had enjoyed their light and easy banter at the Alexander III Bridge. At the next bridge, they ascended the steep stairs back up to street level. On impulse, they crossed the street and entered the *Tuileries* gardens. Once inside, they left the hustle and bustle of the city behind. The gardens were lovely. Roses bloomed everywhere. As if reading each other's minds, they decided to stop for refreshments at one of the cafés under the chestnut trees. They chose a quiet table at an outdoor restaurant.  Kate finally resigned herself to hearing about their assignment.  Reluctantly, she asked Henry to tell her what he had learned.

# Chapter 33

## Henry

*A*s he sat relaxing at the restaurant in the *Jardin de Luxembourg*, Henry reflected on their day. He could not have imagined a better way to start a Sunday morning than with services at *Notre Dame*. He remembered the play of light and sound with genuine admiration for the medieval builders. *La Sainte-Chapelle*, the sun glistening through its windows, provided a scene of unimaginable beauty.

His two tense hours at the embassy were ultimately unfruitful. The man Henry had captured the evening before refused to speak to them. Henry questioned him repeatedly about his actions toward Kate and his presence at the embassy. The man gave no reasons for his attack on Kate. Eventually, he let slip that an assassin would be taking the Simplon Orient Express that evening. He failed to divulge who he worked with or for. Nor would he tell them the name of the assassin's target. Nothing in his pockets provided any information about the man's identity. He would not admit to making the phone call to Henry's room. Henry, seething with frustration, finally gave up questioning the man as a lost cause.

It pleased Henry that no other incidents had occurred to spoil the remainder of their day in Paris. Kissing Kate at the top of the Eiffel Tower had definitely been the high point for him in more ways than one. He knew he probably shouldn't have kissed her so fervently. It was all for the sake of appearances, wasn't it? Kate's downcast face at the base of the tower made him wonder what was wrong. In an attempt to cheer her up, he had bought her flowers. Perhaps roses weren't the best choice. Henry recalled his conversation with the flower peddler.

*"Quelques fleurs pour votre petite amie, Monsieur?"* the man had asked as he cast a pleasant smile at Kate sitting in the distance.

Though he obviously wanted flowers for Kate, Henry had mixed feelings about the man's suggestion that Kate was his *petite amie*, his girlfriend. If the Princess, Monsieur De la Roche, and a street flower vendor had noticed, the entire world must be aware of his feelings for Kate. Perhaps Princess Lazio was right, he might be exposing Kate to grave danger. The idea unsettled him.

Henry pushed aside these perilous thoughts and focused on the present. He enjoyed sitting in the shade of the chestnut trees, quenching his thirst with a refreshing drink. His view included his charming Kate framed by the outline of the elegant restaurant building. No more than twenty feet square, the dark green structure was topped with a dark green metal roof. Fretwork had been added to the edges of the roof to enhance the appeal of the utilitarian construction. Through the large rectangular windows that surrounded the building on all sides, Henry could see waiters bustling about filling their orders. Dozens of small dark green square tables stood clustered around the little building. Each was occupied with couples, friends, or families, enjoying the lovely late afternoon weather.

"Henry, is there anything more I should know before we board the train?" Kate asked, breaking into his mental review of the architectural details. "What did your captive have to tell you this morning?"

"Not much. The only really good information I got from him is that the assassin is taking the Simplon Orient Express Sunday night just like we are. Despite our efforts, he wouldn't say anything more."

"Did the people in Paris tell you more about our assignment? Surely they have more information about the threat to King Alexander's life."

"The information they provided is anything but complete. Besides a plan of the train and information about the occupants of our coach, they gathered more information about the threat to King Alexander," Henry began. "I'll try to be brief. There are definitely three factions interested in King Alexander and his policies. First, there are his countrymen. If you remember what I told you earlier, the Kingdom of Yugoslavia is the result of decisions made following the Great War. Yugoslavia, as we know it today, is actually a combination of many smaller states including the Serbs, Croats, Slovenes, the Dalmatians, and the Montenegro. It is quite a mixed bag of people, nationalities, religions, language, and culture."

"Was Alexander regent or did he inherit the throne? I can't remember what I read," interjected Kate.

"Alexander had been appointed regent in 1914 and he inherited the throne in 1921 upon the death of his father, Peter I. Shortly after the Great War, he declared the areas ceded to him by the Treaty of Versailles to be the Kingdom of Serbs, Croats, and Slovenes. Things became more difficult for the King throughout the 1920s. Both the Serbs and the Croats desired autonomy. There have even been proposals for separate countries. In response to these difficulties, in January of 1929, King Alexander abolished the Constitution and appointed himself dictator."

"He essentially created the nation of Yugoslavia."

"Since that time, there has been significant agitating among his people. As I said before, some want a strong central government and others want regional autonomy. His declarations, such as the one ordering the use of the Latin alphabet in place of the Serbian Cyrillic, were designed to unify the country. Much to his consternation, they have had the effect of further inciting the people. Regardless of what he does, King Alexander seems to kindle hostility in the hearts of his people. In 1931, King Alexander went even further and created a new constitution in which the provision for secret ballot elections was dropped. So you can see that there are many reasons that different factions within his own country would be upset with him."

"You enjoy knowing all these details, don't you?" Kate asked when Henry paused to gather his thoughts.

"The answers often lie in the details," he answered quite seriously.

"Refresh my memory on current events. I know I read about happenings at the time but I don't remember it all," she said to placate him.

"Yugoslavia has entered into several diplomatic pacts with neighboring nations. Some of those pacts displease a few of Yugoslavia's allies. They form the second group of people who might desire the death of the King. In early February of this year, King Alexander participated in the creation of the Balkan Pact. By uniting the Turkish, Greek, Romanian, and Yugoslavian governments, the pact is designed to protect the Balkans from encroachment by more powerful neighboring nations. Tensions ran high among the nations united by the pact when King Alexander announced on June 1$^{st}$ that he had entered into a trade agreement with Germany. There is a belief among some diplomats that Yugoslavia is tying itself to Germany in response to the Italian-Austrian-Hungarian alliance. This action is at odds with what the King previously agreed to. The representatives of some countries believe the new alliances carry things a bit too far. Radical factions might wish to put an end to King Alexander's inconsistent actions." Henry took a sip of his drink.

"You said there were three groups."

"Since April, King Alexander has been touring Europe visiting various heads of state. Through these visits, the King hopes to improve international relationships and create alliances against Germany. Despite the recent agreement with the German government, King Alexander's efforts to ally other nations against Hitler have drawn the anger of those in power in Germany. King Alexander may be seen as more of a liability than an asset."

"Well, it's ever so kind of you to give me all this useful information," she said, her head reeling with facts and figures.

Henry knew he had talked too long about topics unsuitable for a gloriously sunny Sunday afternoon in Paris. He couldn't help himself; the complexities of international diplomacy intrigued him. He was pleased when Kate asked him a question that showed she really had been listening.

"Henry, what will happen if King Alexander dies?" she inquired.

"King Alexander married Princess Maria of Romania in 1922. They have three sons, Crown Prince Peter, and Princes Tomislav, and Andrai. The Crown Prince is now twelve years old, too young to take the throne himself. If his father dies, a regent will be chosen. That man would probably be Prince Pavle Karadordevic, Alexander's first cousin. Unless the regent exerts enough power to hold this struggling nation together, there will be a great deal of civil unrest. The area has always been a bit of a powder keg. Assassinating the King could touch off a crisis. That is why it is so important to ensure the safety of the King."

Henry took a deep breath before continuing.

"That should be enough for now about who we are up against. Though we have uncovered evidence of a plot against the King, not enough information is available to help identify the parties involved. The only thing we know for certain is that the attempt will be made some time during French diplomat Louis Barthou's upcoming visit to Belgrade," Henry said. "Barthou will arrive the day after we do. There will be a welcoming party at the train station in Belgrade which will be followed by a parade from the station to the palace. King Alexander will ride through the parade with Barthou at his side."

Henry's desire to talk about plots and plans diminished. The warm afternoon sun and Kate's alluring presence distracted him. He wanted to move on to more pleasant topics. As he finished with his narrative, he noticed Kate looked worried. Henry certainly could understand her fears. They were going across a continent to stop an assassination by persons unknown, at an unknown time, place, and date. Henry searched her face carefully remembering how just forty-eight hours ago he had had to beg her to accompany him.

"Actually, Kate, now that we are about to embark, I am concerned for your safety. Perhaps it would be best…"

"You're not planning on leaving me behind, are you?" Kate asked indignantly, cutting him off. "I must go, if for no other reason that it would look very awkward to back out now. As your wife, my departure from our honeymoon would surely draw attention to you. We must carry on." The sound of conviction in her tone startled both of them.

What pluck she had, throughout all their adventures, Kate had kept her wits about her. Despite the risks, Henry realized he could not imagine completing this assignment without her aid. He could feel the weight of responsibility settle on his shoulders as he recognized how careful he would need to be for Kate's safety. In the meantime, he decided he needed to be more business-like and professional in his interactions with Kate. Tonight they would be leaving on the Orient Express and he had a job to do.

# Chapter 34

## Kate

*E*arlier, while they had packed their bags in preparation for their Sunday evening departure, Kate had carefully taken one of the blooms from the nosegay that Henry had given her and pressed it between the pages of the London guidebook. Kate smiled thoughtfully at the idea of preserving such a fragile memory of her time with Henry in Paris. She wondered if he would want her to return the emerald ring. Would a postcard, a guidebook, a faded flower and the memory of a few marvelous kisses be all she had left? Pushing thoughts of the future out of her mind, Kate changed into evening wear appropriate for fine dining and a departure on the Orient Express.

Once they reached the *Gare de Lyon* train station, Henry had arranged for a porter to ensure that all their bags made it safely on the Orient Express.

"What is all this?" asked Henry, incredulous over the pile of luggage at his feet.

Kate chose to ignore his comments about the large number of Louis Vuitton cases she had amassed in Paris.

"I don't think it amounts to all that much; four hat boxes, a dressing case, a small suitcase, and a travelling trunk," Kate said in response to his glare. "You just don't understand what it takes to prepare for a trip like this."

"Madame, which luggage cases will you register to go straight through?" the porter asked.

"What do you mean? I don't understand," Kate said.

"Madame must decide which pieces would be registered to go straight through to their destination," the man answered. "These pieces will be locked away in the baggage car. The others can be kept in your compartment on the train."

"Hurry up my dear, the man has a job to do," Henry said impatiently as he stood nearby.

"Don't rush me. I need to make careful selections. A girl has to be prepared, doesn't she?" Kate countered. "Our adventure begins again this evening. I want to be dressed just right."

"You mean you want to have just the right hat!"

By eight o'clock, they were seated at *Le Train Bleu* restaurant, sipping champagne, about to enjoy a marvelous dinner. The opulent décor of *Le Train Bleu* literally left her speechless. Built for the 1900 Paris exhibition, the large restaurant ran the entire front of the train station. The large ornate rooms housed forty-one gigantic paintings of the beautiful sights reached by the railroad. More than thirty years later, the restaurant retained its charming *Belle Epoque* atmosphere. Kate tilted her head back and looked at the vaulted ceiling soaring twenty feet above her. The waning evening light filtered in through the huge windows framed in red velvet curtains. Glorious gilt-framed paintings covered every available inch of the walls and ceiling. Each was an invitation to travel. They depicted destinations throughout the world. The artists had captured the adventure, mystery, and beauty that awaited the traveller willing to leave the comforts of home for places unknown. How Kate would like to venture to each and every one of those locations. Would she and Henry be seeing sights like these on their travels together? And, if not on this trip, what about on others? She craned her neck to find paintings that might resemble where they were bound. Kate caught Henry smiling at her and she sheepishly opened her menu. It wasn't long before her gaze drifted to the lovely huge crystal chandeliers hanging at intervals throughout the cavernous room. She hadn't expected to find such a beautiful setting in a train station. Certainly the curved staircase required to reach *Le Train Bleu* gave few clues to the luxurious world in which she now found herself in. Kate's attention lingered on the ornately carved booths with their handsome leather seats. The booths provided a good deal of privacy between the patrons, allowing conversations to remain private. Despite the large number of patrons, the restaurant was relatively quiet. Kate admired the monogrammed dishes and crystal goblets. Everything spoke of care and attention to detail. Out of keeping with the room's décor, huge clocks hung at the end of each room in order to remind people of the time. The designers of the restaurant obviously understood that it wouldn't do to have sated diners miss their trains.

When the immaculately dressed waiter approached their table, it was Henry who placed their order. Kate hadn't concentrated on the menu long enough to make up her mind.

"To begin this evening, the chef recommends *Asperges Mousseline*, fresh asparagus in season."

"Yes, that sounds very nice," Henry responded. "Would you like that as a starter too, Kate?"

Kate nodded her head yes absentmindedly.

"For your main course this evening, the chef recommends the *Agneau a la Mosaique,*" said the waiter. "Spring lamb prepared with a mosaic of vegetables."

"Yes, that would be fine for me," said Henry. "What would you like, my dear?"

"Oh, I'm sorry. I have been so busy admiring the lovely paintings. I haven't spared a moment to look at the menu."

"Perhaps Madame would like to sample the *Perche du Loire Meuniere.* Perch from the Loire prepared with a butter cream sauce."

"That would be fine," she answered.

"What wine do you recommend to accompany it?" asked Henry.

"I will send the wine steward to your table, Sir."

During a quiet moment while Henry discussed wine selections with the steward, Kate studied his face. Such a handsome man he was, she thought proudly. She glanced around to see if anyone was watching them. Kate hoped so. She had never worn such a beautiful dress in such a fine restaurant with such a wonderful man. She wanted the whole world to see her tonight. Kate thought she would burst with happiness.

When their meal arrived, Kate marveled, "Henry, the *Asperges Mousseline* is wonderful! It positively melts in your mouth."

"I am surprised you have taken your attention away from the room long enough to taste it."

"Henry, you're a bit grumpy this evening."

"Grumpy, no. Feeling a bit left out? Yes."

"I promise I will focus my attention on you throughout the entire *Agneau a la Mosaique de Primeurs du Jardin*," Kate answered with a laugh.

"Darling."

"Yes, dear."

"About your hat."

This statement certainly got her attention.

"What about my hat?" Kate said as she narrowed her eyes at him.

"Well, for starters, can it really be called a hat?"

"I think my hat is a perfect accompaniment for my dress." She touched the tiny riot of shell-pink flowers that perched on her chignon. Was there no pleasing the man?

"Another Chanel?" said Henry, trying to sound terribly blasé just to annoy her. "It suits you, deceptively simple."

Kate's dress was deceptively simple. Her right shoulder was bare except for a single narrow shoulder strap that held the bodice in place. A band of sheer fabric began below her right arm and rose gracefully to drape over her left shoulder. There, she had the option of tying the remaining fabric in a bow or allowing it to flow over her shoulder and down her back. She liked the way it flowed behind her as she walked. Tonight, she had chosen to allow the fabric to hang free. Below a tight bodice that ended at her hips, the skirt of the dress swirled softly around her calves.

"The French certainly knew how to bring out the best in spring lamb and vegetables," he said with satisfaction in his voice.

"Just be sure to save some room for the *Les Fraise Sauvage au Vin Rouge*."

"Wild strawberries for dessert! How delightful!" Henry exclaimed.

"I could certainly get used to dining this well at every meal."

Though she tried hard to concentrate on what Henry was saying about the people travelling on the train, Kate could not help but notice a few of the diners around them. One couple in particular would have been hard to miss. Their loud British voices carried over the sounds of crystal, silver, and china clinking; diners conversing in many languages; and the hurried footsteps of white-jacketed waiters. In between their disparaging comments about the richness of French cuisine, the couple discussed their upcoming trip to Istanbul and beyond. Kate smiled to herself. Many people would have loved to have the experiences this couple shared. When she glanced back toward Henry, Kate saw he was smiling too.

"Perhaps they want the rest of us unlucky souls to know what we are missing," he laughed. They looked at each other, their eyes silently acknowledging that they were the lucky ones.

Next to the British couple sat a group of men dressed similarly in grey suits with conservative ties. They behaved very business-like as they focused on their meals and little else. Across the room from them sat a rather exotic-looking couple. The woman was dressed in finery reminiscent of the 1920s. Kate thought she detected Russian words when they spoke. She began to imagine lives for them as white Russian refugees wandering around Europe in search of a home.

"Henry, are you as curious about the people around us as I am?"

# Chapter 35

## Henry

"*C*urious about our fellow diners? I should think so. Many of them are joining us this evening on the Orient Express. I can see several of them from where I am sitting," Henry began after he placed their dessert order. "This is the perfect opportunity for me to tell you about some of our fellow passengers on the train and how they might play a role in our assignment."

"Oh, Henry, must we?" moaned Kate. "I've been having so much fun. Must our last evening in Paris focus on work?"

Kate leaned toward him causing Henry to catch the scent of her perfume. Violets and springtime. He looked away while he struggled to maintain his composure.

"We are on assignment," Henry said rather sternly though he could feel his resolve to be more business-like weaken.

"But we are surrounded by such beauty, can't we just enjoy it?"

"Really my dear..."

"Very well, if you must be a beast and ruin my evening, go ahead," Kate said in a huff.

Determined to focus on their assignment, Henry forged ahead.

"Let's begin with the people you met at the embassy reception. Princess Lazio, an Italian, is married to an Austrian. She retains her hereditary Italian title and name. Her husband, Herman Kline is pro-Nazi and holds a position fairly high in the new German government. The Princess is popular in both Italian and German society. These connections allow her many opportunities to pass information along channels outside the normal circuits. While no proof has been found to substantiate that she has ever done so, there is some question about the timing of this trip on the Orient Express. We will need to ascertain whether or not her ultimate destination is Belgrade. She has stated that the purpose of her trip is to travel to Istanbul on her way to visit friends in Cairo. This may or may not be true. So far we have not received any confirmation."

"The Princess seemed so nice when I met her. You danced with her. What did you think?" Kate asked.

Henry, still uncomfortable about the Princess' comments at the reception, did not want to answer that particular question just yet. So he continued the conversation by discussing Monsieur and Madame De la Roche.

"Monsieur and Madame De la Roche. Did you meet them at the embassy? I only spoke with them briefly. They are also on the train, in the same coach as we are, as a matter of fact. De la Roche is considered a patriot by all who know him. He is a decorated veteran from the Great War. His wife served as a nurse very near the front lines. They both come from wealthy and well-respected families. Though they keep an apartment in Paris, their primary residence is a chateau in the Loire Valley."

"They sound perfectly wonderful. Why should we even consider them?"

"Monsieur De la Roche is well known in diplomatic circles. The only anomaly in his life is his undisclosed source of income. When questioned about it, he responds with vague references to a job with the French government, but we haven't been able to determine what branch employs him."

"Who else besides the Princess and the De la Roches is of interest to us?" Kate asked as she ate another bite of dessert.

"Perhaps, from where you are sitting you can see the Count di Cosimo?" Henry said looking forward over Kate's shoulder.

"No, the back of the booth is blocking my view," Kate answered.

"You won't be able to miss him when we are on the train. He is a very handsome Italian with a reputation for being quite a lady's man," said Henry.

"I can hear by the tone of your voice that you don't care for him already," said Kate.

"I have my reasons," Henry responded. "Besides being a notorious rake, the man has no visible means of support. He runs with a wild crowd of young continental people. He's had several run-ins with the law in several countries. Count di Cosimo appears to be taking this trip as a lark, rather than for any genuine reason."

"Is that all you know about him?" asked Kate reasonably.

"The embassy briefing material does not say much about the Count," said Henry truthfully. "I suppose we will need to watch him just like we do everyone else."

"Henry, what about that couple seated to our right? The ones who look like white Russians? Could they be involved, you know, some sort of plot to regain their homeland?"

"Kate, are you letting your imagination run off with you here?" said Henry, a bit crossly.

"Well, you are the one who is talking about mystery connections and unknown sources of income," Kate answered, a bit miffed that Henry rebuffed her attempt to join in.

"Let's continue with our analysis. We have representatives from a wide variety of nations," Henry continued a bit pompously. "You can hear one of them right now." They both listened as a very British voice rose over the sounds of the room to complain about the sauce covering their dinner.

"You know why the French use so many sauces, don't you?" the voice asked imperiously. "It's because they are trying to hide the origin of the meat."

Henry and Kate cringed simultaneously. So much for enhancing Anglo-French relationships.

"The voice you hear is that of Colonel Forsyth, late of His Majesty's Armed Forces. Colonel Forsyth fought in the Balkans region during the Great War. In the past 15 years, he has been quite outspoken about English government policies. The Colonel's views are not always appreciated by our government's officials. We have reason to suspect that the length of his journey to Istanbul, ostentatiously to visit friends, will be extended by a stopover in Belgrade. While there, he may try to reacquaint himself with former army comrades. Several who fought with him during the war have risen to positions of power in King Alexander's government."

"So, he definitely merits watching," Kate said.

"A second French couple is also on the train. Their names are DuBois. He is active in the French government. Madame DuBois' background is a bit confusing. Her family is from the Alsace region and has at one time or another been required to switch from being French to being German. Such is the fate of the people living on the border of the two countries. French until the Franco-Prussian war, the area came under German control when hostilities ceased. Following the Great War, the area returned to French rule. Her family is well-connected in the current German government regime. On the surface, the chief occupation of the DuBois is spending money. You will probably be able to recognize them by their clothing," said Henry, unable to resist a small jibe at Kate. She smiled with exaggerated sweetness to acknowledge his comment.

"An American couple has booked a compartment for this trip. Inquiries revealed that they appear to be on vacation. Rumors of ties to the communist party are all our research department was able to come up with."

"Italians, British, French, American, that's quite an eclectic passenger list," said Kate.

"Let's not forget the Germans and the Swiss. We don't know anything about him, but a Herr Altmann, from Frankfurt, Germany, is also taking the train. Sources believe he has some connection with the German government, but no one has been able to pin down the details. That leaves us with four Swiss."

"Tell me about them."

"They will be joining us in Lausanne. Two are businessmen involved in mining and tunnel construction. Given the sorry state of road and train tracks in Yugoslavia, the two men may be interested in doing business there. The two bankers accompanying them are known to invest aggressively in foreign mining and construction projects. That is about all we know about the passengers on the train," concluded Henry.

"Surely there are other passengers on the train," Kate said in a surprised tone.

"Definitely yes, there are the usual envoys and attachés, French, British, and Italian. Their credentials check out, and as a group, they are altogether unremarkable. We are also aware of another vacationing couple from France who is returning to their posting in the Near East. They, too, have been thoroughly checked out. They are not of interest to us. Didn't the list I gave you just now satisfy you?" Henry asked with an impish smile.

Before she could answer, he continued.

"Wonderful, here is our waiter.  Darling, would you like an after dinner drink?" said Henry, effectively shutting off further discussion.

# Chapter 36

## Kate

*W*hat could Kate say to all that? Henry certainly had given her a lot to think about. As Kate drank her cordial, she considered who would be on the train. Two women stood out in her mind; Princess Lazio and Madame De la Roche.

Kate remembered her meeting with Princess Lazio in the ladies retiring room while they were both freshening their makeup. She had complimented the Princess on her stunning jewelry. A necklace designed as a shooting star of diamonds and platinum wrapped around her neck, the star at one end and the tail of the comet at the other. Diamond pendants graced her ears. Her tiara, also of diamonds, had an emerald as its center stone. The Princess gown glittered and sparkled as she moved. Its fabric had been scattered with beads that resembled tiny little dew-drops of diamonds. Taken altogether, the effect was dazzling. The brightest light of all was the Princess herself. She radiated confidence and good breeding. Kate could not imagine this polished woman being involved in anything as sordid as an assassination attempt. The Princess swept from the room before Kate could bring up their encounter at Chanel.

Kate remembered that Henry had danced with Princess Lazio early in the evening. Aside from a few jealous pangs she got whenever he took another woman out on the dance floor, she had not thought anything of it. After all, it was part of his job as a government employee to be an asset at embassy functions. The only odd note was his reluctance to tell her anything about his conversation with the Princess.

Though her introduction to Madame De la Roche had been very brief, the elegant French woman had left an indelible impression in Kate's mind. To Kate, the woman represented all that was stylish and sophisticated about French women. Again, Kate could not visualize this woman as a threat. She had been looking forward to studying Madame De la Roche more closely on the train. If anyone could give Kate fashion advice, it was her.

"I am worried about you," said Henry, breaking into her thoughts. "I think that while we are on the train, you should spend your time in our compartment."

"Stay in the compartment? During the entire journey? You can't be serious?" Kate exclaimed.

"Yes, well, I think it would be wise," he said.

"Don't you feel I'm capable enough to help you with our assignment?"

"Well, no, not exactly," Henry reluctantly admitted.

Kate stared at him, hurt and angry.

"Are you worried that people will realize we aren't married? Did anyone at the embassy guess that we aren't really married?" she asked angrily.

"No, no, not that I know at least," Henry said. After a moment, he added. "The concierge at our hotel certainly questioned our status."

"I don't suppose it was really too hard to guess," Kate said. "We still act uncomfortable with each other when in close proximity. I can work on that if that is what is worrying you."

In her case, it was because Kate found Henry quite desirable. The first time he had held her hand while they walked along the *quai*, her knees went weak at his touch. Kate had caught herself gazing at him adoringly when he would not notice. When he took her in his arms, desire coursed through her veins. She had better make that part of the new wife routine, even though she didn't think that Henry shared her feelings. Whenever they even approached what could be called an intimate moment, he segued into one of his history lessons.  He acted like a walking history lesson, certainly not like a new husband.  She wouldn't mind trading a few more newlywed kisses with him.  He kept saying it was all in the line of duty.

"No, that's not really the problem."

"Henry, what is it then?"

The giant clock on the front of the train station struck the half hour.  Kate heard the characteristic chimes signaling the boarding process for the Orient Express. Her spirits lifted.  She could hardly wait to sample the glamorous carriages, sumptuous cuisine, and personal service it offered.  Putting their conversation behind them, Henry and Kate proceeded to the train platform in good spirits.

# Chapter 37

## Henry

*O*n his way to the platform, Henry kept his eyes open for anything or anyone out of the ordinary.  Kate, he noticed, had focused her attention on the glamorous people boarding the train.

"Henry," she said excitedly as she touched his arm.  "Do you see her?  I wouldn't be surprised if she and her companion have just come from dining at the Ritz.  Are you going to take me to the Ritz one day?"

How innocent Kate looked when she clapped her hand over her mouth, thought Henry.  Obviously, she hadn't meant to ask that question.  He said nothing to add to her discomfort, all the while thinking he would very much like to take her to the Ritz one day.  If nothing else, Henry wanted to see what sort of hat she would wear.  This evening's little profusion of tiny pink flowers certainly suited her bubbly personality.

"Her companion doesn't look like a man to be trifled with," remarked Henry, taking in the man's narrow eyes and hard face.

"And those two over there, they certainly are having a hard time parting.  What a kiss!  Who do you think is leaving who?" she giggled.

"There are Monsieur and Madame De la Roche from the embassy reception.  Do you see them?" asked Henry.

"Are they in our car?  I would so like to meet her again.  She is so very chic!"

"There are ten compartments in each coach.  From what I learned at the embassy, we are sharing the car with the De la Roches, Princess Lazio, four Swiss bankers who will join the train in Lausanne, Colonel and Mrs.

Forsyth, two French attachés, and an American couple," said Henry. "I wasn't able to find out about the last two compartments."

"That man over there can only be Colonel Forsyth. What an awful man, so hearty and full of exaggerated bonhomie. He is like a walking cliché," said Kate mischievously.

"Who else can you point out?" Henry asked, challenging her. "I daresay they will all be here soon."

"That must be the American couple there. It is their clothes that make them stand out. Quite colorful, aren't they?" Kate laughed.

As Henry boarded the handsome navy blue Wagons-Lit coach on the Orient Express Sunday evening, he instinctively knew that this journey would be a personal test of his own resolve and initiative. This adventure would liberate him from his former life, from his environment, from his own limitations. From this point on, Henry could choose to cling to the familiar routines of his previous life, or decide to make a new path with his life. Soon, Henry believed, he would be finding out what sort of person he really was. Henry, in a moment of honest reflection, knew that this assignment would either make or break him as a man. When she spoke, it was as if Kate read his mind.

"Don't you think travelling opens a person to new dimensions, directions, and possibilities in their lives?" Kate said breaking into his thoughts. Without waiting for him to answer, she continued, "I do."

"Tell me."

"You have the opportunity to leave behind your old self, your background, how you dress, how you act, and create a whole new persona. You can't rely on how you used to do things because each moment holds a new adventure. It's like being set free from the past."

They both mulled this over for a moment.

"Every moment on this journey will be a new experience. We will have to adapt a little bit at a time," Kate added, as if trying to keep her courage up in the face of all this daunting freedom.

Henry couldn't agree with her more. The whistle shrilled again and there wasn't any more time for reflection. He hoped they had left any pursuers behind and that the passengers on the train were unaware of his mission. On a personal note, he hoped Kate noticed the flowers he had ordered for their compartment. For some silly reason, he wanted to please her, very much.

# Chapter 38

## Kate

*N*othing could have prepared Kate for the luxuriousness of the train. The navy blue Wagon-Lits coaches with their elaborate crests and polished brass looked like candy boxes too pretty to open. Even the access corridors were paneled with rich hardwoods. Crystal ceiling lights gently lit the space. Their cabin, though tiny could only be described as luxurious. The decorative treatments were unlike anything she had ever seen before. The dominate color in their small room was a pale green. The linens and window shades were in complementary hues. Together, they produced a quiet, restful effect.

Excitedly, Kate explored their compartment. Thoughtfully placed cubby holes carefully concealed in the paneling provided extra space. Opening them, she could see how each had been designed for special uses, such as narrow shelves for their toiletry items. There was even a small drop-shelf for writing letters. When she turned around, she saw that a cheval mirror graced the backside of the door. Already made up for the night, the sheets were the softest she had ever touched. Kate bounced on the spring mattress and patted the down pillows.

"Look at how they carefully concealed the washstand behind this rosewood paneling," Henry exclaimed. "These ornate brass fittings allowed access." He demonstrated by pulling on them.

"Look at us acting like school children on holiday," she said laughing.

"I suppose you will want this entire closet for your clothes," he said gesturing to the small closet.

"There is room to place your suitcase under the bed," Kate pointed out helpfully.

"Every square inch has been carefully planned, hasn't it?" Henry marveled.

Next to the bed, a tiny nightstand held a petit crystal table lamp with a silk shade. Someone had placed a lovely bouquet of flowers on it. They filled the room with their scent.

"Henry, did you order these flowers?"

"Yes, I thought you might like them."

"How thoughtful of you." Kate looked at Henry with renewed appreciation. Perhaps her plan was working. Certainly flowers didn't fall into the category of "all in the line of duty."

Everything was perfect about the cabin, everything except floor space that is. If she and Henry both stood on the floor at once, they couldn't help but touch. Standing nose to nose with Henry in such an intimate space left Kate breathless.

Kate heard the two long shrill whistles signaling the train's departure. With a gentle tug from the engine, they got on their way. When the train swayed, Henry put his arms around her to steady her. His eyes laughing, he took the opportunity to pinch her waist lightly.

"Henry!" Kate squeaked. "Please! Don't! Leave me alone!" Blushing furiously, she mustered as much dignity as possible and took her robe, nightgown, and toiletry case with her to the ladies lounge.

Kate took as long as she could to change and prepare for bed. She didn't quite know how to behave. Part of her wanted Henry to take her into his arms as soon as he saw her in her lovely new nightgown, her sensible side sternly reminded her that she shouldn't get involved with a man who she probably wouldn't see again following the completion of their mission. In her nervousness, Kate blurted out the first thing that came to her mind.

"Henry, I'm not sure how well I will sleep tonight. I am so excited! After all, you never know what might go on during the night when you're on the Orient Express."

So much for trying to be nonchalant. Her first attempt wasn't very successful. There they were in their tiny cabin preparing for their first real night together. She discounted the disheveled night they had spent together in the garden shed in London. Kate carefully took off her new robe and laid it on the end of her bed. She slid quickly into her berth. After a few awkward moments, Henry turned off the light and climbed into his bunk.

How do you like that? Alone in our own compartment and Henry didn't even try to kiss her goodnight. That thought irritated her a bit. She had hoped her lovely new nightgown and robe would break through his reserve, at least enough for a kiss. Kate wondered if he realized that the soft peach silk confection was a far cry from the flannel robe and nightgown she normally wore. She sighed. She would gladly wear pretty things if they would interest Henry. How she longed to kiss him, really kiss him. Kate knew, of course, that she wasn't helping matters by telling him to stop each time he did try something. She couldn't make up her mind. Should she give in to her desire, knowing that their relationship would last only the few short days of their assignment or should she keep Henry at a distance?

Kate knew what she really wanted. She wanted a husband who would put his arms around her when she needed it the most. She wanted a man who would be there in the wee small hours of the morning to hold her when fears and worries about the future crept in. Kate wanted someone who would hold her and tell her she wasn't alone. Would Henry fill that need for her?

Despite her disappointment over Henry's lack of interest, the thrill of beginning the trip welled within her. She looked forward to lying in her bed watching the lights of passing stations reflect in the window. She imagined the gentle rocking of the train as it rolled through the dark countryside punctuated by the lights of the towns they traveled through. Surely there wasn't anything more romantic than being on a train at night. As Kate lay there in the silence, she could hear the distant murmurings of her fellow passengers bedding down for the night. The rhythmic clacking of the train combined with the gentle rocking quieted all her fears and Kate fell asleep.

# Chapter 39

## Henry

*W*here had she purchased that nightgown? It was positively indecent, covering everything yet leaving nothing to the imagination as it draped itself over her curves. The peach color definitely flattered her delicate skin. So what had Henry said or done when she stood there looking so lovely? Nothing. All confused and embarrassed, he stood there in their tiny cabin not saying anything at all. His tongue seemed all tangled up in his mouth. He had been as mute as a fish. Suave, very suave.

When the movement of the train going around the corner threw them against each other, he should have at least kissed her. Any sane man would not have missed an opportunity like that when it presented itself. Instead, Henry had let her go the moment she protested. He should have kissed her. Who knows where that kiss would have led? Henry certainly knew where he wanted their passionate kiss in the hallway of the embassy to lead. Now, he was going to be awake all night with the image of her in that nightgown burned on his retinas. Just as well, Henry thought. He shouldn't be having these sorts of thoughts about a woman who was merely playing a role. Kate was, first and foremost, only present on this train to provide cover for his real mission. Instead of considering how and when he should romance Kate, Henry should stay awake and keep an eye out for trouble. Not that he expected any difficulties so early in the trip, but one never knew.

The delicate scent of her French perfume swirled around him. Henry leaned out of his bunk and stared down at Kate. Asleep! They had barely left the station and she was asleep already! He burned with desire for her and Kate had had the audacity to fall asleep!

Henry lay there awake for quite a long time. Earlier in the night, through the ventilation panel in the door, he watched the feet of fellow passengers as they moved up and down the corridor. Now, the train was silent except for the clacking of the wheels against the rails and the occasional sound of the train whistle. Henry had learned to recognize that two long blasts, a short blast, and another long blast signified that the train was crossing a road. Eventually, he drifted into a light sleep.

Henry awoke from his light sleep with a start. He could swear he had heard the squeaking of a shoe in the corridor. Was it his imagination or had someone hesitated briefly outside their door? Henry knew from his interrogation at the embassy that the assassin might be on this particular train. He wondered if the assassin knew of Henry's presence or his mission. Part of the reason he attended the embassy function and toured Paris with Kate was to give the impression of a man on his honeymoon. He and his superiors hoped that these activities would throw the opposition off balance. If he was honeymooning, surely he couldn't be planning to stop an assassination attempt.

Dawn came early this time of year as the summer solstice approached. Just as light began filtering in around the window shades, Henry fell into a deep sleep.

Monday morning, a loud pounding on the door of their compartment brought him awake instantly. Henry jumped down from his berth as Kate flung on her robe. Henry opened the door to face several official-looking men in uniform.

"*Bonjour Madame, Monsieur. Guten Morgan. Bon giorno.* Good morning," said the conductor officiously as Henry opened the door to admit him to their compartment. "*Nous sommes desole*...Oh, excuse me, *vous parlez Anglais*, you speak English. We are sorry to disturb you at such an early hour, but during the night, the French diplomatic pouch was stolen from a locked cabinet in the forward luggage car. We discovered it missing when we stopped for customs at Frasne. Officers representing both the Swiss and French governments boarded the train at Frasne so as not to delay our progress. No one will be allowed on or off the train until we have searched every inch of it. We must insist that we be allowed to inspect your cabin immediately. *Vous permittez? Ca ne vous fait rien?* You don't mind? *Votre billets, piece d'identites, passeports?* Would you also please provide your passports and travel papers, *s'il vous plait*?"

The flow of the man's words immediately came to a halt when his eyes came to rest on Kate.

"*Desole Madame*," he murmured. "*Pardonez-moi.*" At least the man had the good manners to shift his eyes away immediately. Though she had had time to slip on her robe, Kate was still tousled from sleep at this early hour.

Henry, sensing her discomfort at allowing strange men to peer into their compartment while she was dressed in only her nightgown and robe, protectively shielded her as he handed her his overcoat to use to cover herself. Grateful, Kate sent him a silent thank you. Seeing it, Henry told the conductor they would wait in the corridor until the officers completed the examination of their compartment. In the corridor, impulsively, Henry took Kate in his arms and kissed her on the top of her head.

Pushing him firmly away from her with her hands, Kate told Henry she preferred to use this time to freshen up rather than participate in such a public display of affection. Evidently, she wasn't a morning person, thought Henry. As she left, Henry handed the men his papers, including a copy of their phony marriage certificate. He watched her back stiffen as she overheard their discussion on her way down the corridor.

"Ah, *votre lune de miel!*"

"Yes, our honeymoon."

"*Excusons nous! S'il vous plait.*" Realizing that newlyweds had better things to do than steal diplomatic pouches, the French inspectors departed quickly.

After the men had left their compartment, Henry shaved and dressed. Regarding himself in the cheval mirror, he thought he looked rather dashing in his new navy blue suit. While he waited for Kate to return, Henry pondered the significance of the footsteps he heard in the early morning hours. To facilitate the transfer of train cars along with their passengers to other lines, the train had two luggage cars, one at each end of the train. He puzzled over the memory for a bit but couldn't recall which way the footsteps had been heading. It didn't really matter. He didn't know which car the British diplomatic pouch had been placed in. One bright spot in the morning was that the French, not the British pouch, was missing. Henry knew from discussions at the embassy that the British pouch likely contained documentation for the French Foreign Secretary, Louis Barthou. The material in the pouch would provide information about their discussion concerning their respective countries responses to the Yugoslav-German Trade Agreement. Unfortunately for Henry, it would also contain information about his mission.

The search of the compartments of their train car hadn't taken very long. By the time Kate had returned, the officials were gone. After they had both dressed for breakfast, Henry led Kate to the dining car. Kate positively glowed with happiness when she took in the monogrammed napkins, French Limoges china, crystal goblets and silver. Henry took secret pleasure in her obvious delight. During a breakfast of croissants and baguettes, jam, and strong hot coffee, they made small talk and studied their fellow travellers. As he pointed out the other diners, Henry reviewed with Kate what little background he had on the occupants of the ten compartments in their coach.

"Last evening as we boarded, you identified many of our companions in our carriage," he began. "The De la Roches are the ones you said were obviously French because of their clothes. They live with their three children in the Loire Valley in their family chateau near Tours. From what we have been able to find out, Monsieur De la Roches has no visible means of support except for revenue from their estate. They maintain an apartment in Paris, which they visit fairly frequently."

"We also know she has marvelous taste in clothes," Kate added. Seeing Henry's face as he dismissed this information as unimportant, she pointed out what every woman would know. "It takes a great deal of money to dress like she does."

Henry had to concede that Kate was right about that.

"You may be right. They may require other, less obvious, sources of income to live as they do. We will need to watch them."

"I'm sure it's not them, though. They're such nice people."

"That's a rather broad assumption of innocence to base on such flimsy evidence," Henry said with a smirk.

"Wearing nice clothes does not make a person guilty," retorted Kate. "Who else is on your list of suspects?"

"In the compartment three doors down from us is the Princess Lazio. She comes to our attention because of her interaction with several representatives in the Italian government who are known to favor an Italian alliance with Germany. She maintains a villa in Stresa, on Lake Maggiorie, but apparently has no plans to stop there on her trip from Paris to Istanbul."

"The Princess probably has her reasons for not stopping for at least a few days at her home. I would, especially if my home was in such a lovely setting. I liked her very much. She was very kind to me when we met at the dress shop and again at the embassy ball. You'll never convince me that someone as nice as the Princess would be involved in an assassination plot," declared Kate.

"So you declare her innocent from information you gathered in three minutes?"

"My, my, Henry. Is everyone guilty in your eyes?" Kate responded archly.

"We need to keep an open-mind and base our conclusions on fact, my dear. Let's move on to the others," Henry said, hastily cutting off her protests. "Also in our coach is the American couple you pointed out. We don't have any information on them. They may be taking the train for legitimate travel reasons. We also don't know much about the second French couple, the DuBois. We know he is an official in the French government, but little beyond that. As far as the remaining passengers, it is anybody's guess."

"Look Henry, there's Princess Lazio."

"I'm only mildly surprised to see the Princess at such an early hour. Apparently, the commotion over the missing diplomatic pouch has woken everyone up. Based on the number of people in the dining car, they have all come to be fortified with strong coffee."

"I recognize several people who dined at *Le Train Bleu* yesterday evening," Kate said.

"Fortunately for us, that self-important Englishman and his wife are seated at the other end of the dining car," Henry said. "Unlike last evening, we can only hear snatches of their conversation."

"I pity the people sitting near them."

Henry studied the people in the car. While he couldn't easily see behind him, from where he sat, he could not see that anyone suspicious. Henry chided himself; he was beginning to sound like Kate. It wasn't as if the man or woman, for that matter, was going to make an appearance in the dining room and announce his or her intention to kill the King. He or she would certainly be travelling incognito. The assassin might never even leave his or her compartment. Passengers were welcome to dine in their own cabins. The assassin might plan, except for an occasional nocturnal wandering, to stay hidden in the compartment. Perhaps, thought Henry ruefully, this was all just a figment of Henry's overactive imagination. Who knew? Henry had a suspicion that the assassin would not be anyone they had already come in contact with. He went over the threatening individuals they had encountered thus far. Kate's impressive blow to the head of the man with the long grey overcoat should have taken him out of the game entirely. As for the man in the black suit, the police probably detained him in England. Henry's encounter with the man at the embassy had resulted in his capture. Caterpillar eyebrows, long grey overcoats, black suits, Henry mused. He and Kate needed a shorter system for identifying their enemies. If any more of them popped up, Henry would have to start giving them numbers.

Kate, in her lovely morning outfit, was proving to be quite a distraction. She was wearing another outrageous hat tilted precariously over one eye. Henry realized with a start that he looked forward to seeing her next hat. Her hats gave him a myriad of clues about Kate's true personality. This rakish one revealed her saucy side. He found himself enjoying just watching at her. Certainly, breakfasting with Kate was a pleasant way to start the day.

"Henry," Kate said, interrupting his thoughts. "What do you think of the art of reading people's faces?"

"Reading people's faces? Whatever do you mean by that?" Henry asked skeptically.

"Surely you understand the concept. People do it all the time without realizing it," Kate countered. "We read people's facial features and make judgments about their personalities. For instance, if someone has small beady eyes combined with a tight, pinched mouth, we think of them as mean-spirited."

"Yes, I suppose we do," answered Henry, thinking about it.

"Well, what I was thinking was that we should study the faces of people on the train and use what we see to help us identify the assassin."

Henry's gust of laughter surprised her.

"Another one of your impulsive ideas?"

"Henry," Kate said, stung by his words. "I'm serious. We are hunting an elusive person who we know absolutely nothing about. At least if we study faces, it gives us somewhere to start. Humans learn a lot from watching other people's faces. For instance, we all know the meaning of a smile or frown. But there is more to it than that. A face can tell us about a person's personality, mental attitudes, and character traits. Surely you remember your mother saying to you, 'don't keep making that expression, your face will freeze that way.' Well, that's just it. A person's preferences show up in their facial expressions, gestures, and body language."

"Yes, my dear, I am certain that you are serious. However, I am equally uncertain that face reading will lead us to our prey. It's not like we are playing at cops and robbers with toy guns here. Isn't there some saying about never suspecting the one who looks guilty?"

"I know that. I'm just trying to help. You don't have to be so hurtful in rejecting my suggestion," Kate said as she turned away from him to look out the window.

She was angry that he wasn't taking her suggestion seriously at all. Seeing the hurt in her eyes, Henry backpedaled.

"All right. All right. I promise to take your suggestions seriously. So, tell me, what does my face say about me?" he asked.

"Based on this conversation, I would think the answer would be obvious," Kate said crisply, studying his face. "Your straight forehead, combined with your straight, even eyebrows, gives people the impression that you take a logical approach to problems and that you need facts. It also combines with other features on your face, like those faint lines on your forehead, to say that you are a thinker who pays attention to detail. Your square face, chin, and jaw line point to a man who is not easily intimidated.  You are saved from being too serious by the laugh lines around your eyes and mouth."

"Well, my dear, I hope you like what you see," Henry said smiling.  He knew what he saw in her face, imagination, originality, adaptability, and kindness.  Henry definitely liked what he saw.

# Chapter 40

## Kate

*A*s the waiter draped a crisp linen napkin across her lap, Kate didn't know how to divide her attention: the train, the scenery, the people, Henry. The dining car was a tribute to opulence. Opalescent Lalique glass panels decorated the walls between the windows. The comfortable seats were upholstered in rich velvet. Limoges china, starched white table cloths, monogrammed napkins, and crystal goblets adorned each table. Light reflected off of the highly polished silver tea and coffee pots carried by the waiters.

"*Café au lait*," Kate responded when the server asked her preference.

The fragrant smell of rich, dark coffee helped brush away the last cobwebs of a night's sleep. The delicate scent of the flowers on every table served to enhance the aroma of the light buttery croissants. Creamy French butter melted in her mouth, while the fresh fruit preserves entertained her taste buds. Outside her window, the beautiful scenery unfolded. Enchanting views delighted her eye. She could see church steeples in the distance framed by blue-grey mountain peaks ringed by puffy white cumulous clouds. Her senses kept finding new pleasures to feast upon. Lovely, it was all so very lovely.

"Last night we travelled through approximately 500 miles of eastern France," Henry said as he studied the small trip plan thoughtfully provided by the waiter. "Our path took us through Dijon, Dole, Mouchard, and Frasne. According to this, if you had been awake, you might have been able to discern in the darkness sweeping fields of green, orchards in bloom, grazing cattle, and the rows of vines in a few vineyards."

She could tell he had slept badly the night before. Rather than respond, she let him continue with his travelogue.

"This morning, travelling through the Jura Mountains in Switzerland, our view of the countryside will include forests, streams, rocky hillsides, white and brown chalets, and an occasional small field."

"Henry, what do the train whistles mean?" Kate asked just to be nice.

"At crossings, the train signals with two long, one short, and another long blast of its whistle."

"Oh, I see," said Kate as she waved to those travelling by road as they passed.

"Two short blasts signal that the brakes have been released and the train is going to proceed."

When they descended into Lausanne, Kate caught a glimpse in the distance of the white hooded Mount Blanc towering over the smaller, greener hills across the lake. From their elevated perch on a ridge above Lausanne, Kate could see the nearly unbroken line of hotels fringing the lake shore. The scenery was a study in contrasts: the deep blue of the lake, the green of the foothills, the near black of the conifer trees, the white mantle of snow on distant grey mountains, the brilliant blue of the sky. The tower of a castle protruded above a village of clustered houses. Nearer the train, cows with brass bells on leather collars grazed in the fields.

"It is like a beautiful postcard," said Kate. She laughed when she remembered the unassuming postcard of a red bus that started this adventure. The postcard outside her window now was a sharp contrast to the one of Piccadilly Circus. As if aware of what she was thinking, Henry smiled back at her. Filled with contentment, Kate turned her attention back to the scene outside.

Regardless of Henry's opinion about face reading, Kate knew her job required her to watch her fellow passengers. When they entered a heavily forested section of track, Kate studied the faces of the diners around them. Kate considered herself very intuitive. Just like she told Henry, she had always thought that a person's face provided the viewer with insight into their personalities and moods. There were a few couples scattered about the dining area as well as a few tables of businessmen. She could pick out the diplomats without any trouble at all.

"Henry, are those men over there diplomats?" Kate asked innocently.

"Yes, they are. How did you know?" asked Henry as he looked up from his paper.

"My first clue is their serious faces. Their high foreheads give them an intellectual, cautious appearance that matches their conservative grey suits, ties, and haircuts. What really provides another clue about their profession is the way they keep their briefcases close by their sides. They must be particularly protective of their briefcases following this morning's discovery of the missing diplomatic pouch. I wonder which of the Frenchmen placed the now missing diplomatic pouch on the train last night."

"Not bad. What about those men over there," asked Henry, trying to trip her up.

"They must be bankers," Kate concluded quickly.

"Oh? And how do you know that?" he asked skeptically.

"Their meticulous dress and fastidious motions give me the impression they are the type of men who pay a lot of attention to detail. Their faces tell me that they would be careful in their speech and actions. Notice that they are studying their papers with dedicated concentration."

Before he could make a flippant response, a strikingly attractive couple entered the dining car.

"They're French," Kate said.

"How do you know?  Are you clairvoyant?"  Henry teased.

"No, of course not.  But look at them.  They have such presence.  They can only be French."

"Really?"

"Yes, really.  Only a Frenchwoman could carry off such a daring outfit with such nonchalance.  Surely the outfit has to be couture from the *Avenue Montaigne* in Paris."

"And what about the man?  Is he French too?"

Kate studied the woman's companion.  He dressed quite fashionably in a three piece suit.  Tall and elegant, they both knew the amount of attention their entrance attracted.  Kate could tell they enjoyed it.

"Henry, I saw them at the embassy reception!" Kate realized.  "The man has a very distinctive face.  Notice his dark deep-set hooded eyes set above a prominent nose.  Don't you think his height, broad shoulders, athletic build, and face combine to allow him to present an image of power?"

"More face reading?" responded Henry, unable to keep a note of scorn out of his voice.

As they passed by her table, Kate longed to reach out and touch the soft sable stole draped around the woman's shoulders.  Kate wondered if she could justify such a purchase with the money they had taken from the man in the long grey overcoat. Kate noticed that the man treated his wife with a cold disdain.

"I checked with the porter this morning.  He told me that they are Monsieur and Madame DuBois," Henry said.  "They are in the compartment next to ours."

"Oh my," said Kate. "Imagine us having such illustrious neighbors."

Kate studied the other diners. She noticed that many of them had a copy of Agatha Christie's *Murder on the Calais Coach*. Even though the book had only been published on January 1st of this year, it had already apparently become *de rigeur* reading on the Orient Express. Kate could hear people discussing the intricacies of the plot. Secretly, she hoped to be able to return to her copy soon. It was another one of the purchases she had made before boarding the train to leave London. Kate had just reached the point where Hercule Poirot had undertaken the questioning the suspects in the murder.

Near the back of the car, Kate saw a man dining alone. Hurt by Henry's lack of interest in her face reading, she did not bother to draw his attention to the man. Henry would probably just laugh at her. To Kate, the man across the room looked very much the under-cover agent. His face remained mask-like as his sharp eyes flicked around the room taking in his fellow passengers. Kate was sure he did not miss a thing. Tall and thin, his face had rather harsh features. Bushy, angled eyebrows rested atop hooded eyes. It seemed to Kate that his puffy top eyelids cut his pupils in half, reminding her of the eyes seen on violent criminals or terrorists in the newspapers and news reels. His down-turned, thin, very pointed nose gave him a ruthless demeanor. The older man definitely presented a picture of someone who would prefer to move around in the shadows, thought Kate. His body language signaled that he wished to be apart from the others in the car. She thought the man merited watching. Henry would probably tell her that the man failed the first rule of espionage—the man didn't look ordinary.

As Kate studied the man, he looked her way. He examined her coldly, making her uncomfortable. She quickly turned to look out her window, but not before noticing that he had been studying each table of diners. For some, he merely registered their presence, saw nothing that interested him and moved on. At other tables, his inquiring gaze lingered much longer. Kate was curious about what he was thinking. She wondered how long he had been observing their table. Would she and Henry appear like newlyweds? The next time she dared to look at him, the man had a newspaper covering his face.

"Princess Lazio is holding court at the table in the center of the dining car," remarked Henry.

"How appropriate," said Kate. "Princess Lazio certainly knows how to draw people to her."

"Yes, I suppose she does."

"She definitely knows how to wear jewels too," said Kate as she admired the ropes of pearls adorning the neck of the Princess. "Those pearls are large, at least 10 mm. Can you see the shortest pearl necklace? Look at the baroque pearl as big as a man's thumb hanging on it."

"Are you more interested in clothing, hats, and jewels or in our assignment?" Henry asked as he looked up from his newspaper.

"Oh, go ahead, make fun of me. At least I don't have my head buried in a newspaper."

The English couple seated at the far end of the car could be heard arguing loudly about the coffee. Despite their discontent with the food, Kate wanted to meet them. Their natural enthusiasm for travel spilled over into her. Having overheard much of their conversation last night in *Le Train Bleu*, she knew they had gone to so many interesting places in the world. Kate hoped there would be time during the trip to visit with them. She'd like to hear more about their exotic travels to the near and far East. This morning, the man sat with his back to her and Kate was surprised to note that with his dark hair and medium build, the man resembled Henry. Thoughts of Henry obviously invaded her mind, now she saw a bit of Henry in every man.

Shaking her head over her folly, Kate knew she had to keep her mind on the business at hand. In reality, all she really wanted to do was spend her time gazing at Henry. Kate watched him across the table. Henry didn't seem to be having any difficulty staying focused. Ever conscious of their roles as newlyweds on their honeymoon, Henry was going on again about travel on the Orient Express.

"Would you like to hear what I learned about the engine that pulls our train?" Henry asked earnestly.

Listening to Henry with half an ear, Kate wondered why he hadn't even noticed her new outfit. She had carefully chosen the belted, tailored jacket in loden green with a tweed skirt that draped skillfully to mid-calf to show off her small waist and long legs. Kate thought that the little Tyrolean hat complemented the suit rather well. She particularly liked the large feather rosette that nearly covered the entire left side of the hat. It saved the hat from being ordinary. Kate broke into his monologue to redirect their conversation.

"Henry, do you like my hat?" she asked.

"It's very nice dear," he said without looking up from his notes.

He is playing the longtime married husband role a bit too well, thought Kate.

"You don't think it's a bit too ordinary, do you?" she inquired innocently.

"None of your hats could ever be called ordinary," Henry said dryly. "In fact, some of them could hardly be called hats."

So Henry had noticed. His amused scrutiny of her hat secretly pleased Kate. When he began to speak again about the specifications of the engine, she didn't really listen to what he said. She just sat back and let his voice flow over her. She could, Kate suddenly realized, listen to that voice every day of her life without ever growing tired of it. It soothed, refreshed, and entertained her all at the same time. Unexpectedly, Kate didn't want the trip to end. She didn't want life to move on beyond these wonderful moments in an elegant train car with Henry. Kate wanted them to stay here, on the train, cocooned against the threats of the outside world forever.

# Chapter 41

## Henry

*P*rincess Lazio beckoned Henry and Kate to her table with a faint nod of her head. As they joined her, the Princess extended her hand graciously to welcome them.

"*Boungiorno* Princess. Thank you so much for inviting us to join you," said Henry with a formal bow. "You remember my wife Kate. You met briefly at the embassy ball in Paris."

"Pleased to meet you again, Katherine," said Princess Lazio gesturing for Kate to sit down. "It appears we are having our own little mystery on the Orient Express, the disappearance of the diplomatic pouch."

They nodded in agreement.

"One only has to look at the faces of the French attachés to know whose diplomatic pouch is missing," continued the Princess as she gestured toward their table by inclining her head almost imperceptibly in that direction. "Henry, from where you sit, you can see that the Italian attachés are positively gloating. Not that I am proud of the behavior of my countrymen."

Henry was too relieved that the lost pouch was not the British diplomatic pouch to answer the Princess. He knew there was a high probability that the pouch contained information concerning his mission and identity. He wondered what the French pouch contained.

Just then, the inspectors arrived in the car. The protests and questions of the French diplomats could be heard throughout the car. Despite the pandemonium of voices and gesticulations at their table, the arrival of the authorities had the effect of silencing everyone else in the car. Even the servers exerted great care in order to minimize the sounds of china and cutlery. Everyone waited to hear news of the missing diplomatic pouch. Although the men conducted their conversation in French, Henry, Kate, and the Princess possessed the language skills necessary to follow the conversation.

Apparently, the conductor, in preparation for customs inspection between Frasne and Vallorbe, went to his office to collect the keys to the luggage cars and lockers. Oddly, they were not hanging in their usual place. He searched the office for them. Not finding them there, he went to his private compartment to look for them. They were not there either, so he returned to his office. Though he thought it a bit unusual to have misplaced the keys, he had not been particularly worried. The station official had a master set, for just such cases. Back at his office, he rummaged around again and found them amidst the clutter on his desk. The whole process could not have taken more than fifteen or twenty minutes.

The luggage cars are kept locked during the trip, though if a passenger needs something in one of their cases, the conductor can open the car for them. No such request had been made during the night. The train, and its passengers, had made the first leg of their trip quietly. The diplomatic pouch had been found missing when, during the customs inspection, the conductor noticed the lock dangling from the door to the storage cabinet. The man had a habit of checking the cabinet locks while the customs inspectors inspected the luggage. He had never before, in his 10 years with *Wagon-Lits* on the Orient Express, found it unlocked.

Despite intensive demands, the French attachés refused to divulge the contents of the French diplomatic pouch. After further discussion, the officials departed.

When they were gone, nearly everyone in the car speculated about what might have been in the pouch. The Princess proposed that the contents may be plans for the visit of Barthou. This made sense since protecting such an important personage would be of prime concern for the embassy staff.

"Enough mystery for one day," said the Princess. "It is not a subject suitable for a young couple on their honeymoon. But, Belgrade and Istanbul are no place for a honeymoon either. I suggest that you leave the train in Milan and from there go to Rome or Capri. Rome is marvelous. The wonders of ancient Rome, the Coliseum, the Pantheon, the Forum, the Piazzas. In Rome you should dine at Alfredo's. Do not miss his signature dish, Fettuccini Alfredo. Have you been to Rome?"

"No, I have never even been to Italy," answered Kate.

"You've never been to Italy? Then you must leave the train in Milan. Do not miss Capri."

Henry wondered whether it was his imagination or did the Princess place a good deal of emphasis on the words "leave the train?"

"Capri?"

"Yes, Capri is a perfect place to visit on your honeymoon. How vividly I remember my own honeymoon to the Isle of Capri. So many flowers in bloom," reminisced the Princess with a sigh.

"Please tell me of your stay in Capri. I have never been there and have heard of its beauty," encouraged Kate.

"Ah, Capri. Capri represents the best of Italy; simplicity, kindliness, and naturalness. There are a number of palaces and villas on the island, each with a breathtaking view of the sea. On our honeymoon we stayed near the Grande Marina. Now when we visit, we prefer to stay in *Ana Capri*. It is great fun to take the steamer from Naples, cross the Mediterranean and watch the island grow larger. How exciting it is to leave the dock and join the other passengers for a ride up the funicular railway to the town. It is like disembarking on an enchanted fairy island. There are fewer day tourists there, so it is very peaceful. When you are in Capri, the worries of the world seem far away. In Capri, you can just be. Certainly, the spell Capri places on you makes even reading a thrilling detective story too exhausting to contemplate. How about you, Henry, do you enjoy mysteries?" the Princess inquired.

"Well, yes, as long as they aren't too far-fetched. I am enjoying Agatha Christie's *Murder on the Calais Coach* right now," said Henry, a bit disconcerted by the abrupt change in the direction of the conversation.

"I imagine one's taste for excitement depends on whether or not you are reading the mystery or living it," said the Princess.

As they spoke, the waiter arrived to refresh their coffee cups and set down a plate of *patisseries.* The silver tea and coffee pots flashed in the sunlight that filtered into the car. They sat quietly for a moment while the man served them. Henry could not decide if the Princess was hinting at something. But before he could contemplate her words further, the Princess continued.

"We always hire a *sandolin,* a type of sailing boat, to explore the caves that dot the island. The water takes on the loveliest colors—blue, red, and green, depending on the light refracted by the sun. My favorite is the blue grotto. When you go to Capri, be sure to see it. Be careful though. The seas around the island can become rough very quickly. If you are not an expert sailor, you should hire a boat with a guide. Of course, it goes without saying that it is never wise to endeavor something dangerous without appropriate training, is it, Henry? It is not only seas that can become rough."

Now, Henry thought, there was a leading question. He tried to read her face, but the Princess merely looked pleasantly at her audience as she stirred her coffee. Kate would probably have been able to tell him volumes from one quick glance. Henry, on the other hand, thought he might be imagining things. Henry had the uncomfortable feeling that they should never have departed from the relatively safe conversation about the diplomatic pouch.

"Do not forget to visit the *Castiglioni*, Capri's ruined medieval castle. Of course, you must not miss the *Palazzo di Timberio*, the villa of the Roman emperor Tiberius. You will find them both interesting," the Princess said, sounding as if they had already changed their intended destination.

Henry could tell by the tone of her voice that she enjoyed her visits to Capri. Any innuendos must have been all in his mind. While the Princess continued to chat with Kate, he turned his attention to the other diners, keeping an eye out for anyone acting oddly. At this point in time, Henry was uncertain about how he would judge suspicious behavior. People had been drifting in and out of the dining car since morning. The disappearance of the diplomatic pouch brought them out of their compartments. Henry turned his attention back to the Princess in time to hear her say something very revealing about her philosophy on life.

"Truly successful people are the ones who manage to land on their feet like cats when placed in awkward situations. Don't you agree?" said Princess Lazio. "Personally, when difficulties arise, I try to remain at peace and rely on my wit to rescue me. It is important to remain tranquil in spirit when confronted with the folly of life."

"Yes, I suppose that is a good philosophy. I can see it working in all but the most trying of circumstances," said Henry.

"Remember, Henry, you are a married man now. You should find ways to avoid unpleasant situations," the Princess warned.

# Chapter 42

## Kate

$\mathcal{A}$t lunch, Kate and Henry joined Colonel and Mrs. Forsyth at their table. Since she couldn't help but overhear their conversation at dinner and again this morning, the arrangement pleased Kate. She looked forward to hearing about their various travel experiences. Kate knew that all she had to do was give him a leading question and Colonel Forsyth would carry the conversation.

"Tell me, Colonel Forsyth, what was your most interesting experience?" Kate inquired.

"Well, my dear, let me consider for a moment before answering. Let's see. I'd have to say that the most challenging moment came during the Great War. While stationed in the Balkans, I was there at a time when it seemed as if we were being besieged by Germany, Austria-Hungary, and Bulgaria all at the same moment. It took all the courage we could muster to regroup and drive the invaders out. As a matter of fact, one of the men I fought alongside with is on this train. Decent enough chap. Spoke to him this morning. He's returning to Belgrade following a visit to Paris. I had an interesting chat with him about the current state of affairs in the Balkans."

The Colonel paused for a moment and Kate could see that his mind was busy making connections. She noted his petulant expression. His thin lips pursed in anger. His face at that moment certainly revealed his mean-spirited character. He gave the impression that he was struggling with what to say next. Since the Colonel never seemed to lack for words, Kate thought it must be because he didn't know where to begin his tirade. Unfortunately for those nearby, he found his voice.

"What are those fools at Whitehall thinking?" the Colonel thundered. "Don't they realize this has all happened before? Haven't they considered the effects of the tensions between Germany and Italy over the future of Austria and the Danube region? Even the meeting in Rome in March did little more than make Austria more reliant than ever on Italian protection against Germany. And those conferences in Geneva designed to reduce and limit arms in Europe? Worthless! Most nations have begun re-arming, regardless of what they say in public. What about the nations who are entering into non-aggression pacts, like Germany and Poland and the Soviets and Poland? Seems to me, Poland has placed itself between a rock and a hard place. Can't they see the similarities between events preceding the Great War and those today? What could they possibly be thinking? But, of course, do you think they take the time to listen to old soldiers like me? No, good heavens, no. That would make too much sense." The Colonel glared around their table belligerently, waiting for someone to contradict him.

"Now dear, don't let yourself get so upset. Things aren't really all that bad," said Mrs. Forsyth in an attempt to sooth her husband.

"Confound it woman! Don't you understand anything I have been saying?" asked the Colonel in a strident voice. The Colonel pounded on the table making the silverware jump. Obviously he was in no mood to stop his tirade. "What about the abolition of the Reichstag in Germany? Do they think Hitler will stop there? The Balkan Pact, bah, what has that bought but more weak alliances between weak countries. And our own Anglo-Russian Trade agreement, that's nothing but an ineffectual attempt to improve relations between the two countries. Doesn't solve any problems or deal with the real issues of the day, does it?" the Colonel asked rhetorically. He was nearly purple with rage.

Neither Kate nor Henry wanted to ask him what the real issues were. On the whole, they were both regretting their decision to have lunch with the couple. Instead of an entertaining discussion of where the couple had travelled, they were being treated to a lecture on what was wrong with the world. Kate tried to concentrate on her food as the Colonel continued shouting his disgust with current events. She had had enough of politics.

"Are you aware of all the assassination attempts?" the Colonel soldiered on brusquely. "That should give anyone in politics a clue about how people feel. Who was it that said even bad men seldom get murdered without a good reason? Or was it *with* a good reason? Can't remember."

As the Colonel carried on with his monologue, Kate couldn't help but notice how his voice became more and more virulent. He sounded so disgruntled by the end of his dissertation; Kate shifted her concentration from her delicious meal to study his face more closely. The ripples in his jaws stood out and made him appear as if he was holding in repressed anger. In the center of his forehead, he had a single deep line running from his brow to just between his eyebrows. It reminded Kate of a railroad track and showed her that he let nothing stand in his way. His chin had a tense, bumpy appearance that Kate always equated with obstinacy. He looked like a very determined and exceedingly bad-tempered man. However much the shape of the Colonel's head was similar to Henry's from the back, there was absolutely no resemblance from the front.

"I say," continued the Colonel, "these pacts are futile. Not necessary. Not at all."

At that point, Kate was no longer listening to his ranting and raving. It wasn't until he looked directly at her that Kate was able to put her finger on what else was bothering her about the Colonel. She did not like being unable to see his eyes, hidden as they were by the reflection on his glasses. Kate always thought that the eyes told a lot about a person. She hated to stereotype people, but to her, the Colonel seemed like an overly-hearty, angry, portly, middle-aged caricature of a man.

As they dined, the train skirted the edge of *Lac Leman*, better known outside Switzerland as Lake Geneva. The sight of Castle *Chillon* thrilled Kate while taking her mind off the Colonel. Reflected in the glassy surface of the lake, the medieval castle looked enchanted. Romantic thoughts of princes and princesses filled Kate's imagination until she remembered reading of the turreted castle in Byron's *Prisoner of Chillon*. His work was based on the true story of Bonnevard, a patriotic Swiss friar, who had been imprisoned in 1526 by Duke Charles of Savoy. The poor man had been left to languish in the dungeon, a deep windowless black hole beneath the castle, without hope for ten long years. Kate had always considered the French word for forget, *oubliette*, far more descriptive of the actual prisoner conditions than the word dungeon. The idea of being forgotten in the dark horrified her. Kate shivered when she recalled that the castle had a grim torture chamber. So much for enchantment. Pushing the gloomy thoughts away, she ignored the Colonel and concentrated her attention on the intensely picturesque scenery.

The nearly 150 miles the train traveled through Switzerland included some of the most majestic scenery that Kate had ever seen. The train took them past blue lakes as smooth as glass. High mountains rose on each side of the tracks. Glimpses of villages peeked out from the wooded hillsides as the train snaked through the long narrow valleys. As the day progressed, the houses began to look more and more alpine in design. Each had wooden balconies, steep roof tops, and deep overhanging eaves. Now, spring had melted their covering of snow and they were decorated with a profusion of bright red geraniums framed at the windows by wooden shutters or suspended from the railings of balconies. In small pastures goats and cows grazed among the wildflowers. High up one hillside, Kate could see a little village. The few white and brown buildings seemed to hang on the hillside, very small and very brave, encircled by forbidding mountains.

"Katherine, wherever did you find such an outrageous hat?" Mrs. Forsyth's voice broke into Kate's reverie.

"Kate has always had a penchant for unusual hats," said Henry, saving Kate the need to answer. It wouldn't have mattered anyway; Mrs.

Forsyth took advantage of a momentary lull in her husband's monologue to begin one of her own.

"I find Switzerland so confusing," she complained. "So many languages! To the west they speak French, to the east, German, in the south near Lugano, Italian. Did you know they have a fourth language? Romansch. Why once, while I spoke with a shopkeeper, the man used words from all four languages in one sentence!"

"I daresay that's typical," interjected her husband.

"As if a person could follow that!" Mrs. Forsyth continued unaware that her husband had even spoken. "It boggles the mind. Such a confusing country. Have you ever visited Switzerland?"

Without waiting for Kate to nod yes or no, Mrs. Forsyth forged on.

"Good heavens, when you visit a town, it will often have two names: Morat, Murten; Neuchatel, Neuenburg; Solothurn, Soleure. One town even has three names: Bale, Basle, and Basel! And why don't they decide what to call the lake at Geneva, Lac Leman or Lake Geneva. Pick one! They really should simplify it all for us visitors." complained Mrs. Forsyth. "Honestly, there are limits!"

Kate noticed that at first glance, Mrs. Forsyth had a round open face that welcomed the viewer. Up close a person could see the tiny lines around her mouth that showed her dislike of the world in general. She certainly was expressing that disapproval now as she spoke to the waiter.

"See here, young man, why haven't you brought us any fresh tea?" the Colonel's wife demanded of the unfortunate waiter. Her querulous voice rose easily above the noise of the dining room. She persisted with her litany of complaints, real and imagined. Kate realized that Mrs. Forsyth rather enjoyed taking people to task, expressing her discontent, and in general making mincemeat of those less powerful than herself.

As Mrs. Forsyth droned on, Kate let her attention drift around the dining car. As she did, the waiter approached the older man sitting all by himself. She could see him more clearly now and she noted the hair streaks of grey in his hair. She shivered as she took in his lean, irritated face. She overheard the sallow-faced porter addressing the man as Herr Altmann. Henry was right about the Orient Express, people from all sorts of different countries and walks of life traveled on it. Henry, apparently as bored with Mrs. Forsyth as she was, pinched her waist under the table. She squealed, turned to him, and saw the mischief in his face.

"Henry!" she began. Seeing his face, Kate laughed involuntarily.

"I know, I know. Leave me alone," Henry said, smiling as if he had won a small victory.

Kate couldn't help herself, she grinned back at him.

# Chapter 43

## Henry

*M*ercifully, after lunch, Colonel Forsyth and his wife returned to their compartment. Kate and Henry stayed in the dining car to watch the scenery through the large windows. For a few moments, they sat in silence as the panorama unfolded. Before they left Switzerland behind, the train would stop briefly at the small neat stations of Montreux, Martigny, Soin, and Brigue. As they passed through the area around Sion, they would see the vineyards that made the area the winegrowing capital of the Valais region. Henry explained to Kate that the grapes were first introduced into the region by Charlemagne hundreds of years ago. They would also see the ruins of Tourbillons castle built in 1294. Perched on top of another hill, they could see the castle Valere. Henry relaxed into the unaccustomed luxury of sitting in a rhythmically rocking seat while watching some of Europe's finest vistas slide by.

Framed in their window, the Alps, lit here and there by the sun, thrust their peaks through scudding clouds. Now that the train traveled closer to the mountains, the travellers could see how the snow, ice, and wind had sculpted the landscape, allowing only the strongest and most hardy vegetation to survive. Henry hoped he had the strength of character and body to endure the challenges that lay ahead. He switched his gaze from the majesty of the mountains to the face of the woman who sat across from him. He found this view even more breathtaking than the one outside. Henry found himself thinking of entering something deeper than a flirtation with Kate.

At the table next to them sat the French couple, the DuBois. Madame DuBois appeared ravishingly beautiful in a simple day dress, her luscious deep brown sable thrown casually over her shoulders. Both Kate and

Henry were surprised when Monsieur DuBois turned towards them abruptly and began to speak to them in lightly accented English.

"You are British, are you not?" Monsieur DuBois asked in a condescending tone. The Frenchman waited only briefly for them to nod yes, before he continued. "Are you travelling all the way to Istanbul?"

"No, not immediately, we are stopping in Belgrade for a few days," Henry answered smoothly. "We are on our honeymoon and want to visit the sights the city has to offer."

"Ah, we are also stopping in Belgrade. We want to see the museum there. More importantly, we plan to hear what the French foreign minister, Louis Barthou, has to say about the future of Europe. Were you aware of his State visit? Certainly the city will be crowded with country representatives and their retinue this week. I understand tomorrow's diplomatic train will be heavily guarded."

"Really, we were only vaguely aware of his visit. Our minds have been on other things," said Henry, reaching across the table to give Kate's hand a squeeze. "Can you tell us a bit more about him?"

"Our foreign minister, Louis Barthou, is making quite a name for himself," said Monsieur DuBois. "He has raised fears in France concerning the Yugoslavian-German Trade Agreement. Barthou thinks that Yugoslavia will defect from the Balkan Pact. He makes this visit in hopes of cementing relationships between Yugoslavia and France."

"How interesting," murmured Henry encouragingly.

"Yes, Barthou is an outspoken opponent of Hitler's rise to power. Minister Barthou statements concerning Hitler's state visit to Italian Premier Benito Mussolini caused much tension between the French and German governments. Fortunately, for the French, the German and Italian leaders made a poor impression on each other," said Monsieur DuBois, warming to his topic.

"Given all of the events so far this year, there are tensions between many people and many governments right now," commented Henry, careful not to make any inflammatory remarks.

"I am sure Monsieur Barthou is not a favored person in Germany at the moment," remarked Monsieur DuBois a bit harshly. "However, world leaders must strive to pursue the wisest course for their country." Without warning, just as unexpectedly as the conversation had begun, Monsieur DuBois turned away from Henry and Kate. "Come along dear, we have no more time to spare." Monsieur DuBois extended his hand to his wife. Madame DuBois gave Kate a cold look as she turned to leave the table.

"Aren't they a pair?" whispered Henry conspiratorially as he and Kate watched the couple leave the car.

"Most definitely," responded Kate. "That woman makes me uneasy."

"I couldn't agree more."

"Henry, I'm a bit chilly. Would you be a dear and fetch my cashmere shawl? I left it lying on the table in our compartment."

On his way past the table where Monsieur and Madame De la Roche sat, the Frenchman signaled for Henry to stop. He and Kate had spent a delightful few minutes visiting with the couple while waiting for the Forsyths to appear for lunch.

"*Pardonnez moi*. Excuse me, may I have a word with you?" asked Monsieur De la Roche politely. Henry stopped and waited for the man to continue. "Would like to join us for supper this evening?"

"Yes, that would be lovely," said Henry.

"I couldn't help but overhear part of your conversation with the French couple, the DuBois. I see, Henri, that you have mastered the French art of speaking eloquently without actually saying anything," said Monsieur De la Roche, smiling enigmatically.

Henry did not know how to answer that. Around De la Roche, he felt a bit unsure of himself. Awkwardly, Henry excused himself and went to fetch Kate's shawl. As he left their table, Henry could not help wondering about Monsieur De la Roche's small curious smile.

On his return trip down the corridor, Henry paused at a window to consider their route to Belgrade. Soon they would leave Switzerland to travel through 260 miles of Italy. Henry marveled at the information he had learned about the Swiss rail system from the conductor. The Swiss had converted from coal-fired trains in the early 1920s. By 1924, Swiss trains were all electric. With no smoke from coal, Switzerland had singularly pure air. The Swiss rail system contained some of the finest examples of railway engineering in the world, especially their tunnels. The Simplon tunnel opened in 1906 and, at 12 plus miles, it was the longest tunnel in the world. Switzerland also had the second longest tunnel in the world, the 9 ½ mile long 1882 Gotthard tunnel. In a few moments, the Orient Express would enter the Simplon tunnel near the town of Brigue, an important railway junction in southern Switzerland.

According to the brochure, on the Italian side, they would emerge from the Simplon Tunnel into a vastly different world as they left the harshness of the Alps behind. Once through the tunnel, the mountains would be greener and not as threatening as the tall, forbidding Alps. Travellers could expect to see more small villages, farms, and lakes dotting the landscape. They would exit near Domodossola, stopping briefly for customs. The train would probably be detained and passengers questioned about the missing diplomatic pouch when they entered Italy at Domodossola. Henry had not heard that it had turned up.

Henry knew that after Domodossola, the train would stop for several minutes at the fashionable lakeside town of Stresa. Several passengers would be disembarking there, but not the Princess. She mentioned at lunch that she would not disembark at Stresa to go to her villa on Lake

Maggiorie. Odd, Henry thought, that she would be continuing her trip instead of taking time to stop at her home. The Simplon Orient Express stopped at Stresa regularly, so she could easily resume her trip following a few days rest. Henry had not been able to determine whether or not the Princess planned to travel to Istanbul or beyond.

Now that he had had a chance to look over the passengers on the train, Henry began to doubt if the assassin had really joined the train in Paris. No one fit neatly into his idea of what an assassin should look like. Henry contemplated where someone could enter the train along its route. It wouldn't be easy when the train crossed the frontier in Frasne or Domodossola. The stations were too small, no one entering and leaving the train would go unnoticed by the customs agents or border guards. The other stations were also rather small and since the disappearance of the diplomatic pouch, well-guarded. Besides, at each station, Henry had watched everyone who had boarded or left the train.

Stresa might work. Some passengers would be leaving there to holiday at the lovely lakes. *Lago Maggiore, Lago di Como* and *Lago di Lugano* all attracted well-healed visitors this time of year. *Lago Maggiore*, where the Princess had her villa, was surrounded by peaks of over 3,000 feet. These peaks protected the lake and kept the weather relatively mild. Stresa served as a fashionable resort for the smart crowd who enjoyed sunning themselves on the lakes' lovely beaches.

Henry wondered which of the islands the Princess's villa overlooked; *Isole Borromeo, Isole Madre*, or *Isola Bella*. One day, Henry thought, he and Kate would return to Stresa to stay at the sumptuous Regina Palace Hotel, with its magnificent views of the lake. They could try some of the lake district's famous fish dishes like *Trota di Lago or Pesce Persico*. Maybe he would take Kate to see the famous waterfall at Fiumelatte. The nearly 800 foot drop of water was made even more mysterious because it began to flow each year around March 25 and stopped flowing each year around September 8. Kate might enjoy attending one of the festivals marking the waterfall's appearance or disappearance. Henry shook his head. He wondered what had got him thinking of a future life with Kate. Henry pulled his attention away from Kate and back to his assignment.

Following Stresa, the train would stop briefly at Milan before continuing on to Venice. They would cover the 800 plus miles from Paris to Venice in less than 24 hours. As the largest and most modern train station in Europe, Milan presented more opportunities for people to join the train. The station served nearly 350 trains per day. There were so many different ways for people to take a train to Belgrade.

Henry worried about his assignment. How would he ever find the assassin among all these people? SIS knew of the assassination plan and its proposed date, but had only the sketchiest of details about the people involved. Granted Henry was skilled at arranging chaos into order, but this situation presented him with quite a challenge. Henry had so little information to go on. Why had they sent him virtually alone to deal with such a complex problem?

As he puzzled over this question, standing in the corridor, Henry looked out at the snow, blue-white in the sun against the harsh grey granite. The train gave a haunting shrill whistle signaling that they were about to enter a tunnel. As the train plunged into the darkness of the Simplon Tunnel, the lights suddenly went out, leaving the car as black as pitch. Henry jumped when a momentous crash occurred immediately around him. Moments later, the lights flickered back on to reveal a man lying prostrate on the floor near him. The man, obviously a porter, had just emerged from a nearby compartment carrying a tray of dishes. Kneeling beside him, Henry noted the man had been struck from behind. Blood flowed from a nasty blow to the back of his head. The prostrate porter groaned as Henry fingered the man's neck for a pulse. Henry heard movement behind him. He turned to see a second porter at his side. Henry thought he saw a brief fleeting expression of panic cross the man's face.

"*Qu'est-ce-qui ce passé?*" asked the porter. Recognizing Henry, the man switched to English. "What happened? I heard a crash as I came in to the car. The lights were off. Someone had disconnected the electricity supply to this car. I reconnected the switch by the door and they came back on immediately, as you can see." Cautiously, the porter helped his comrade to his feet.

Henry studied the porter's sallow face carefully before answering. Henry realized he could trust no one but Kate.

"I don't know, either," said Henry. "I was standing here gazing out the window, wool-gathering, when the lights went out. The crash came from behind me. For a moment, I couldn't see a thing. Fortunately, the lights came back on quickly. You said you turned them on at the switch?"

"Yes, sir, there is a switch at each end on the car, right next to the door. They are covered to prevent accidental operation. Most people don't notice them, they blend in so well with the wood paneling," the porter told him.

"Will you see to your colleague? I will go and see if I can find the conductor. I think this man was deliberately struck from behind," said Henry.

Other travellers began to emerge from their compartments, murmuring about the faulty lights. Henry moved past them in search of the conductor. Relieved the man was still alive; Henry considered whether the blow had been meant for him. If the porter hadn't emerged from the room in the darkness of the tunnel, Henry would have been alone in the corridor, his back facing away from the source of the blow. A very unpleasant thought.

As he passed by the compartment of the Princess, her door opened quietly.

"Ah, Mr. Littleton," the Princess said as if she had been expecting him.

"Princess," Henry said a bit breathlessly.

"What has happened?" Princess Lazio asked in a worried tone. "You appear less than your calm self."

Henry quickly explained the recent events. He was about to say something more, to tell her about his suspicions concerning who the blow to the head was really meant for when she stopped him with a wave of her hand. The Princess looked at him gravely for a long time.

"I like you, Henry, very much." Princess Lazio said. "Take care. Take great care. Don't tell me your secrets."

Before he could ask the Princess what she meant, she walked past him toward the dining car. As Henry continued his quest for the conductor, the same question went round and round in his head. Was the Princess an ally or an enemy?

# Chapter 44

## Kate

While Henry went to get her shawl, Kate spent the time enjoying the scenery passing by her window. Earlier the scenery had been neat and orderly, the mountains serving as a distant backdrop. Now as they travelled deeper into the Alps, the landscape became rougher. The view from the window showed exposed rock, tumbling streams, and smaller rock-strewn pastures. Only occasionally did a rustic farmhouse appear, towered over by the surrounding mountain peaks. Kate could see foaming streams plunging through gorges on their way to the valley below. Glaciers appeared in the distance. The track had changed too, its path rougher. The train twisted left and right as it wove its way between steep mountains on both sides. Small tunnels permitted passage through some larger mountains. Overhanging shed roofs protected the train from falling rocks.

Several other tables in the dining car were occupied, though the Colonel and his wife had left the car earlier. She had seen him patting his pockets as if in search of his pipe tobacco. Kate had also noticed the sallow-faced porter following close behind.

Kate had hoped to see more of the impossibly elegant French couple, the DuBois, but they kept to themselves and returned to their compartment following a late breakfast. Kate enjoyed studying the woman's clothing. That morning, Madame DuBois' elegant deep burgundy travelling suit went well with her dark coloring. The Frenchwoman had artlessly draped a luxurious sable shawl over her shoulders. Her carefully careless appearance made Kate green with envy. Maybe her husband was the assassin, Kate thought spitefully. That would be quite a comeuppance for this woman. She considered the other occupants on the train. It takes a devious mind to plot a murder. Kate couldn't fathom hurting someone for money, profit, glory, or ideology. She had yet to meet someone on the train she felt would go to such an extreme as murder.

Kate decided to practice her spying in the form of eavesdropping. Maybe she could find out something that would help Henry. Maybe then he would take her seriously. At the table nearest to her, four Swiss businessmen were deep in discussion about rare metals, mining, railroad tunnels, and investments. Her German was a little rusty and she missed much of the conversation when they switched into Swiss German, but she understood words here and there.

*"Permesso? E solo?"* said the stunningly handsome man who appeared as if by magic at her side. "Oh, *mi scusi. Parla Inglese?* Do you speak English?"

*"Non parlamo Italiano,"* Kate stammered. *"Inglese."*

*"Scusi. Scusi.* I am sorry. I did not mean to startle you. Please allow me to present myself; I am Count Vincente di Cosimo." The Count extended his hand to take hers. Bowing, he placed a kiss gently on the back of her hand. Kate had only seen that sort of thing happening in the movies. The Count's action seemed as natural to him as breathing.

"How do you do," Kate replied a bit breathlessly. "I am Miss...Mrs. Littleton."

"I could not help but notice such a lovely young woman sitting all by herself," said the Count with a dazzling smile. Gesturing to the seat opposite her, he asked again. *"Permesso?* Do you mind if I join you?"

Caught off guard, Kate merely gestured to the seat next to her. The Count had the fluid grace of a cat. His dark hair and good looks could seduce any woman. Kate studied his face, noticing that it lacked guile. Its tanned complexion made him look like a man who spent a lot of time enjoying outdoor pursuits.

"Such a charming hat," the Count complimented. "And you wear it so cunningly."

"Thank you," said Kate in a surprised tone. As she involuntarily touched her hat lightly, she studied the Count's face. She could see the admiration in his eyes. Maybe he really does like my hat, she thought. How very flattering of him to notice.

"My friend...husband thinks it is a bit over the top," Kate said. Inside, she chided herself for her inability to remember to refer to Henry as her husband. She hoped the man sitting across from her hadn't noticed her double error. Kate probed the Count's handsome face for a cynical or questioning expression. Finding none, she relaxed perceptively.

Behind him, Kate noticed the Princess Lazio glaring at the Count as she entered the dining car. The expression on the Princess's face caught Kate's attention. The Princess's finely arched eyebrows were raised in a look that conveyed mingled dislike and contempt. Obviously, Kate was showing a significant lack of judgment being seen with the Count. Kate's face fell. She liked Princess Lazio and didn't want to offend her.

"*Scusi.* Excuse me," said the Count. "Have I said something wrong?"

Kate flushed and said, "No, of course not. I am the one who is sorry. I have allowed my attention to wander. Please excuse me."

"A beautiful woman needs no excuse," said the Count, his eyes sparkling with good humor.

Kate could feel herself relaxing. Count di Cosimo seemed like such a very nice man.

"Would you like some refreshment?" Count di Cosimo asked solicitously. Without waiting for an answer, he summoned the waiter.

"*Due Cappuccino,*" he said to the waiter, taking charge.

Kate's eyes wandered around the dining car before coming to rest again on the nearby table of Swiss business men.

"Ah, I see you are interested in our Swiss friends. May I translate for you?" said the Count *sotto voce*, his eyes twinkling mischievously. "You never know, we might learn something interesting."

What a strange thing to say, thought Kate. While Kate, herself, had been eavesdropping, at least she hadn't had the audacity to do it so blatantly. It was almost as if the Count had specifically chosen to sit at her table for the express purpose of listening to the conversation of the Swiss gentlemen. She frowned.

"You do not approve of eavesdropping on our fellow passengers, do you?" he asked as if reading her mind.

"Well, it is just that I..." Kate began reprovingly. Her voice trailed off. After all, she had been trying unsuccessfully to eavesdrop.

"I, too, do not listen to idle gossip. However, in this case, their conversation may entertain us. At the very least it will be informative," said the Count favoring her with a disarming smile.

Kate couldn't help herself, she smiled back.

"They are speaking of Yugoslavia's natural resources. Brown coal, bauxite, silver, and copper. Besides these, the mines that produce silver and copper also provide small amounts of lead, zinc, chromium, antimony, and cadmium," he said after pausing to listen for a bit. As an aside to Kate, he added with a hint of a wink, "that is quite a list of key mineral deposits for such a small country, don't you think? It could make Yugoslavia very interesting for their larger, more industrialized neighbors, such as Germany. Of course, this is all just conjecture on my part." Returning to listen to the conversation at the other table, he continued.

"Now, their conversation becomes interesting. The man with the black hair is Herr Bauman. He is president of a mining company. His company is skilled at mining ore, yet it is not the mining he is concerned about, it is transporting the minerals out of the mountains to be processed. Herr Bauman proposes financing a train line to reach some of the distant mine locations. According to him, the road and rail system in Yugoslavia leaves much to be desired. The man sitting across from him, Herr Christoff, has commented that his company would like to be involved. Herr Christoff would use Swiss tunnel building technology to construct the necessary tunnels. The two of them think it would be a highly profitable business venture, except..." the Count trailed off as he listened more intently to the conversation.

"The other two men at the table, Herr Schmidt and Herr Fullbeck, are bankers. They are concerned that the policies put in place by King Alexander will limit any effort on the part of outsiders to profit from the development of Yugoslavian natural resources. King Alexander believes that only Yugoslavian companies should be involved and therefore prefers to maintain things status quo. Apparently, the King's cousin, Prince Pavle, is much more open to investment by foreign firms. The Swiss are speaking heatedly about the difficulties of dealing with King Alexander. Herr Christoff and Herr Baumann want to meet with the King to try to convince him of the benefits of allowing their companies to develop transportation lines to the mines. Herr Schmidt and Herr Fullbeck want to approach Prince Pavle. They cannot seem to agree on which approach is the most likely to result in profits for the four of them," Count di Cosimo translated.

The Swiss business-men concluded their business discussion and moved on to the sporting opportunities in Yugoslavia. Aside from each man proclaiming a certain amount of skill with either a pistol or a rifle, their conversation appeared to hold no more interest for the Count.

"Ah, they have moved on to discuss where they plan to hunt and shoot in the Yugoslavian mountains. Surely, all this talk of business transactions and hunting must bore you, my *Bella*. Shall I leave you in peace to enjoy the lovely scenery outside our windows?" the Count asked in his most charming manner. Without waiting for an answer, di Cosimo stood abruptly and bid Kate good-bye.

"*Arrivederci, Bella*. I am sure we will meet again in the near future. Perhaps even in Belgrade. Please give my regards to your husband," he said.

Kate cringed with embarrassment as she couldn't help notice the inflection the Count placed on the word husband.

The Count hesitated a moment, studied her face intently, and added one word before he left. "*Coraggio*."

Kate had little time to think about what he meant by the word courage. Immediately after his departure, Princess Lazio gathered her book and reading glasses in preparation to leave the car. As she passed Kate's table, the Princess paused briefly. Her countenance gave the impression she disapproved of what had just passed between Kate and the Count. The Princess' verbal warning left no doubt in Kate's mind.

"My dear, you should not associate with the Count. He is not received in the best circles," said the Princess haughtily.

As Kate watched the Princess' receding back, she couldn't help thinking to herself, "neither am I." So what was it about the Count that the Princess did not like? Kate wanted to talk to Henry about it when he returned.

"Where have you been?" Kate asked when Henry finally arrived. Her eyes rested on her crumpled shawl. "Oh, Henry, not again. What happened this time?"

"Let's go back to our compartment, I'll tell you there," Henry responded.

"Can't we stay here? I have so much to tell you," Kate said, loathe to leave the Swiss businessmen in case they mentioned anything else interesting.

"What's this?" Henry asked, picking up a book from the table.

"Oh, that must be Count di Cosimo's book," Kate said, taking the copy of *Murder on the Calais Coach* from him. She fingered the folded piece of paper marking his place.

"Count di Cosimo? He was here at the table with you? Did you allow him to sit down? That slimy Italian pretending to be to the manor born," sneered Henry.

"Henry, that's not a very nice thing to say," Kate protested, her welcoming smile fading quickly.

"Come now, Kate, you weren't taken in by that Casanova, were you?" Henry remarked caustically.

"Taken in? Henry, what on earth are you talking about? He is a very nice man," Kate responded, surprised at the anger she heard in Henry's voice.

"Don't tell me you fell for his smooth compliments? The man chases anything in a skirt!" exclaimed Henry.

"He does not. The Count was very nice to me. Besides, he has a kind face."

"Don't tell me, more face reading! Haven't you got anything better to do than flirt with strangers?"

"You're the one who has been ignoring me! You could take a few lessons from a man as nice as the Count," Kate said heatedly. Aware of the volatility of the Italian character, she had not expected to find it in Henry.

"Nice? Ignoring you? Take lessons?" Henry said incredulously. "What has gotten into your pretty little head? Has your silly hat addled your brain?"

"Henry, how can you be such a brute? Why are you being so beastly?" Kate said, tears pricking her eyes.

"Me? A brute? Just how have you arrived at that conclusion in the space of time it has taken us to have this silly conversation?"

"Oh, Henry...our first quarrel!" cried Kate, jumping to her feet and running toward her compartment.

# Chapter 45

## Henry

*A*s Kate ran out of the car, Henry stood there flabbergasted. At that moment, Monsieur De la Roche appeared at the table.

"Young love is very fragile, Henry. You must treat it with care," the Frenchman said quietly.

"I...she...we..." stuttered Henry. "You've got this all wrong."

"Jealousy can trick even the smartest of us to say things we regret," Monsieur De la Roche said with feeling. "I do not mean to intrude, but, man to man, I suggest you follow your young lady and apologize."

Feeling a bit foolish, Henry thanked him and departed for their compartment. He wondered how things had gone so wrong so quickly. Certainly he wasn't jealous as Monsieur De la Roche suggested. He was merely annoyed that she hadn't played her role as his loving, newlywed bride. Henry reviewed the conversation in his mind and recognized it for the disaster it was. He couldn't help but be a bit peeved with Kate. Why had she allowed the Count to sit at their table? How had Kate known Henry had been involved in some sort of incident? No sense wasting time with unanswerable questions. He had better concentrate on framing his apology. Their compartment was too small for two angry people.

"Kate," Henry said, tapping at the door to their compartment. "Let me in?"

"I really have no choice, do I? You'll seem rather silly standing in the hallway on your honeymoon," Kate answered curtly as she opened the door.

He could tell by the look on her face, she wasn't about to forgive him just yet.

"Kate," Henry began. "We've got a job to do here. We're supposed to be newlyweds. Flirting with potential suspects won't help our cover at all."

"Flirting! How dare you accuse me of flirting? You weren't even there to see it," Kate said crossly, her back turned partially toward him. "I was engaging in business. Remember, we have been sent to find out who might be interested in killing the King."

"By flirting?" said Henry, temporarily forgetting that he was supposed to be the one apologizing.

"I was not flirting with the Count, I was gathering information," she said with as much dignity as she could muster.

"Very well, what did you learn?" Henry asked equally as stiffly.

"Whether you believe me or not, I learned quite a bit thanks to the Count's knowledge of the Swiss German language. The Count helped me eavesdrop on the conversation of the four Swiss men," Kate said, aware of Henry's feelings about listening in on others. "Henry, did you know that Yugoslavia is rich in nonferrous metals like lead, zinc, chromium, and copper?"

"Yes, I mean, I have read reports about it," Henry answered. "But there are significant issues related to mining and transporting the ore."

"That's where the Swiss come in. They are travelling to Yugoslavia to meet with either King Alexander or Prince Pavle, or both of them, to see if they can put together a deal involving Swiss investment in railroads, tunnels, and mining equipment. Apparently, King Alexander has limited interest in their proposals. The king would prefer that companies within his own country develop Yugoslavian natural resources. Prince Pavle, on the other hand, is very interested. Didn't you tell me that the Prince would become regent if anything happened to the King? And Henry, all four men claim to be excellent shots with either a pistol or a rifle," she finished with a flourish.

"Well, now, that could be important, though. You may be taking a big leap to connect potential business deals with assassinations," Henry said. Seeing her miffed look, he quickly added, "We'll have to investigate those four men further. What were their names again?"

"Herr Schmidt and Herr Fullbeck are bankers. Herr Christoff and Herr Bauman are in tunnels and mining."

"I received very little information on them from the embassy. Let's see," said Henry consulting a paper from his briefcase.

"Where were you for such a long time?" Kate asked, as if she had just remembered how long he had left her.

Henry told her about the incident in the tunnel. Kate burst out laughing.

"It's like something out of a mystery novel! The lights going out as the train enters a tunnel! Someone striking someone else in the dark! Oh Henry, are you making this up to hide something? Who have you been flirting with," Kate teased. "Surely it must have been an accident. The porter must have tripped and hit his head."

"An accident? An accident? Has anything that has happened to us on this trip been an accident?" Henry said, obviously upset by her attitude. "Don't be so skeptical. It really happened."

Kate's laughter bruised his ego. Henry wondered why she was not more worried about him. She actually laughed.

"Don't be silly. Surely you are overreacting about this particular incident. You sound like one of those people who keep seeing the Loch Ness monster whenever a ripple appeared on Loch Ness," she countered, laughter lingering in her voice.

"What will it take for you to believe me?" Henry said in a hurt tone. "Oh I know. You want a photo just like the one taken of Nessie by Surgeon R. K. Wilson on April 19th of this year. Haven't we been through enough adventures together by this time that you realized the truth in what I told you?"

"Oh, Henry, I'm sorry," Kate said soberly. "You're right."

"Let's forget about it and get back to work," he said, somewhat appeased. Though still a bit put out by her lack of concern over his safety, Henry was not immune to the glow on her cheeks her laughter had created.

As he prepared for dinner that evening, Henry thought back to their mid-morning visit with the De la Roches. Henry had enjoyed spending time with the Frenchman. They had discovered their mutual interest in fly fishing and had spent some time discussing the merits of various different styles of rods and flies. Henry looked forward to dining with the couple that evening. He realized with a start how much he liked the quiet, intelligent Frenchman despite his concern about their odd conversation earlier that day. Though it had begun normally enough, its topic puzzled Henry or at least the tones and inflections used seemed strange. While he dressed, he reflected on their conversation.

Shortly before lunch with the Forsyths, Henry had approached the couple to formally introduce Kate.

*"Bonjour Monsieur et Madame. J'aimerais vous presenter ma femme, Madame Katherine Littleton,"* said Henry with a flourish. *"Kate, je te present Antoinne et Juliette Rose De la Roche."*

Following the introductions, both couples had made small talk about the weather to the opulence of the dining car. As often happens on a train, the discussion had turned to travel.

"So, you are on your honeymoon. Wonderful. Are you planning to leave the train in Venice? Yes, you should stop in Venice. Venice is a perfect place to visit on your honeymoon," Monsieur De la Roche had said.

Was it his imagination or had the Monsieur placed a good deal of emphasis on the word "leave the train?" First suggestions about Capri from Princess Lazio, now Monsieur De la Roche focused on Venice.

"*Venizia*, the pearl of the Adriatic Sea. Have you been to Venice, Kate?" asked Madame De la Roche.

"Oh, no, I haven't really been anywhere," said Kate shyly.

"Wonderful, you are unaffected by memories of other journeys. Venice is the perfect place to begin your exploration of faraway places. We will be stopping at the *Sainte Lucia* rail station. It would be quite easy for you to disembark there. I am sure they would change your tickets to rejoin the Orient Express a few days later," said Monsieur De la Roche.

Henry thought the man was making it all sound so simple. Of course, Monsieur De la Roche didn't know the real reason he and Kate were on the train to Belgrade.

"Let's see, should you stay at the elegant Londra Palace? You would have beautiful views of the lagoon and it is near the *Piazza San Marco*. Though being young and in love, you might prefer to stay on the Lido. Imagine, from your hotel on the Lido, you can step right out onto the beach and into the sea! There your sole criterion for each would be only what you yourselves feel like seeing or doing. You should definitely consider stopping in Venice," said Madame De la Roche.

"The Lido sounds truly delightful, but tell me more about Venice," said Kate.

Henry watched their faces as the De la Roche told Kate about Venice. Why were they encouraging him and Kate to get off the train at their next stop?

"Some think that Venice is nothing more than dirty water and old stones, but I assure you it is full of many treasures. The Doge's Palace, San Marco's Cathedral, the Palazzo Ducale, the Bridge of Sighs, so many wonderful sights to fill your days. Enjoy having coffee at one of the *trattorias*. You could try *Trattoria del Elefante or Trattoria della Vida*. Those are two of our favorites. Do not forget to climb to the top of the Campanile tower to survey the city. That is, if you are not afraid of heights. But, you are not afraid, are you Henry?" Monsieur De la Roche added while staring steadily into Henry's eyes. Before Henry could answer, the man continued.

"Kate, be sure that you lure Henry into a gondola. If you have not glided through the Venetian *rios*, the canals, on a moonlight night with someone you love, you cannot really say that you understand the true atmosphere of this wonderfully romantic city. For 12 *lire* you can hire a gondola for the evening. Imagine, my dear, floating along in a gondola through the maze of Venetian *rios*. Henry is very good at finding his way out of mazes, is he not?" said Monsieur De la Roche as he stared pointedly at Henry.

What was going on here? Surely Henry's imagination was running away with him again. Monsieur De la Roche could know nothing of their adventure in the Hampton Court maze. Henry remained expressionless as Madame De la Roche turned her attention to Kate.

"Of course you will want to take a *vaparetto* to Murano. Henry can buy you some lovely Murano glass there as a wedding trip souvenir. Convince Henry to invest in a set of goblets. They are quite beautiful. Have you seen any? The colored glass is chased with designs in silver and gold. Ceramic flowers in pastel colors complete the decoration," Madame De la Roche said with enthusiasm.

Kate shook her head no.

"And the nights! You would surely be invited to one of the many balls and receptions held this time of year. You are quite good at dancing, are you not Henry? Even on the crowded dance floor at the embassy, I noticed you waltzing Kate out of danger. You wouldn't want to collide with anyone, would you?" Madame De la Roche said as she arched her eyebrows knowingly.

243

As he changed for dinner, Henry felt a pang of disquiet as he remembered the conversation. Once again, Henry thought the speaker had placed significant emphasis on her carefully chosen words. What was she trying to tell him? Was she in on this too? Had the comments obliquely referred to Henry's assignment? Henry had had to be very evasive when asked what he did for a living. He remembered the look that passed between the couple when he had said he had a small job in the government. He could tell Kate couldn't quite follow their curious repartee. Henry hoped to keep it that way. He had grown quite protective of Kate.

# Chapter 46

## Kate

$\mathcal{F}$or cocktails and dinner that night, Kate chose to wear a lovely dress created by Madame Vionnet. The black dress, with its halter-neck and bias cut, a signature style of Madame Vionnet, was designed to mold itself to a woman's body. Soft folds of creamy white fabric graced the neckline at the front of the dress. To complete the outfit, Kate had chosen a black hat as round and flat as a plate. The cunning veil covered her eyes giving her an air of mystery and adding to her allure. The hat perched on the side of her head nearly perpendicular to the floor in a manner that caused people to wonder what held it in place. Kate knew the secret. The clever hat designer had placed nearly invisible elastic that could be attached to and hidden by the wearer's hair.

Kate liked the effect the dress had on Henry. She could tell by the look of appreciation in his eyes that her appearance met with his approval. And when Kate turned around, she smiled at the shocked expression on his face in the mirror when Henry realized her shoulders weren't the only thing revealed by the dress. From the look on his face, he would be thinking about something else besides their assignment tonight. The dress was low-cut in the back, daringly so. From its widest point at her shoulders, the delicate fabric flowed down the back of the gown to the center of her lower back. The design exposed a V-shaped wedge of her skin from shoulder to waist. At her waist, the fabric had been formed into tiny pleats that flowed to the floor like a train behind her.

"Thank heavens we won't be dancing this evening, darling. There isn't anywhere safe to place my hand at your waist," Henry said, his eyes lingering like a touch on her bare skin. "On second thought, perhaps we should be dancing this evening."

Kate heard the catch in his voice and smiled with satisfaction. Finally, she thought happily, Henry noticed her as an attractive woman. It had been maddening the way he ignored her, saying it was all in the line of duty.

Despite their quarrel and his lack of sleep, Henry insisted that they return to the dining car for cocktails, rather than nap. As part of their plan to investigate everyone on the train, Kate and Henry sat together at the bar with the American couple, Mr. and Mrs. Johnson.

"Walter, do you mean to tell me that we will be travelling through Hungary and Yugoslavia during the night?" queried Mrs. Johnson.

"Yes, my dear Minnie. According to the time-table, we stop for a few minutes in Venice at six this evening. From there we continue on to Trieste. It should be light enough for you to see a good deal of the countryside while we have dinner," her husband answered.

"It's just that I have heard so much about the scenic mountains, I did so want to see them," she said.

"I know dear. That's why we took the train across Europe instead of going by sea to my appointment in Cairo. We won't travel by boat until Istanbul, then, we'll complete our journey by sea," Mr. Johnson explained to Henry and Kate.

Mr. Johnson seemed to be on a roll, because he continued, "Did you know that Yugoslavia is only slightly larger than our American state of Kentucky."

"Imagine that," responded his wife. "I hadn't really thought about it at all. Kentucky is not all that impressive, though they produce excellent race horses. We're from New York. We keep our race horses at Saratoga. Do you have race horses?"

Kate could see that Henry was nonplussed by this question, so she returned the conversation to the original topic of Yugoslavia.

"Mr. Johnson, tell me, what else do you know about Yugoslavia?" Kate asked disarmingly.

"Well," Walter said in his clipped New York accent. "The climate sounds similar to what we experience in New York. The winters are cold and damp in most parts of the country. Temperatures vary depending on where you are. For instance, along the coast, summers are usually hot and dry. In the mountains, the summers tend to be more humid. From what the guidebook tells me Yugoslavia is a country of contrasts. The scenery includes everything from snow-capped peaks to gorges and waterfalls. Montenegro is supposed to be covered with sheer barren rocks, giving it a rather primitive ruggedness. The seashores are supposed to be some of the loveliest in the world."

"Walter, I never realized you knew so much about Yugoslavia," Minnie said, earning herself an intolerant look from her husband. Oblivious to his poor temper, she continued. "But when I asked about stopping along the way, you said we will be going straight through to Istanbul. Listening to you speak now, you make Yugoslavia sound worth visiting. Why don't we stop in Belgrade and look around? What do you think dear?" Mrs. Johnson asked her husband. Rather than answer her, he turned his attention to Henry and Kate.

"What does the country have to offer besides scenery? What do they produce here? Raspberries, plums, nuts, corn, pigs? They don't even have significant natural resources. It's not worth our time," Mr. Johnson said sharply.

"From what I understand, they have significant deposits of coal, bauxite, silver, and copper," Kate said, remembering what she had overheard earlier. "They are currently trying to create the transportation network necessary to access these resources." Kate noticed Henry gave her an incredulous look. He obviously didn't know as much about Yugoslavia as she had learned.

Her comment seemed to remind Mr. Johnson of his manners. In a calmer voice, he added, "I understand you are stopping in Belgrade."

Kate wondered how he knew that.

"Why, yes," said Henry. "We plan a short stop before continuing on to Istanbul. We want to take in the quaint old town, spend some time boating on the Danube and the Sava rivers, that sort of thing. We understand there was quite a Roman presence in the town. There is an old Roman well and fortress at the park where the Danube and Sava join that I wouldn't mind seeing. I've always been interested in Roman history. I've been told the park is quite lovely and romantic at sunset." Henry put his arm around Kate, acting the part of a young man on his honeymoon.

"We could do the same thing," exclaimed Mrs. Johnson.

"I don't think we will have time," said Mr. Johnson flatly.

The conversation began to dwindle at that point to the usual platitudes about travel and weather. Later, it struck Kate that the Johnsons had talked about everything and nothing at all. Only Mrs. Johnson seemed quite interested in including a stop in Belgrade on their trip east.

When Monsieur and Madame De la Roche entered the dining car, Henry and Kate left the bar to join them at their table. Kate noted that, once again, Madame De la Roche was stylishly turned out in a *Parisienne* haute couture gown. Really, thought Kate, the woman's elegance could be so intimidating. However, Kate's fears were put to rest when the impossibly chic woman greeted her with a compliment.

"*Bonsoir, ma Cherie.* Such a cunning *petit chapeau.* Surely you found it in Paris?" Madame De la Roche said as she greeted them warmly. "I simply must know where you buy your divine hats!"

"I do hope my wife's enthusiasm for hats does not intrude on your honeymoon," said Monsieur De la Roche as he smiled at his wife affectionately. He reached over and took his wife's hand, squeezing it gently. "After our short visit this morning, Juliette insisted that we share a table this evening."

Kate, still a bit awestruck at being placed at a table with these elegant beings, found herself tongue-tied.

Fortunately, Madame De la Roche went on. "I can see that you visited the shops along Avenue Montaigne and in the Rue Royale. Delightful, aren't they?"

"*Oui,*" stammered Kate.

"I commend you on your excellent taste in clothing. You are young and slender. You can dare to wear clothes that are a little ingenious. Madame Vionnet is a master at the art of draping fabric, isn't she?"

"The French designers are talented at adding the small touches that give *Parisienne* clothing a certain *je ne sais quoi*. Those little additions change a garment in ways that are as hard to define as intuition," Kate said, finally managing to find her voice.

"A dress from Madame Vionnet is a dress for eternity," Madame said in typical French overstatement. "Sometimes, I prefer *chez Molyneux* for a smart, yet slightly unconventional afternoon suit. Where did you happen to find that charming little suit you were wearing today?"

Kate was loath to admit she had picked it up at *Printemps*. It was obvious to her that Madame De la Roche shopped at only the finest haute couture establishments in Paris. The white satin evening dress with black appliqué worn by Madame De la Roche was one of the most striking Kate had ever seen. "I found it at a boutique on the Boulevard Haussmann," Kate said to cover her discomfort. To deflect further attention, she hazarded a guess and said, "Your lovely evening dress, is it from *Chez Lanvin*?"

"*Mais oui*! How observant you are about fashion. I find Jeanne Lanvin a remarkably creative dressmaker. Would you believe she started out her career at a very young age as a seamstress? Now she is one of the premier designers in Paris," said Madame De la Roche. "As much as I love our chateau in the Loire, I enjoy visiting Paris. We always take a suite at the Plaza Athene. Not only are all the best shops in Paris within walking distance, the views of the Eiffel Tower from the balcony of our room is magnificent."

"And the damage to my bank account equally magnificent," Monsieur De la Roche said under his breath to Henry.

Kate couldn't help but overhear that comment and wondered how Henry would explain her extravagant gown. She needn't have worried; Henry was up to the challenge.

"I have only just begun to understand the needs of a woman shopping in Paris. We are, after all, on our honeymoon," Henry said smiling.

"Have you been to Worth?" Madame De la Roche asked, pointedly ignoring her husband's comment. "You simply must have your evening wraps and day coats made at Worth. There, they respect tradition while adding modern touches." Continuing on with the topic of shopping, Madame De la Roche wanted to know if Kate had selected her travelling luggage at Louis Vuitton. "Personally, I use my mother's 1911 *wardrobe en toile monogram* whenever I travel. It is perfectly designed for travelling," said Madame De la Roche.

Tiring of fashion, Monsieur De la Roche changed the subject and began to talk about the joys of champagne. Picking up his crystal goblet, the Frenchman held it toward the light. There, the golden liquid fizzed and sparkled.

"Dom Perignon, my personal favorite," said Monsieur De la Roche. "Did you know that champagne is best served as an aperitif? Yes, it stimulates the appetite. Me, I prefer to drink champagne with smoked salmon or *foie gras*," Monsieur De la Roche said. He sipped his champagne appreciatively before continuing.

"Ah, *parfait*. So *delicats et raffine*. So delicate and refined," he said appreciatively.

"*Seduisant*," agreed his wife.

"Champagne should be served chilled to between 45 and 50 degrees Fahrenheit." Holding the glass to the light again, Monsieur De la Roche continued educating them about champagne. "This one is particularly nice. Notice the fine, small, tight bubbles." He waited while they all lifted their crystal goblets to the light to see the bubbles. "Small bubbles extend the flavors." He sipped again. "Ah, *magnific*!"

"Did you know that champagne was a favorite beverage of Napoleon I?" Monsieur De la Roche made a grand gesture with his glass. "The Emperor once said: '*when I win, I drink champagne to celebrate, and when I lose, I drink it to console myself*'." All of them laughed at the rightness of this statement.

"Did you know that champagne is made with three grapes?" Henry asked, wanting to add something to the conversation.

"Yes, and one of them is chardonnay," responded Monsieur De la Roche who watched Henry intently.

"The others are pinot noir and pinot meunier," volunteered Kate, eager to join in. It was Kate's turn to be carefully studied by Monsieur De la Roche.

"Did you also know that Dom Perignon considered champagne a mistake?" Now Monsieur De la Roche had everyone's attention. "He spent his life trying to get rid of the bubbles in his wine. Still wine was more practical. At that time, bottles were not strong enough to hold the pressure of sparkling wine. The yeast in the wine caused pressure to build that would pop the corks out of the bottles."

"Imagine going to the cellar to retrieve a bottle and having corks shoot out at you."

"Isn't that one of the things we love about champagne? The pop of the cork when we open it?" said Madame De la Roche.

"It's such a happy sound," agreed Kate.

"Did you know that the original corks in a bottle weren't corks at all, but wooden plugs?" Monsieur De la Roche continued. "Dom Perignon, in search of a solution to his problem, began to use cork to cap a wine bottle. He also perfected the metal caging we remove with dramatic flourish from the bottle before easing out the cork. His corking system worked very well, corks no longer shot out of the bottles when stored in the cellar. Unfortunately, champagne refused to be held in a bottle. When popping corks could no longer be used to relieve the pressure, the sparkling wine shattered the bottles, usually by breaking off the bottom." That brought a smile to everyone's face as they pictured the consternation of the monks faced with bottles exploding around them.

"Fortunately for us, glass bottle makers in Newcastle, England figured out how to make more robust bottles," Monsieur De la Roche said with a nod to Henry. "They used coal-fired furnaces to produce stronger glass, thus enabling us to enjoy champagne today." He replenished their glasses with the bubbling gold liquid. "Undeterred, Dom Perignon continued his quest for still wine. He experimented with ways to make the wine purer, thus preventing excessive fermentation. He even developed a gentler process for pressing the grapes so the skin would not be mixed in with the flesh inside. This enabled him to make white wine from red grapes, thus the appellation, *blanc de noir*, white from black."

"You certainly know a lot about champagne," exclaimed Henry. "Tell us more."

"All right, just one more bit of information," said Monsieur De la Roche to his captivated audience. "True champagne can only come from the

Champagne region in France, a minor result of the Treaty of Versailles following the Great War." Seeing the disbelief on their faces, the Frenchman continued.

"It is true! The land around Reims and Epernay had been badly scarred by the war making it difficult to produce any champagne. During the negotiations following the end of the war, the French government wanted to protect the region and allow it time to recover. You can imagine what would have happened if sparkling wines from Germany, the United States, Italy, or even other regions of France had been able to fill the gap left by low grape production in the Champagne region." Seeing that they all agreed that this was true, Monsieur De la Roche went on with his narrative. "Article 275 of the Treaty of Versailles protects champagne as a product produced solely in the Champagne region of France. All other sparkling wines must be labeled as sparkling wines or *methode Champagnois* to denote that they are not from the Champagne region."

"How fascinating," said Kate. "I had no idea there was so much history behind champagne."

"I have a question for you," said Henry. "What is the difference between *Cremant* and sparkling wine and champagne?"

"That is actually two questions, my friend," said Monsieur De la Roche with a smile. "*Cremant* is a sparkling wine made in the Burgundy region of France. So, a sparkling wine cannot be a *Cremant* unless it is made in Burgundy. In answer to the second part of your question, *Cremant* is a sparkling wine with only two-thirds of the bubbles of traditional *methode Champagnois* wine. We could try some this evening except we are dining on Italian food. It would be more appropriate to have an Italian wine. A *Prosecco* would be perfect to begin with."

The remainder of the evening passed quite merrily. Their conversation ranged from fine French food and wine to fascinating descriptions of faraway places. They dined on Italian food. After the champagne, the delectable meal began with *fettucini alfredo. Fritto misto con fagiolini* followed as the next course. The two couples lingered over coffee, expressing their delight in the Orient Express and all it had to offer. Kate was glad their supper conversation had not been filled with suggestive statements. No more comments were made about Venice. Kate wondered whether that was because they had already passed Venice. Certainly Trieste held little attraction for a honeymooning couple. Either way, no one had made any further veiled suggestions about leaving the train. Thinking back, Kate remembered how both Monsieur and Madame De la Roche started ever so slightly when an older man entered the dining car. She had heard their whispered *"Que veut dire ca?"* What does it mean? Kate wondered what they were referring to.

It had been a long and exciting day. As it grew later, Kate looked forward to going back to their compartment to compare notes with Henry about all the people they had seen and met during the day. She found it peculiar that when shaking hands before separating for the evening, Monsieur De la Roche had wished Henry *bonne chance*. Good luck.

# Chapter 47

## Henry

*B*ack in their compartment following dinner, Henry wasn't sure if it was the effects of the champagne, the gentle rocking of the train or Kate's halter-necked dress revealing the honey-colored skin on her soft shoulders, that made him sweep Kate into his arms.

"You are as radiant as the full moon," Henry whispered into Kate's auburn hair.

"Henry," Kate began.

"Shh. Don't talk, just let me hold you."

For a moment, they just stood quietly wrapped in each other's arms. As their heart beats quickened, they turned their faces toward each other. The kiss that followed was sweeter than Henry could have imagined. He wrapped his arms tighter around Kate, crushing her in his embrace. She ran her fingers through his hair, pulling him to her to deepen the kiss.

"Dearest, loveliest," Henry began, his voice soft and warm.

Unexpectedly, a loud commotion could be heard in the corridor outside their compartment. Voices raised in anger accompanied the sounds of scuffling. Remembering that he was on the train to do a job, Henry sighed and released Kate. Together, they placed their ears close to the door in an attempt to overhear without disturbing the people arguing nearby. Henry and Kate looked at each other with raised eyebrows when they realized that one voice sounded distinctly like the Colonel. Two men were obviously quarreling. Oddly, the Colonel was speaking with someone in Yugoslavian dialect. Though they could not understand what he was saying, the anger and contempt in his voice were evident. Further along the corridor, a door opened, instantly cutting off all conversation. Only the sounds of departing footsteps remained. Cautiously, Henry opened the door to their compartment and quickly glanced around. In the corridor, Monsieur DuBois walked calmly toward the washroom facilities. As he passed Henry and Kate, Monsieur DuBois barely acknowledged them with a nod of his head.

"Have you noticed how Monsieur DuBois seems angry all the time?" Kate asked Henry when they were once again alone. "And the Colonel, was it really him we heard in the hallway speaking Yugoslavian?"

"The Colonel did tell us that he spent time there during the Great War," mused Henry.

"Do you think he was talking to DuBois?"

"I don't know. DuBois may have just opened the door to his compartment."

"Oh, Henry," Kate said with despair. "This is all so complicated. There are so many questions we don't have the answers to. Is this what it is like to work in espionage? I don't like not knowing at all."

Despite his annoyance at being interrupted mid-kiss, Henry knew his most immediate concern was keeping Kate out of harm's way. They sat side-by-side on the lower berth.

"You're right," Henry said. "There have been too many small incidents. It's only becoming more confusing. Nothing adds up. So many questions! How did enemy agents find us in Piccadilly Circus?"

"How did they find us at the British museum?" Kate countered

"How did they track us to Paris?"

"How many people have followed us?" Kate wondered aloud.

"Was the man at the embassy, the man with the caterpillar eyebrows, connected to the original two in London in any way?"

"Was he working for a different faction? Did he reveal else anything during his interrogation in Paris?"

"No, his answers told us nothing except that the assassin would be on this train. Even that bit of information I got out of him under duress."

"What about the passengers on the Orient Express? Why are so many people making leading and misleading statements?" Kate asked, surprising Henry. He hadn't thought she had noticed. She certainly played her cards close to her chest. Her face had given nothing away during their conversations with others. He deliberately chose not to answer the question and posed one of his own.

"I don't know what to think of Monsieur and Madame De la Roche. They certainly seem sincere. Didn't you think so?"

"I thought it odd that they talked about Venice this morning, but then said nothing more about it at dinner."

"Perhaps that is because we are already in Hungary."

"What did you think about Colonel Forsyth?" she asked.

"Grim chap."

"Horrid company," Kate agreed. "Did you see the expression on the Colonel's face during dinner?"

"More face reading?"

"Don't start picking on me again. Besides, can't you see the anger in his eyes?"

"He's just an arrogant old man. What about the earlier incident with the porter in the hallway? Why did the lights go out? Was it a fluke of electricity on the train or deliberate?"

"It had to be deliberate.  How else would the person know to try to strike you at that time?" Kate answered logically.

"So you think the blow was meant for me, not the porter?" Henry asked Kate.  He yawned widely.  The lack of sleep over the previous few nights was catching up with him.

"Why, yes, of course.  It seems a bit far-fetched that someone would go after a porter just when he is leaving a compartment.  Why was he in an empty compartment anyway? Who struck the blow? That is the real question."

"We seem to be surrounded by people who were definitely not friends of ours.  Is there anyone we can trust?"  Henry asked while he tried to cover another sleepy yawn.  He turned and lifted his feet up on the bunk so he could rest his head against the back wall of the compartment.

"Well, let's see.  We have quite a list of characters in this little farce, the Princess, Monsieur and Madame De la Roche, Monsieur and Madame DuBois, four Swiss businessmen, Colonel and Mrs. Forsyth, that secretive man Herr Altmann, Count di Cosimo, Mr. and Mrs. Johnson, and probably countless others.  Who are we looking for?"

She received no answer to her question.  Though he tried to pay attention, Henry, tired from so many sleepless nights, lay down on his side and promptly fell asleep.

# Chapter 48

## Kate

*K*ate tucked Henry into bed in the lower berth. After she had climbed into the upper berth, she lay there a while staring out the window. The countryside the train passed through glimmered in the moonlight. She could see lights of villages twinkling in the distance. Kate contemplated the list of characters on the train. Her tired mind had spun with the memories of conversations heard throughout the day, but she came to no conclusions. After restlessly tossing and turning, Kate finally fell asleep.

Now, as their train drew nearer to Belgrade, Kate had been up since dawn preparing for their early Tuesday morning departure. Kate didn't really want to leave the train. The truly challenging part of their adventure would take place in Belgrade. Would Henry be able to prevent an assassination? Would she be of any help? Her mood darkened, as did the skies outside the window of their compartment. It had begun to rain, first as a fine mist, now in full force. It slashed against the window and reduced the view to a harsh grey watery landscape. The weather matched her mood, she thought grimly.

As she packed, Kate picked up her copy of *Murder on the Calais Coach*. It was only when she saw the piece of paper marking a page that Kate realized it was Count di Cosimo's book. She would need to make sure she returned it to him. Was he getting off the train in Belgrade? Kate couldn't remember. She could always ask the porter to return it for her. Idly, she opened the book to the marked page. A passage had been underlined. Kate fingered the piece of paper and finally her curiosity got the better of her. She unfolded the paper and examined it quickly. She nearly gasped out loud when she realized it was a map of Belgrade. So di

Cosimo was disembarking in Belgrade after all. Studying the map more closely, she realized a route had been marked on the plan of the city. She would give it to Henry when he returned from checking on their bags with the porter. He would understand whether or not it was important. In the meantime, Kate tucked the map back in the book and put the book in her small suitcase.

Henry had gone to confirm that their luggage would be taken off the train in Belgrade. Before he returned, Kate could hear Mrs. Forsyth wailing in the hallway. The woman sounded positively frantic. Kate opened the door and was instantly engulfed by the large sobbing woman.

"Billy is gone," Mrs. Forsyth managed to gasp out between sobs.

"Billy?"

"My husband! My Billy! He's gone," she said upon seeing Kate's blank face.

Soon Kate had the whole story. Late last night, Colonel Forsyth had told his wife he was going to get some air on the platform before retiring for the evening. At first Mrs. Forsyth had waited up for him, but soon she fell asleep. It wasn't until waking this morning, finding his bed untouched, that she realized her husband had never returned.

"Where could he be?" cried Mrs. Forsyth.

When Henry reappeared, Kate filled him in on the Colonel's disappearance. He set off to find the conductor. When the conductor arrived, he questioned Mrs. Forsyth.

"Was your husband in the habit of retiring later that you did?"

"Not usually."

"Did the Colonel seem to be bothered by anything yesterday or last night?"

"No."

"Did you and your husband have an argument?"

"We most certainly did not!"

"Had the Colonel mentioned anything that might have a bearing on his disappearance?"

"No."

"Had she seen the Colonel following the train's brief stop in Zagreb?"

"Yes."

"What had the Colonel been wearing when she last saw him?"

"Blue pajamas with red piping and a matching dressing gown."

The answer to this last question really caught Kate's attention. According to his wife, the Colonel wore blue pajamas with red piping and a matching dressing gown. Henry's pajamas and gown matched that description exactly, Kate realized. Hadn't she, just the previous morning, thought that from the back, Henry resembled the Colonel?

At a comment made by the conductor, Kate looked up sharply. What was that she just heard the conductor say? May have disembarked in an unusual manner from the train last night? Had she heard him correctly? Had something happened to that over-bearing man? Why him? Was the Colonel involved in something clandestine? Did he know something he shouldn't? In the dark of the night, had someone mistaken him for Henry? So many questions!

At the idea of her husband making an unscheduled departure from the train, Mrs. Forsyth began wailing again in earnest. Despite Kate's attempts to sooth her, the woman would not be comforted. Henry and the conductor went to signal previous stations along the lines to instigate a hunt for Colonel Forsyth. The two of them would search the entire train for the missing man.

What was it about the Orient Express that invited mystery and murder? Kate changed her mind and was suddenly glad they were getting off the train in Belgrade.

# Chapter 49

## Henry

*H*enry caught his breath as the thought came to him that the Colonel, wearing a dressing gown similar to his own, might be mistaken for him. Henry's attention had been consumed with the disappearance of the diplomatic pouch. Now the Colonel had vanished from the train dressed in an outfit identical to Henry's. First London, then Paris, then the porter on the train, now this! Someone was definitely trying to put Henry out of the picture. Who was behind all this? Who knew about his mission? Who was after him? Were the events of the past few days related or isolated incidents? Or was Henry allowing too much Agatha Christie to cause him to see mysterious behavior about every occurrence? He was used to dealing with rational things like numbers and invoices and accounts. The current situation presented him with too many questions and too few logical bits of information.

Henry tried to sort out all the players in this espionage game. He still had no clue just who the assassin was. Had he really travelled on the train like the man at the embassy had said? Their captive may have said that as a red herring to throw Henry off the scent. Despite their efforts on Sunday in Paris, the man had not told them anything else.

Henry's mind moved on to Princess Lazio. The comments made by the Princess continued to puzzle him. Had her meeting with Kate at Chanel been accidental? What about her warning during their dance at the embassy? Was she just being friendly to a honeymooning couple or was she trying to get him off the train? What about all the cryptic comments she had made? Henry had seen her speaking to an older man earlier in the day. There was something about the way they had their heads together that suggested more than a casual acquaintance. Added together, the evidence pointed to her being involved in some way.

Henry had seen the same older man speaking in low tones with a porter. They had pulled apart quickly when Henry approached. A bit too quickly, now that he thought about it. That had happened shortly before his near miss in the darkened corridor. Reviewing the scenes in his mind, Henry was sure it was the same sallow-faced porter who had found him in the corridor with the injured man. Had Henry heard the man's shoe squeak? For the life of him, he could not remember.

As much as he liked them both, Henry also questioned the behavior of the De la Roches. Certainly their conversation the previous afternoon had been full of suggestions and innuendos. Monsieur DuBois was another Frenchman that bore watching. The man was abrupt and abrasive. There were the Americans too. When Henry went to check on their luggage, he learned that the Johnsons had unexpectedly changed their travel plans to include a lengthy stop in Belgrade. Their quickly invented interest in the cultural delights the region had to offer worried Henry.

Then there were the more innocuous travellers on the train, the bankers, the diplomats, even the porters. Henry could not remember any of them behaving suspiciously. But he might have missed something.

His heart pounded as he examined every inch of the train with the conductor. This had become such a routine that their intrusion into each compartment merited only minor protests from the occupants. So far they hadn't had any luck finding the Englishman or the diplomatic pouch. The train had not made any stops since early in the evening the night before, long before Colonel Forsyth disappeared. Therefore, unless he had been thrown off the train, the Colonel had to still be somewhere on the train, but where? As the train drew hissing and puffing into the station at Belgrade, Henry and the conductor brought their unsuccessful search to a close.

# Chapter 50

## Kate

*G*ratefully, Kate sank into the bathtub of warm water. It had been a long and trying day. After arriving in Belgrade, the train and its passengers had been delayed while every square inch of each car had been searched. Though a thorough inquiry had been made of the passengers on the train before it departed, no trace of the Colonel could be found. After being questioned by the authorities, Kate and Henry had spent the morning trying to help Mrs. Forsyth. First, they met with Belgrade police officials at the train station. Later they discussed the Colonel's disappearance with representatives of the British embassy. Most of their conversations were fruitless conjectures about what might have happened. Mrs. Forsyth alternated between loudly demanding action and weeping copiously. When questioned, the woman had had nothing new to add. Throughout the day, at the embassy, via telegraph, they had received information from line stations. Fortunately, no bodies had been found beside the track. Unfortunately, by late in the afternoon, they were no closer to discovering the Colonel's whereabouts than they had been that morning.

At the embassy, they had been given a meager lunch but none of them had been very interested in eating. Eventually, Mrs. Forsyth regained her composure enough to spend the afternoon badgering anyone and everyone about her missing husband. Much to Kate's dismay, Henry had left Kate alone with Mrs. Forsyth while he went to confer with his official counterparts. His relief at having somewhere else to go was palatable. Late in the day, Kate convinced Mrs. Forsyth that they would be more comfortable waiting for news of the Colonel at the hotel. The staff at the embassy gratefully thanked Kate as she pushed the reluctant woman toward an awaiting cab. Honestly, the woman was a trial.

Kate left a message for Henry saying she would wait to dine with him on his return. In the meantime, she planned to put her few moments alone to good use. First a long soak in the tub. When she finished with her bath, Kate dressed in a dark blue suit. Since Henry had not yet returned, Kate spent quite a bit of time at the dressing table mirror brushing her hair, applying her new make-up, and dreaming of him. She wanted to be looking her best for dinner that night, potentially one of their last together. Kate could tell that she had captured his interest. She hoped to signal her willingness to deepen their relationship. Kate also knew that, despite his teasing, Henry enjoyed her hats. She tried on several before settling on one that was merely a small suggestion of a hat with a veil that covered her face. She pinned it securely in place. Studying her reflection in the mirror, Kate decided that the suit needed just a little bit of excitement. Sorting through the few pieces of costume jewelry she had purchased in Paris, she decided on rhinestone collar clips that added just the right touch.

Tomorrow morning, she and Henry would be attending the parade honoring the visiting diplomats. King Alexander would be riding in one of the open cars. Kate would finally get to see the man Henry had been sent to protect. Henry had shown her the intended parade route on a large map at the embassy. Thoughts of the parade and its route got Kate to thinking about the map she had found in Count di Cosimo's book. She removed the book from her suitcase and pulled out the map. She speculated about its importance. While she couldn't be positive, to the best of her knowledge, the Count's marked map matched the plan for the parade. That was a curious coincidence. Kate pondered this for a while. Count di Cosimo struck her as a womanizer, but she could not visualize him as an assassin. She doubted he would have the stomach for it. She wondered what Henry would make of the map when he got a chance to study it. Though she had given it to him on the train, Mrs. Forsyth's crisis had taken his full attention.

Kate spent a few moments considering who else would be watching the parade. She had seen the De la Roches and the Johnsons earlier in the hotel lobby. She had exchanged greetings with each couple but they made it clear that they wanted to spend as little time as possible with Mrs. Forsyth. Kate couldn't blame them. It was all she could do not to leave the woman right there in the lobby.

Kate hadn't seen the Princess or the Count at any time during the day. Hadn't they each said something about taking the train to its final destination? Kate couldn't remember. Another person she thought she had seen earlier was Herr Altmann. He had been across the square as she entered the hotel. It had been getting dark, so she might have been mistaken. Though Henry would never believe her, Kate still thought the man had a suspicious air about him.

When Henry still hadn't returned, Kate turned her attention to her selecting her outfit for the next day. Her outfit of choice, a conservative dark brown suit, flattered her figure, without drawing attention to her. She chose another small hat to compliment the quiet elegance of the suit.

Her planning complete, Kate glanced at the clock and wondered why Henry wasn't back yet. Her face brightened when she realized that, given the late hour, he might be crossing the square in front of their hotel right now. Kate went to the small balcony and watched the activity in the square below. Unexpectedly, she had felt hands grip her from behind.

"Henry!" Kate said exasperated, "Stop that! Please! Don't! Leave me alone!" She turned around to discover it wasn't Henry.

# Chapter 51

## Henry

$\mathscr{I}$t was late when Henry finally got back to the hotel. He was looking forward to dinner with Kate. It surprised him to discover that she was not in their room. Since he was so over-due, perhaps Kate went to the dining room with Mrs. Forsyth for a bite to eat. Somehow he doubted it. They had both had enough of the Colonel's wife for the day.

Henry made his way down to the dining room at the hotel to check for Kate. The room contained only a few late diners. The maître d' politely informed him that, no; he had not seen Mrs. Littleton that evening. The man also verified that Kate had not requested that any food be sent up to her room. As he left the dining room, Henry met Monsieur and Madame De la Roche returning from dinner. From them, Henry found out that Kate and Mrs. Forsyth had indeed arrived at the hotel earlier in the evening. Kate had made a comment about looking forward to spending a few hours resting before dinner.

Strange, thought Henry. Kate wouldn't have left the hotel without leaving him a note. She wouldn't have left without her purse either.

Perhaps Kate had stepped out for a moment to check on Mrs. Forsyth. Reluctantly, Henry made his way up to Mrs. Forsyth's room. There, he wasted precious time in his quest to find Kate when the woman became hysterical again. Henry finally convinced the hotel management to send the doctor to care for the Colonel's wife before making his way back to his hotel room.

The room was depressingly empty. Where had Kate gone? Henry couldn't decide whether or not to be angry or disturbed over her disappearance. He prowled the room looking for any clues for where she might be.  He hoped wildly that she had left him a note and that he had merely overlooked it.  A complete circuit of the room revealed no more information than he had when he had first arrived.  Kate's clothing and hats had been placed neatly in the closet.  She had been thoughtful enough to unpack for him.  On the dressing table, her usual collection of cosmetics and perfumes showed signs of use, as did the bathroom.

On the nightstand, he found a copy of *Murder on the Calais Coach.* Hadn't she said something about that being Count di Cosimo's book?  He remembered that she had shown him the map that she had found inside. He had been so caught up in his own adventures that he had virtually ignored her find and the information that she had uncovered.  Henry's expression became a grimace when he remembered that they had both laughed when she called him a magnet for trouble.  The crystal bright sound of her laugh echoed in his head.  Henry picked up the book and looked for the map.  It wasn't there.  Why would she have left the room without her purse but with the map?  Standing there in the middle of the room, Henry knew without a doubt that Kate would not leave without telling him where she went.  Had he, the human magnet, drawn trouble to Kate?

Henry took his pistol out of his briefcase.  He checked it thoroughly.  As he placed additional bullets in his jacket pocket, he reviewed the passenger list from the Simplon Orient Express.  The information from the embassy contacts, the interview with the man from the embassy ball, and the strange behavior of the passengers on the train, all pointed to an assassin on the train.  But who?  Who had he met or seen on the train fit the profile of an assassin?  Henry wondered how the map that Kate found in Count di Cosimo's book fit in.  The plan of Belgrade had shown a route very similar to the proposed parade route that Henry had been briefed about in Paris.  Had someone given the map to di Cosimo or was he supposed to give it to someone?  Di Cosimo could be the assassin or he might be only a messenger.  Henry tried to decide if di Cosimo had given any indication on the train that linked him to another individual.  So many questions and no definite answers ran through Henry's mind.  Henry turned these puzzle pieces around in his mind for a while before deciding to ask at the front desk if anyone had seen Kate leave the hotel. He took the stairs to the lobby two at a time.

"*Oprostite*. Excuse me."

"*Dobro vece.* Good evening Mr. Littleton, how may I help you?"

"My wife and I were supposed to have dinner together this evening but she is not in our room. Have you or anyone else seen her?"

"She and Mrs. Forsyth came in together earlier this evening, sometime around six, I believe."

"Have you seen her since then?"

"No sir."

"Would you mind asking your colleagues?"

The man left to find an answer to Henry's question. A few minutes later, he returned shaking his head.

"I am sorry to say, Mr. Littleton, that no one has seen your wife tonight. Are you sure she is not with friends?"

"No. We don't know anyone in the hotel besides Mrs. Forsyth and the De la Roches. I have spoken with each of them and they have not seen my wife."

Henry paused to think about what to do next.

"I believe my wife has disappeared from our room, perhaps against her will. Who do you suggest I speak to at the hotel in order to arrange a search?"

"Surely you understand Monsieur that we cannot search the guest rooms of the hotel. It would be quite unpleasant for the guests and there is the late hour. . ."

"There must be something we can do to find out if my wife is here in the hotel."

"At the moment, no. Perhaps the day manager can be of some assistance. I am sure your wife will return before then."

"But..."

"*Laku noc*, good night Mr. Littleton," said the concierge firmly.

Henry had wasted several more precious minutes arguing with the man, but the night manager remained adamant. No effort would be made to explore the hotel for Kate. Henry stood in the center of the lobby considering his next move.

"Mr. Littleton. I apologize for failing to give you this message. It was left in your box. Perhaps it is from your wife." The night manager handed Henry a plain envelope before walking quickly away in order to avoid another argument. Henry tore it open and rapidly read it.

> "We have your wife. Leave Belgrade at once. Allow us to complete our plans. It would be a shame for an obituary to follow a wedding announcement so quickly."

Henry froze. He merely stared at the note, unable to breathe as his mind struggled to make sense of what he had read. A cold sweat broke out on his brow. Kidnapped. Someone had kidnapped Kate. Heart in his throat, Henry read the note again. So it had come to this. This was how they would stop him in the end, by using his concern for Kate. He should have left her in Venice.

Henry ran his hand over his face. Until now he had not realized how strong his feelings were toward Kate. He had ignored what was happening between the two of them, shrugging off his feelings as a fun flirtation to pass the time. Reading the note again, Henry knew better. Henry knew he loved Kate and Kate alone. The Princess had asked him if he could imagine life without Kate. Henry realized that he could. Life without Kate would be a long progression of cold, dark, lonely days.  It would not be a life, only an empty shell.  His heart froze at the bleak emptiness he contemplated.  Kate, he must find Kate.  His own life depended on it.

Henry read the note again.  It said that they had her.  They.  Who were they?  Who had sent the note?  He remembered his joking response to Kate's earlier question; kingdoms, republics, powers, individuals.  Had that only been five days ago?  Henry realized he really didn't know the answer any better now than he had in London.

Henry's mind went back to the people on the train.  Who among them had the ability to take the life of another person?  He considered the thinly disguised hints he had received from the Princess and from the De la Roches.  Since they had been unsuccessful at getting him and Kate off the train, was either of them responsible for Kate's disappearance?  The kidnappers were in Belgrade somewhere, if Henry could find them, he could find his Kate.

His Kate.  That is how he had come to think of her.  Imagining a day without her and her crazy hats in it made his heart clench.  The events of the past few days were like a fast-moving stream, dragging him along, bashing him against hidden rocks.  He needed things to slow down.  He needed more insight into the problem.  Henry felt like an impostor, a fool, in a world full of real spies and agents.  Who was he to think he could save the world?  He was on his own, no one to help him.  How he longed for one vital piece of information: who.

Out of the corner of his eye, Henry caught a glimpse of Monsieur De la Roche walking swiftly toward the rear entrance of the hotel.  How odd, thought Henry, the man had specifically said that he and his wife were going to their rooms for the night.  Now it was closer to morning than night.  Hesitating only briefly, Henry set out in pursuit.

As he trailed behind the Frenchman through the deserted streets of Belgrade, Henry reviewed recent events in his mind.  From his interrogation at the embassy, he knew that the assassin had probably left Paris on Sunday like he had, possibly on the same train. The Orient Express Arlberg had left the day before. The Orient Express through Vienna left the day after. From a timing point of view, the Simplon Orient Express made more sense. By taking the Simplon Orient Express at the same time he and Kate did, the assassin would be sure to arrive the day before the French Foreign Minister, Louis Barthou, giving him time to prepare. Henry knew from his briefing with the embassy representative that Barthou and other key representatives had taken the Orient Express through Vienna. That particular train would be so heavily guarded that an assassin would not have wanted to risk taking it. If all this were true, then it was highly probable that one of the people Henry and Kate met was the assassin. De la Roche, with his questionable sources of money and shrouded past, certainly was a candidate.

Henry felt that he might make better headway by approaching the problem from a different direction, starting with the timing of the assassination. Assuming the assassin was here already, all Henry had to do was figure out when and where the attack would take place. Piece of cake thought Henry. His superiors had only said that it would occur sometime during Barthou's visit to Belgrade. The visit began with welcome speeches in the plaza across from the train station. Following the speeches, in honor of the visiting diplomats, a parade through the city would take place at nine o'clock. King Alexander, together with the visiting dignitaries would ride through the streets in open cars. Suddenly, a few of the puzzle pieces finally clicked into place.

The welcoming ceremony or the parade! That's it! Either event would provide excellent cover for an assassination attempt. The assassin could easily blend in with the crowd. As big as the attendance was projected to be, it would be incredibly easy to disappear. However, that same crowd would make it difficult to attain just the right vantage point for a killing shot or to plant a bomb. If Henry's hypothesis was true and the assassin planned to attack during the opening ceremony or the parade, then there were really just two questions. Where would the attempt be made? And what weapon would the assassin use? Bomb? Gun?

The more Henry thought about the possibilities of a bomb, the more he was inclined to discard it as an appropriate method of killing the King. Bombs were cumbersome to carry and difficult to set in place. Often, explosives were more dangerous to the person setting it than to the intended victim. It took time to install a bomb, time in which the assassin could be spotted. On the other hand, there was also the difficulty of concealing it effectively from the guards who inspected any area before the King was allowed to enter. Bombs could do significant damage and they were effective for killing large groups of people randomly. In this case, however, only one man had been marked for death. An expert marksman with a pistol or rifle would be far more likely to hit its target. Henry turned his attention back to the parade route.

Henry's briefing had provided details the parade route and photographs of the areas. All of the buildings were going to be under heavy guard. He knew sharpshooters from the King's guards would be placed on all roof tops to protect the diplomats. This left the assassin with shooting two options: somewhere on the sidewalk along the route or in the square at the welcoming ceremony. As Henry considered the photos of the square, he couldn't see any place where a shooter could get a clear shot. The King and diplomats would be on an elevated platform, but seats arranged around the platform and other obstructions prevented a clear line of sight from nearly every angle. Henry would need to arrive early and determine the best location for him to watch the people in the square in hopes of spotting his man.

Anyone familiar with the parade route would know that it would be very difficult to secure the safety of the participants for the entire route. Guards mounted on horseback would proceed and follow each car. Each car would also be flanked by horse guards. While their presence might discourage the crowds from surging onto the parade route, Henry did not think they would deter an expert marksman intent on his task. The convoy of vehicles would be progressing very slowly allowing ample time to take steady aim at the King.

Where would the most advantageous place be to set up for a shot? In his mind, Henry shuffled through the photos of the parade route again. One in particular caught his eye. All of a sudden, it came to him. The square in front of their hotel! The columns of the surrounding buildings would provide a measure of cover and a steadying force against the flow of the crowd. Their broad bases, often used as a seat to rest on could also serve as a stand to permit a person to see over the heads of the crowd. To see over the heads of the crowd and sight a well-aimed shot at the King, repeated Henry as the importance of this thought sunk in. That could definitely work in the assassin's favor. He would have to get to the square quickly following the speeches. Henry coldly considered the man he had been following for the last hour and a half. Where was the man's random path leading them?

# Chapter 52

## Kate

$\mathcal{D}$azed, Kate shook her head to clear it of the fog that wrapped itself around her brain. The dull ache that resulted told her she must have been drugged. She remembered reading somewhere that chloroform left an odd taste in a person's mouth. She could not understand what had happened. Groggily, she shifted her position. Kate thrashed violently when she realized she was bound at the wrists and ankles. A gag tied tightly over her mouth strangled the scream that rose within her. Where was she? How had she gotten there? Panic surged through Kate like an out-of-control train. Kate's eyes searched the inky blackness surrounding her. Nothing penetrated the complete darkness to tell her where she was or what time of day it was. Kate stared out at the impenetrable gloom as thoughts of the prisoner of Chateau *Chillon* haunted her. Please, she prayed, don't let this be an *oubliette*. Please don't let anyone forget her. Please let someone find her. Tears coursed down her cheeks. She closed her eyes tightly against the panic rising within her.

Kate had been such a fool. Despite being pursued around London and Paris, she had refused to acknowledge their tenuous situation. For two days, she had been happily cocooned on the train feeling safe against the problems of the outside world. Now Kate realized that they had never been out of danger, not even on the train. Danger stalked them. It always had. She hadn't wanted to believe Henry when he told her about the porter. Nor did she feel that the disappearing diplomatic pouch had anything to do with them. If she was honest with herself, Kate had to admit that until the Colonel, who resembled Henry from the back, had vanished, she believed that she and Henry would come out of this adventure just fine. Kate had even imagined telling her grandchildren about her little espionage adventure. Given that she had been kidnapped and no one knew where to find her, children and grandchildren were not in her future. She might not even have a future, Kate thought despairingly.

Just five days ago, in Piccadilly Circus, Kate had met a man in the grey suit and black Homburg who stood with his back to the viewer, his hands clasped behind his back, looking neither left nor right. Just five days ago. Kate could hardly believe the course of her life had altered so much in just five days. The fortune teller had been right in one respect, her life had changed. Once it had been orderly and calm, now it was chaos. Here in this darkened room, not a trace of her former life remained. What had she been thinking that afternoon as she made her way to Piccadilly Circus? Why hadn't she ignored her desire for adventure? The postcard, the red bus, and Henry, it was all their fault! Yes, Henry. It didn't matter that she loved him, he was the one who got her into this mess, he better just well get her out of it. Would Henry find her in time? Would he get her out of this mess? Kate's throat constricted in fear for her future. It could have been minutes, it could have been hours, but eventually she opened her eyes as her tears ran their course.

Struggling to check her wildly racing thoughts, Kate chided herself forcefully. Oh, for heaven's sake, she told herself, get a grip on yourself. Giving into fear only made matters worse. She could not afford to lose control. Kate knew that if she was going to get out of this mess she would have to save herself. She needed to stay calm otherwise she would be too pathetically frightened to do anything. She wiped her cheeks on her shoulders. Her eyes search the gloom again and she realized she could discern faint outlines of objects around her. Her spirits lifted when she recognized that the first rays of dawn had begun to illuminate the room. Eagerly Kate waited and watched the room slowly brighten. In the dim light permitted by the tightly drawn curtains, she could see that she was in a hotel room. Relief flooded through her. Surely someone would eventually check on the status of a hotel room. Sooner, rather than later,

Kate hoped. Rather than dwell on that thought, she chose to shift her attention to the key question. Who had left her here?

By the meager light from the window, Kate noticed a lumpy shape silhouetted against the wall. Her heart jumped into her throat when the lump moaned. There was someone huddled in this dark room with her. Friend or foe? There was no way she could possibly know. Why had she ever answered that advertisement and accepted a position with SIS? How many times had she asked herself that question in the past five days? As her mind raced through possible scenarios, Kate's heart pounded loudly in her ears.

Seconds ticked by as Kate held her breath but the bump in the corner didn't make any new sounds. When would the person regain consciousness? Kate considered pretending to be unconsciousness until she ascertained who it was. In the meantime, she moved her legs to ease a cramp. Her toe came in contact with a heavy object. Using her feet, she kicked the item closer to her bound hands. Feeling like a contortionist, she explored the object with her fingertips. Nearly 15 inches square, its surface was stiff and rough, like canvas. She could feel several leather straps securing a flap and a lock too. The diplomatic pouch! It had to be. That brought other possibilities to mind. If the diplomatic pouch rested at her feet then the lump in the corner could be Colonel Forsyth. Somehow they managed to conceal him somewhere on the train and transfer him to Belgrade. She wondered where they could have hidden him. Every square inch of the train had been searched thoroughly.

In the gloom, she continued her slow exploration of the wall behind her and the radiator she was tied to. The bindings on her wrists and ankles made movements difficult. Her investigation didn't reveal any way to free herself or any more information about where she was. Disappointed, Kate sank back down onto the floor. She let her thoughts drift over the strangers she had met on the train. Businessmen. Bankers. Diplomats. Travellers. Who among them would want to hurt her? Kate bit back the fear rising in her throat. If she could live with this terror, Kate knew she could face anything the future had to offer.

Nearing tears, she sought to stave them off by thinking of her life in London. She cursed ever having visited the fortune teller that precipitated the answering of the SIS advertisement. She was stuck in the dark somewhere in Belgrade all because she answered Henry's postcard. How exquisitely comforting it would be to be in Henry's arms right now. Henry, the older man who would change her future. Well, her future had certainly changed and it wasn't proving to be for the better. What a joke. He was only two years older than she was. She distinctly remembered the fortune teller describing an older man. Her mind went in circles. An older man. The postcard. An older man. If Henry didn't qualify as the older man, then who in her recent acquaintances did? It nagged at her, a vague memory that wouldn't surface. She wished she had told Henry about the tarot cards and the older man who would change her future. She had hesitated because she was afraid Henry might laugh. He probably would have, just like he laughed at her clever hats. But if Henry knew about the prediction for an older man, he might have been able to figure out who the man was. And if Henry knew who the man was, he might be able to find her. These thoughts were getting her nowhere. The fortune teller's prediction probably did not even have a place in this nightmare. The woman doubtlessly just made it all up. Kate knew her panicked mind was grasping at straws.

Kate looked up to see a face peering at her out of the darkness. Instinctively, she recoiled, cold fear coursing through her. The gag caused her scream to come out as a squeak. The face in the corner began to speak.

"Good heavens! They have you too?"

Kate breathed a sigh of relief when she recognized the Colonel's petulant voice.

"By thunders, what is going on here? Harassing English citizens on holiday! What is the world coming to? You can't imagine my consternation! Can't say exactly as how I got here myself. I remember staying up late in the night on the train. On my way back to my compartment, I took a minute to look out a window. Must have been at the end of the corridor. Could smell the coal burned to heat the water for the sinks. The last thing I remember was hearing a quiet shuffling noise behind me. Thought it was the night porter. Woke up all trussed up like a Christmas goose. Couple of unsavory types in the room with me. Roughed me up a bit, they did. Going on about spies, secret documents, assassinations! What a bunch of nonsense! Wouldn't believe me when I told them I had nothing to do with any nefarious schemes! Just hit me again. Don't know exactly when I passed out. Not very strong of me, I must admit. Don't know who they were, couldn't place the accent. Reminds me of dicey times during the Great War," babbled the Colonel.

Unlike Kate, the Colonel had not been gagged. How odd, thought Kate. Wouldn't kidnappers have gagged them both? Kate, with her mouth covered, was powerless to stop him as he droned on. Even in a time of crisis, the man wouldn't shut up, thought Kate a bit uncharitably. You'd think he would at least call for help.

"Shouldn't shout for help. Could bring the wrong team. Morning comes, someone will check on this room," said the Colonel as if reading her mind.

She chose to ignore him and asked herself again, what would the heroine in one of her mystery novels do at a time like this? The obvious answer, escape. But how? She wanted one of those convenient solutions that mystery writers dreamed up just in time to save the heroine. Courage. *Coraggio*, that was what she needed now.

Kate knew her connection to Henry had placed her in this situation, but what about the Colonel? What had he done to get kidnapped? Had he simply been in the wrong place at the wrong time? Was it because he wore a dressing gown like Henry's? Kate's mind whirled around and around. Kate regarded the Colonel. Despite the low light level, she noticed that, not for the first time, the Colonel's eyes were hidden by the reflection of his lenses. How very fortunate and surprising for him that he still had his glasses on after all that had happened to him. Yet, somewhere in the back of her mind, things did not make sense.

# Chapter 53

## Henry

*I*n the pre-dawn darkness of Wednesday morning, Henry continued to follow the Frenchman through the streets of Belgrade. Henry had worked out that they were now going in the direction of the train station. Was Monsieur De la Roche the assassin? Where would he choose to set up for a shot at the king? Unexpectedly Monsieur De la Roche stopped abruptly and crouched down as if to tie his shoe. To avoid being seen, Henry retreated to safety in a deep doorway. From there, Henry watched the man as he knelt half-hidden by the corner of a building. Henry surveyed the layout of the buildings around him. If he moved fast enough, by moving off to his right, he could skirt down an alley and come up behind Monsieur De la Roche. Henry could taste revenge for Kate's kidnapping. Swiftly Henry approached the Frenchman from behind and punched him hard in the kidneys. As the man fell to the ground, Henry grabbed his arm and twisted it behind him.

"Where is Kate? Tell me now or I will break your arm," Henry raged.

"*Henri*, I am on your side," gasped the Frenchman through gritted teeth.

"Don't lie to me! Where is Kate?" Henry said, tightening his hold on the man's arm.

"I don't know," Monsieur De la Roche answered again, clenching his teeth against the pain in his arm and shoulder.

"What are you doing here?" demanded Henry in a strained voice.

"Just as you are here to protect the King, I am here to protect Barthou."

"No more lies! Tell me what you are doing here!"

"My government sent me to protect the French Foreign Minister Barthou," said Monsieur De la Roche.

"I said no more lies!" said Henry angrily.

"Your contact from the French embassy is called Balzac. Your code name is Westminster. Am I right?" grunted Monsieur De la Roche.

Henry hesitated a minute.

"Our recognition phrase is 'champagne is made with three grapes.' During out dinner, you used it yourself in the form of a question. Since you and Kate answered together, I assumed you were working together."

This information caught Henry by surprise. He had, quite mistakenly, during their conversation about champagne, used the code words. Henry remembered now that Monsieur De la Roche had responded correctly with "yes, and one of them is chardonnay." But it had been Kate who supplied the final phrase "the others are pinot noir and pinot meunier." She had done so quite unwittingly, Henry had never told her the code phrases. Given the setting and the involvement of all three of them, Henry hadn't even realized the entire code had been given and received. Henry slackened his grip perceptively, but wanted more proof.

"Who is Rabalais?" Henry asked.

"My wife," chuckled the Frenchman.

"Your wife?" Henry asked incredulously, releasing his grip. His anger toward the Frenchman dissipated despite his suspicions about the man's activities.

"What is the fun of life without risks?" responded Monsieur De la Roche philosophically rubbing his arm. "I give you my word of honor as a gentleman that I am on your side."

This old-fashioned comment, harkening to a time when honor had been enough, had the effect of balm on Henry's strained nerves. He helped Monsieur De la Roche to his feet.

"Our countries have been fighting with or at least aggravating each other for the past one thousand years," said Monsieur De la Roche smiling. "Perhaps, just for today, we can cease hostilities and work together."

"Kate is missing."

"So you told us last night. Yet you have chosen to follow me?" The Frenchman made the sentence into a question.

"I saw you sneaking out of the hotel the back way."

"Before our little meeting here, I have been following one of the porters from the train for the past two hours."

"We were told that none of the train staff left the train in Belgrade."

"Yes, I know. That is why I chose to follow him when I saw him out the window of our hotel room. The man must have traveled on to the next stop and taken a return train."

"There is something else you should know. A note I received points to the assassin as the culprit in Kate's disappearance. We've got to stop him before he hurts Kate or kills the King. Have you any idea who we are seeking?" Henry asked, thankful to have help.

"No, my superiors have not been able to tell me. I spent yesterday at my embassy trying to figure out who we might be after. There seems to be some confusion over whether the actual target is King Alexander or Louis Barthou. Some people think both may be targets, two assassins," said Monsieur De la Roche. The Frenchman thought for a moment. "It might be best if we split up to cover the welcome reception. I have a suspicion that the attempt or attempts will take place this morning, either at the reception or during the parade."

"Yes, probably," Henry answered. "Tell me, have you considered the parade route? Kate found a map of Belgrade in di Cosimo's book. The Count left it at our table accidentally. I am not sure if it means anything. The route marked in pencil on the map is similar but not exactly the same as the parade route."

"What do you think?"

"The parade route is almost impossible to guard. Of all the potential locations for an assassin, the columns in the square in front of our hotel make a nearly perfect place for a gunman to wait."

"You don't think he would try from a window in a building along the parade route?" queried the Frenchman.

"I wondered about that, but the buildings will have guards on top and at all entrances. If someone did shoot from a window, the shooter would have little chance for escape, providing he wanted to escape. There is the problem too of the distance of the shot. The streets along the parade route are broad. In the square, a single gunman can get much closer to his target. The surging crowds provide cover both before and after the shooting," said Henry thoughtfully.

"Let us hope we have thought this through, my friend. We have been given a very difficult task to do. Come, it is nearly time for the speeches to begin," said Monsieur De la Roche. "Let us see if we can find the porter again."

They made their way to the plaza, checking positions and sightlines along the way. Dawn had begun to lighten the sky by the time they reached the plaza. There they separated, agreeing to meet near the side entrance to the train station. Within minutes of their arrival, the square began to fill up with workmen and people seeking to claim their viewing spot. Neither man saw anything suspicious in the crowds gathered to welcome the diplomats. Nor did they locate the porter Monsieur De la Roche had been trailing. The welcoming speeches were well underway when they met back where they had started from.  Linking up, they both shrugged.  The presentations ended and the diplomats moved toward the waiting automobiles.  Henry began to speak when the Frenchman swiftly pulled Henry out of sight behind an advertising sign.

"What's the matter?  Who did you see?" asked Henry.

"The porter from the train, the one with the sallow face.  Let's follow him and see what his plans are," said Monsieur De la Roche.

Henry and Monsieur De la Roche tracked the man to the square in front of their hotel.  Along their route, the man exhibited very suspicious behavior.  However, thought Henry ruefully, so had Monsieur De la Roche.  For all Henry knew, the man was another red herring leading them away from the real assassin—leading them away from the men who had Kate.  Anguished, Henry wouldn't let himself think about Kate right now.  He pinned his hopes of finding her on the man who skulked along in front of them.  Every time the man turned to look around, Henry and Monsieur De la Roche had to shrink into the cover of building doorways.

# Chapter 54

## Kate

$\mathcal{K}$ate refused to give up. Grief at the thought of losing Henry spurred her into action. She discovered that by rubbing her face against the edge of the radiator, she could manage to pull down the gag. With a great surge of relief at being released from its suffocating bond, she gulped air before concentrating on her other restraints. Kate used her finger tips to explore the cord that bound her hands. The way it bit into her wrists gave her the impression it wasn't a very thick rope. She moved her fingers around until she could feel the end of the rope. No, not very thick at all. If she could only find something sharp to rub the rope against. Kate moved her fingers around the knots on her wrists but there wasn't enough play on the cord to let her reach them effectively. She had read lots of mysteries. In a situation like this, the heroine always came up with an ingenious solution. Although, thinking about it, it always seemed a bit fishy to her how the answer just presented itself in the nick of time. Kate could use a bit of that nick of time stuff right now. She needed a plan. She needed to take action. She jumped when the Colonel spoke.

"What are you trying to do, my dear?" he barked.

"Shhh! Do you want them to hear us? Why, what a silly question to ask! I am trying to get out of these ropes," she whispered. "How else will we manage to escape?" Kate thought she saw a shadow pass over his face, but she continued. "What about you, can you free yourself?"

"Oh, I'm dizzy," said the Colonel, swaying slightly.

Funny, thought Kate, he seemed fine just a moment ago when he was regaling her with his adventure. Right now, he should be cooperating with her.  She studied Colonel Forsyth closely.  Once again, she couldn't see his eyes hidden behind the reflective glare of his lenses.  Her heart gave a leap of hope in her chest when she noticed them.  Glittering in his glasses, could be the answer to her dilemma, her costume jewelry.  Kate had discovered that one of the clips had a very sharp edge when she had dressed earlier.  She carefully bent her head and plucked at the clip over her right breast with her lips.

"What are you doing?" the Colonel asked in an aggrieved tone.

"What do you think I am doing?  I am trying to get this clip off.  The back edge of it might be sharp enough to cut through the rope on my wrist," Kate explained her plan to the Colonel.

"Are you sure you should escape, my dear?" the Colonel inquired.  "We don't want to upset anyone.  These are not very nice people.  What can a slip of a girl like you do against them anyway?"

"All the more reason for us to escape as quickly as possible."

Colonel Forsyth's comment made Kate angry.  Where was the Colonel's bravado now?  The man had positively disintegrated.  She certainly was not going to surrender, not without trying to escape.

"Us?" the Colonel's voice faltered.

At his tepid response to her escape plan, Kate lifted her head quickly and stared at the Colonel.  Again the thought came to her.  How was it that the Colonel still had his glasses on even though, by his own admission, he had been treated roughly?  She wondered why he had never explained where they had hidden him on the train.  Pushing the thoughts aside, Kate continued to struggle to free the clip.  Yes, it was sharp.  She nearly cut her lip on the edge.  Maybe, just maybe, this would work.  Kate could free herself and join Henry.  Unexpectedly, the clip finally came loose.  She nearly let go of it but managed to hold on to it with her lips.  Now, Kate thought, where was the best place to drop it?  She couldn't move her hands very far from the radiator.  Dropping the clip within reach would be essential to her success. Kate moved her body slightly to the left, toward the Colonel. She looked up in time to see that he was staring at her, hard. Just for a moment, she thought she saw anger in his face, but when she blinked, his face was once again inscrutable. It might have been the play of the dim light from the curtained window.

Breathing deeply, Kate quieted her body and dropped the clip over her right shoulder. It made a perfect landing on her fingertips. She carefully explored its edges until she found the sharpest one. She began sawing on rope that held her prisoner. It was hard work. As her hands heated up with the movement, she could feel them sweat. The moisture caused the clip to slip. Several times Kate worried that she would drop it before she was able to secure a firmer grip. The rope burned her wrists as her sawing became more frantic. She noticed that the Colonel was positively squirming next to her. She wondered if he was making any progress on his own bonds. After what seemed like hours of effort, the rope gave way. Kate rubbed her hands to help the circulation before she could find the coordination to untie the ropes on her ankles. Joy spread through her body as they finally slipped off.

"Don't leave," Colonel Forsyth said with rather more force than necessary. Once again, the sound of the Colonel's voice surprised her. In her effort to concentrate on winning her freedom, Kate had not paid any attention to him.

"Don't leave? Why ever not? We've got to get out of here before they come back," Kate exclaimed.

"Don't play games with me, stay right where you are," growled the Colonel.

At his unexpected command, Kate looked up from untying her feet and saw the pistol in his hand. For a moment, nothing made sense in her mind. The Colonel was aiming a gun. At her. Aghast, Kate came to the realization that Colonel Forsyth wasn't playing for her team. Kate's mouth went dry as the Colonel took a step toward her. Suddenly, a loud noise penetrated the room from the street below. The sound momentarily distracted the Colonel. Acting instinctively, Kate picked up the diplomatic pouch by the handle and swung it full force at the man. The heavy bag connected with an audible thump against Colonel Forsyth's head causing him to drop his gun. Kate scooped up the pistol and bolted for the door.

# Chapter 55

## Henry

*H*enry could not believe the crowd in the square in front of the hotel waiting for the parade. Despite the presence of police on horseback, the mob pushed its way off the sidewalks and into the street. Only a narrow corridor remained in the center of the street. People were everywhere, leaning out the windows, standing on cars, lining the sides of the street. Henry estimated that people stood fifteen deep each side of the square. In the throng, they lost sight of the porter. Henry struggled through the mass of humanity searching for the porter or for any familiar face from the train.

"You take the north side of the square and I'll take the south," he said to Monsieur De la Roche.

Based on what Henry knew about the design of the square, he thought that the best position for an assassin would be atop one of the column bases of the buildings lining the square. Henry bemoaned his inexperience. By this time, he was supposed to have isolated the threat. Amid the swarming crowd, he questioned his ability to take any action at all.

Henry reached the north side of the plaza just as King Alexander's honor guard rode in, their sabers flashing in the sun. Henry climbed the base of one of the columns in order to see over the heads of the crowd. He surveyed the scene in front of him. Henry knew the arrangement of the parade from his briefing at the embassy. Twelve men would ride three abreast in four rows. Behind them would follow three open touring cars carrying the visiting dignitaries. Two armed horsemen would flank each side of each car. Between vehicles, another group of twelve men would ride in formation. King Alexander's car would be the fourth and last car in the parade. The French dignitary, Barthou, would ride next to the King in the backseat of the open car.

Now that Henry had an idea of where and when the assassination attempt may take place, he needed to figure out who would try to do it. It stood to reason that most of the people on the train were innocent. He had to figure out which of them were red herrings that merely threw him off track. The one remaining would be the true assassin. The jumble of ideas and impressions in his head needed to arrange themselves, making order out of chaos by sorting out the clues. He began by listing those he could eliminate.

Henry hadn't seen the Princess when they left the train. He wondered if she had disembarked or gone on to Istanbul. He knew she was involved somehow but he could not picture her firing a gun. Count di Cosimo had not left the train as expected. Henry had seen his face in one of the windows as the train departed. Obviously the De la Roches were in the clear.

On the list of potential assassins, the sallow-faced porter came first. Henry looked around trying to find the man in the crowd without any luck. Henry spent a few moments considering the diplomats on the train. Though he suspected a leak somewhere in the SIS, he did not think any of the men on the train were assassins. More likely the leak was someone back in the home office. Henry wondered who. In his opinion, the Swiss bankers and businessmen appeared too fastidious to be dealing in murder. Their method of persuasion would focus on financial gains. Colonel Forsyth was just a blustering old fool. That left Monsieur DuBois and his elegant wife. They certainly seemed to be able to play it cool, though Henry couldn't picture them dirtying their clothes. Henry paused a moment, he was beginning to think like Kate. The American couple, the Johnsons were also in the running. Wait a minute, there was someone else; the older gentleman who sat by himself at breakfast the morning before. He and Kate had not been able to learn anything about him. Henry had noticed Kate watching the man with interest.

Henry followed this thread of thought further. He remembered his fleeting glimpse of the older man, Herr Altmann speaking with the Princess. Their body language suggested that they were trying not to be seen or overheard by anyone. The older man had spoken with her at length. Interestingly enough, the porter was the same man Henry had seen the Colonel speaking with. Henry remembered hearing a shoe squeak when they separated. A man with a squeaking shoe had stopped in front of his compartment door the night the diplomatic pouch was stolen. It could be that the pouch contained information related to the assassination attempt. That would explain why it was stolen. He could think of no reason for the Colonel's disappearance. Henry put his money on the sallow-faced porter, the one he and Monsieur De la Roche had been following.

# Chapter 56

## Kate

$\mathcal{F}$leeing from the room, Kate fairly flew down the corridor. She recognized the corridors of her own hotel. The woodwork, lighting fixtures, and paint color were the same. She even recognized the artwork! Kate could not believe she was on the same floor. Henry once said that hiding in plain sight was to hide where no one would suspect. It seemed so long ago that they hid in the shed together.

Nearing the stairs, Kate slowed and began to creep down the hallway, expecting to be intercepted at any moment. Hopefully, the Colonel was unconscious and unable to summon help right away. Since returning to her room wasn't an option, Kate decided to leave the hotel and find her way to the embassy. That actually presented a problem. She could not remember the route they had taken the day before. She would have to find someone to help her. In her mind, as she tiptoed down the hallway, she reviewed the phrases she knew for asking the location of the embassy. *Ou est l'embassade de Grande Bretagne? Je cherche l'embassade de Grande Bretagne. Comment faire pour aller a l'ambassade de Grande Bretagne? Wo ist die Konsulat? Wie komme ich nach die Konsulat? Dov'e l'ambasciata? Sto cercando l'ambasciata?* If she couldn't find anyone to tell her where the embassy was, she would go to the police station. She tried to stay calm by reviewing those phrases in her mind. *Ou est le commissariat de police? Ich suche die Polizei. Dov'e la Polizia?* Oh, what was she thinking? They probably would not even understand her French, German, or Italian. She didn't have a map of Belgrade, let alone her papers identifying her as a citizen of Great Britain. Where was Henry when she needed him? Kate longed to see his face.

She wouldn't mind it at all if he appeared, his usual insouciant self, his eyes crinkling at the corners as he mocked her fears.

As French, German, and Italian words streamed through her subconscious, it came to her. Old man, *vielle homme, alt mann*. Herr Altmann, old man. Instinctively, she knew who the assassin was. She just knew. Her intuition took a giant leap of faith and connected the prediction of the tarot card reader with the man who spent most of the time on the train hiding his face. Herr Altmann and Colonel Forsyth. They must be working together. Two assassins!

Kate gripped both the pistol and the diplomatic pouch so hard her hands hurt. Just as she neared the end of the hallway, she saw shadows on the walls of the open stairway leading to the main floor. Two men and they were hurrying. The Colonel must have phoned to his accomplices elsewhere in the hotel. Kate wished she had hit him harder. She hesitated, listening to their voices before she turned to sprint in the opposite direction. Panic seized her when a hand clamped tightly over her mouth. Frightened, she struggled against being dragged into a room. In a heart-beat, she was inside. Only the tiny snick of the door latch revealed that Kate had ever been in the hallway at all. Her capture gripped her so tightly that Kate couldn't even bite the hand that held her or deliver a well-placed kick. She tried to squirm. The only sound she could make was a tiny squeak. Out of the firing pan and into the fire for her, Kate thought.

"Silence. Do not let them hear us," a familiar French-accented voice whispered in her ear.

Madame De la Roche! What was she doing here, holding her so tight?

"Will you be quiet if I let you go?" Madame De la Roche asked very quietly.

Silently, Kate shook her head yes. As the woman released her, Kate turned to look at her. Kate searched her face until the voices in the hall took her attention away. One look told her that her only real enemies were in the hallway. The voices receded down the hall. She heard the sound of a door opening, followed by muffled shouts of alarm. So, it was them. Now they knew she was gone. A few seconds later, she heard the sound of men running by the hotel room door. That was interesting. She had only seen three shadows on the wall. So, she had been right, the Colonel was one of them. As they passed the door, they were speaking in a language she didn't understand, but it sounded as if they were giving each other directions. She turned again to Madame De la Roche.

"The Colonel aimed a gun at me! He must be working with the men who kidnapped me," Kate whispered. "I think Herr Altmann and Colonel Forsyth are assassins sent to kill King Alexander. We've got to stop them!"

Eyes wide with surprise, Madame De la Roche placed a finger to her lips and put her ear to the door. As the voices receded, she spoke.

"How do you know this? It makes sense and explains so much," Madame De la Roche said as she cautiously placed her hand on the door knob.

"I'll explain later. You have some questions to answer too, beginning with, how did you know where to find me?" Kate asked.

As she waited for her to speak, Kate noted that Madame De la Roche carefully examined Kate from head to toe before answering. She noted the bruises and cuts on Kate's wrists and ankles.

"Have they hurt you?" the Frenchwoman asked gently.

"No, I'm a bit roughed up, that's all," Kate managed to say as tears threatened to fall. It was all so trying. Kate had not expected this sort of adventure when she joined SIS. Now that she was away from the Colonel and her captors, fatigue came crushing down on her. She wished with all her might that Henry would appear and take her into his arms. Right now, Kate didn't feel like one of those people the Princess admired, the ones who managed to land on their feet like cats and maintain a tranquil spirit.

A single tear escaped her eye and coursed down her cheek. Madame De la Roche handed her a clean handkerchief and smiled sympathetically.

"They seem to be gone for the time being. Why don't you take a moment to freshen up after your ordeal? See if you can find something to bind your wrists in the bathroom. Hurry, we will leave here soon," urged Madame De la Roche.

Kate did as she suggested. When she returned, Kate cast a questioning glance at Madame De la Roche.

"Henry told us last night that you were missing. We have been very concerned about you. I have been searching for you ever since. I reasoned that, even at night, it would be difficult to move someone in a busy hotel. I wondered if they would hide you near your own room. I was about to go and check around when you appeared," the Frenchwoman said. "Like magic!"

"What are you doing here? Who are you really?" Kate managed to say.

"No time to answer you right now. Come along now, we've got to help *Henri*."

"Help Henry! What's wrong?"

"Nothing is wrong *ma cherie*, at least not yet," Madame De la Roche said in a tight voice. "For heaven's sake, do not panic now. *Henri* can take care of himself. He is a man of courage. We must let him know that you think that there are two assassins, Colonel Forsyth and Herr Altman. *Henri* doesn't know he'll need to watch his back. So we must do that for him." Madame De la Roche noticed the diplomatic pouch and gun still in Kate's hands.

"Ah *bon*, I see you have brought the important items," Madame De la Roche said as she took the pistol from Kate and placed it in her own pocket. "No sense alarming anyone, is there?"

Kate wasn't completely comfortable that Madame De la Roche took the gun away from her. As of yet, she hadn't given Kate any reason to doubt her, but she had been wrong about the Colonel. The Colonel and Herr Altmann. They could be working alone or together. Kate was not sure there was anyone from the train could she trust.

Madame De la Roche listened carefully at the door. Hearing nothing, she opened it slowly and peered out. She stepped into the hallway and beckoned for Kate to follow. They had nearly reached the opposite end of the hallway when they heard the distant sound of a man running up the stairs.

"They must be returning to see if you are still on this floor. *Vite! Vite!* Quickly, this way," Madame De la Roche said urgently.

At the end of the hall, Madame De la Roche pushed Kate through a thick curtain and out onto a balcony. Kate could see a narrow ledge that lead to a nearby fire escape. In their hurry, they had missed the fire escape door. It would have made matters so much easier, Kate thought. She knelt down to take off her high-heeled shoes. She quickly shoved them into the pockets of her jacket. On her next adventure, she would dress more sensibly. She didn't dare look down as she crawled after Madame De la Roche along the ledge. Kate clutched the diplomatic pouch in one hand and held onto the ledge in the other. Her heart in her throat, she gained the fire escape. Any more antics like this and she should try out for a circus high wire act. Kate reasoned it would be safer. The two women flew down the fire escape on feet that barely touched each stair. Fortunately, they made it to the street without being seen from above. For some reason, perhaps because they had not used the fire escape door, their pursuers had not stopped to check outside for them. When they reached the street, the crowd waiting to see King Alexander engulfed them.

# Chapter 57

## Henry

*K*ing Alexander's car rounded the corner and entered the square. From his position standing on the base of one of the columns, Henry could see photographers dashing out into the street. Some of the armed guards struggled to hold back the crowd, others pushed back the photographers. As Henry scanned the other side of the square, a movement to his left caught his eye. He turned to see the Colonel running toward him, two men in pursuit. The Colonel stared straight at him before turning away to look at King Alexander. Henry followed his gaze toward the King. As he shifted his field of vision, Henry saw him, the assassin, right where he thought he would be, standing on the base of a column. The man had his gun aimed at the King's car. In one swift decisive movement, Henry pulled out his pistol, took aim, and fired at Herr Altmann. At the same instant, he heard two simultaneous shouts.

"Littleton, look out."

"Billy!"

Henry turned just as a second shot rang out, then a third. Searing pain filled Henry's being. He gasped for breath. As he fell to the ground, Henry heard the Colonel's voice.

"Confounded woman!"

As if by magic, Kate appeared at his side. She wrapped her arms tightly around him.

"Henry! Henry!"

Henry noticed her tiny hat was askew. The effect was charming. Smiling up at her, he couldn't understand why he had ever found her hats anything but wonderful.

"Henry, please don't ever leave me. Please, please don't leave me alone," Kate whispered frantically in his ear.

"Somehow, this time, those words sound very different."

"Oh, Henry. How can you make jokes at a time like this?" she said, tears glistening in her eyes. "Please don't leave me alone, not now, not when I have found you at last."

"Don't leave you alone?" Henry asked weakly.

"Please don't!" Kate answered fervently.

"Marry me," he said. It was a statement, not a question.

"Yes, just don't ever leave me," she responded lovingly.

# Chapter 58

## Kate

"*J*ust lie still," she said in her most soothing voice. Kate hoped Henry hadn't noticed her voice shaking. She was so frightened. Henry's breath came in shallow, painful gasps. Henry's blood oozed from between Kate's fingers. She held him to her and pressed the wadded up scarf in her hand against the wound in his shoulder hoping to staunch the flow of blood. Henry simply couldn't die now, not now that she knew she loved him.

"Hurry," Kate pleaded to Madame De la Roche. "Get help."

Glancing frantically around to see who else she could enlist to help Henry, Kate could see Monsieur De la Roche busy pinning Colonel Forsyth to the ground. The crowd frantically flowed around her as it sought escape from the shooters. A second group of people stood near Herr Altmann across the street. She didn't know if he had died, but she noticed the people surrounding him were less agitated than those around the Colonel. Shrill blasts from police whistles pierced her ears. Would no one help her with Henry? He just could not bleed to death in her arms. He must live through this so she could hold him to his promise to marry her. Kate desperately wanted him to live, to marry her. Honeymoon on the Orient Express, indeed. Henry even kept his sense of humor while bleeding.

"Henry, stay with me darling. Please, please don't leave me alone. Don't leave me a widow, do you understand me? Don't leave me now that I have found you," Kate said, her voice filled with love, fear, and caring.

"Marry me and I'll never leave you alone," Henry said in a weak whisper.

Kate held the bloody scarf to his wound, pressing hard as she struggled not to cry. Though it seemed like hours, in a few minutes there were men from the nearby hospital lifting Henry into a car. They helped her in alongside. Once at the hospital, they whisked him away from her. As Kate stood there, not sure of what to do, paralyzed with fear for Henry, Madame De la Roche's gently touched her on her shoulder. Kate allowed herself to be taken to a quiet room. There she washed and changed into clean clothes Madame De la Roche had conjured up out of thin air. As she sipped the tea provided, she noted Madame De la Roche spoke to those around her as if she was accustomed to being in command.

"Ah, *bon,* you are coming back to us," said Madame De la Roche solicitously. "It surprises you that a pampered woman like myself knows something about first aid, doesn't it? During the Great War, I served as a field nurse."

Kate nodded. Yes, that would explain a lot.

"Henry will survive this experience easily. He is young and healthy. His wound is not as serious as some I have seen. He is supported by your love for him."

Those words brought Kate's head up.

"You knew I love Henry? I hardly knew it myself until I saw him lying there," she said.

"*Mais, bien sur, ma Cherie.* But of course, my dear. Your whole face tells the world you love him whenever you look at him. He loves you too. You have the glow of a woman who knows she is loved. Trust me on this, we French understand these things," laughed Madame De la Roche.

# Chapter 59

## Henry

"*I*t's good to see you are back among the living, *Henri*," said Monsieur De la Roche.

"Hello," croaked Henry. Though he didn't want to wake up, he turned his head slightly and opened his eyes. Lounging in the chair next to his bed sat Monsieur De la Roche.

"How about you letting me do all the talking? You have been through a lot," said Monsieur De la Roche as he handed Henry a glass of water.

Henry nodded slightly. Even that small movement seemed to take all his energy. Gratefully, he took a sip of the proffered drink.

"Where to begin? First let me congratulate you on your clear-headed tracking and neutralization of Herr Altmann. How did you know he was up to no good? Sometime when you are feeling better, you will need to tell me. Herr Altmann planned with his radical group to kill the French diplomat Barthou and as many of his entourage as possible. Barthou, as you know, is an outspoken critic of Hitler's regime. Your well-aimed shot across the square saved Barthou's life."

"Barthou?"

"Colonel Forsyth took aim at King Alexander after he shot at you."

"Two assassinations at the same time? Two assassins?" Henry said as he tried to struggle upright.

"Rest easy my friend *Henri*. Lay back, it's a long story," Monsieur De la Roche said as he eased Henry back onto his pillow. "Yes, we were actually following two assassins. Colonel Forsyth had been recruited to kill King Alexander. Herr Altmann's targeted Barthou. That is what made everything so confusing. Your Kate is quite a woman. She figured it out before we did. Kate told me about both Herr Altmann and Colonel Forsyth just before I spotted you standing on the base of the column above the crowd. You won't guess where I found our lovely wives. Scampering down the fire escape!"

Henry smiled weakly. Actually, he had no trouble picturing Kate in one of her hats doing just that.

"How did you find her?"

"If anyone can take credit for that it is my wife, Juliette. She reasoned that they had to be keeping Kate somewhere nearby. As she was leaving our room to search for her, Kate appeared in front of her like magic. Juliette heard running footsteps on the stairs and quickly pulled Kate into our room without waiting to find out who they were." Monsieur De la Roche noted the perplexed expression on Henry's face. "What, you don't believe me? Can't our wives be espionage agents too?"

"Her hats would give her away," countered Henry.

"Ah, yes, her charming hats. All the same, Kate identified the two assassins and saved the diplomatic pouch, all while keeping her hat on. Just wait until she tells you about crawling on ledges and sliding down fire escapes. Kate found the diplomatic bag and had the good sense not to drop it while they made their escape. My government is very grateful for her assistance. They will welcome both of you back to Paris for a visit. Although, between you and me," he said conspiratorially, "we will have to keep our wives distracted and away from the Avenue de Montaigne."

Henry smiled at the thought of exerting control over the two women shopping together in Paris.

"So let us return to the Colonel. It seems we all underestimated him, including his own government. He really put one over on us. A very ambitious man, the Colonel is. He's the one who shot you. I apologize for not getting to you a bit faster. I spotted the Colonel just seconds after he shot you. I prevented him from firing again by shooting him myself. Amazing the chaos those shots created in the crowd. Fortunately, the King's guards were able to take everyone in the parade quickly to safety." Monsieur De la Roche said. "By the time I reached Colonel Forsyth, his wife was at his side. She is really the one who saved your life. When she saw her husband in the crowd, she shouted his name. That woman's voice can certainly carry a long distance, even in a mob."

Henry nodded. He remembered hearing her call out "Billy."

"Her shout distracted him, spoiling his aim. Fortunately for you, his bullet struck you in your shoulder and not your heart. My shot stopped the Colonel before he could do the King any harm. By then, the place was a madhouse anyway, following Forsyth's shot and yours. Nothing like three shots close together to panic a crowd. Lucky for us, we were each protected by nearby columns. From what I understand, Altmann's body had been trampled by the crowd before officials got to it." Monsieur De la Roche frowned, remembering.

"Kate ran on to take care of you. Knowing you were in good hands, I stayed with Colonel and Mrs. Forsyth. Mrs. Forsyth didn't really seem to understand what her Billy had been up to. Perhaps for her sake, or maybe just to have the last word, before he died, the Colonel explained his role in this drama."

"It seems that he has been disgruntled with his government for quite a long time. Colonel Forsyth never thought his full talents had been put to use following the Great War. Put out to pasture was how he stated it. After years of disappointment, it wasn't difficult for the King's enemies to recruit Forsyth for this particular task. Right to the end, the Colonel proudly talked about how the Yugoslavians needed a man with his skills. His disappearance on the train served to throw suspicion off of him. Colonel Forsyth hadn't even told his wife. He basically planned a new life in his adopted country without her. As a reward, they had promised him a position high up in the new government that would be formed following the King's death. More than likely, they would have disposed of him, leaving his body to be discovered along the route of the Orient Express. It wouldn't be too hard to believe that he had been tossed from the train the night he vanished and not found until later."

"The Colonel and the porter stole the diplomatic pouch to create confusion and excitement on the train. That way he hoped to draw attention away from himself. The porter also hid the Colonel following his disappearance. Members of the police are now holding the porter we chased through Belgrade. Based on his behavior on the train, we should have been suspicious of him. He broke down under questioning, but it was too late, the shooting had already happened. According to him, it was the Colonel who tried to kill you on the train. The porter's job had been to turn off the lights. A short while later, he would conveniently discover your body. You can imagine his shock to see it was his colleague that the Colonel injured instead of you. The man was afraid you would suspect him of something."

Henry remembered the Colonel saying he had met someone he knew from the war on the train. Henry had incorrectly assumed it was a fellow passenger, not an employee. So it must have been the porter's shoes that squeaked, not Altmann's, thought Henry.

"The Colonel pretended to be tied up with Kate so that he could keep an eye on her. She would also provide him with an alibi. He intended to free himself just in time to shoot the King. He planned to tell Kate that he was going to get help. Where better to find help from one of us than on the square?"

Henry nodded his understanding.

"So that is the story. Two assassins, two planned assassinations. Fortunately for our governments, only the assassins died. By the way, late today, when word became known about the failed attempt on the King's life, the mole in your organization panicked. Given how things turned out in Belgrade, he was worried that someone might talk. Either way, authorities apprehended him trying to leave Britain."

That explained how the three men had tracked them from Piccadilly Circus to Paris. Henry had suspected that there was someone within the organization tipping off their pursuers.

"The mole confessed that he specifically picked you and Kate for this mission. He planned for you and Kate, due to your inexperience, to fail completely in your mission. You rather surprised him."

"The Princess sent a telegram expressing her regards and best wishes. She read about the incident in the papers while waiting in Istanbul for the boat to Cairo. The Johnsons have left Belgrade stating that there is too much excitement here for them."

"What about the DuBois?" Henry asked, seeking to tie up loose ends.

"They have decided to return to Vienna. It seems that riding on the Orient Express has done little to repair their marriage. As for the others, they are going about their lives as if nothing has happened," Monsieur De la Roche finished. "When you are feeling better, King Alexander wants to thank you personally. You can use the opportunity to ask him to help you keep your promise to Kate. Who better than a king to help arrange for a wedding in Belgrade?"

"Will you be my best man?" Henry asked grinning.

"I thought you would never ask," said Monsieur De la Roche with an answering smile.

# 2004

# Chapter 60

## Kate

"*S*o you see, my dear," she said to her wide-eyed granddaughter. "That is how your grandfather and I met all those years ago in 1934. There he was, just like the man in the postcard. A man in the grey suit with the black Homburg standing with his back to the viewer, his hands clasped behind his back, looking neither left nor right."

Kate lovingly stroked the old postcard, the emerald ring on her left hand sparkling in the afternoon sun. Kate watched her granddaughter as she stared disbelievingly at the white haired elderly gentleman sitting across from her. Kate raised her eyes to his. After all these years, one look from him could still send feelings of warmth flooding through her. Her beloved Henry. He winked conspiratorially at her. She straightened her hat. Their matching smiles of understanding lit up the room.

## Epilogue

Though Kate and Henry's story is fiction, in real life, King Alexander and the French Foreign Minister Barthou met with a fateful end. During their joint visit to Marseille, King Alexander of Yugoslavia, along with French Foreign minister Louis Barthou, were assassinated on October 9, 1934, a Tuesday.

# *The Red Bus: A Postcard to an Assassin*

# *Book Club Questions*

1. If you were Kate, would you have answered the postcard?
2. Do you think Kate was a help or hindrance to Henry?  Why or why not?
3. What would you have done if you were being followed in Paris?
4. What do you think of the art of face reading?
5. Whose side is Princess Lazio on?  Why did you come to that conclusion?
6. Does Henry make a believable hero?
7. Does Kate make a believable heroine?
8. Were you able to understand why the characters reacted the way that they did to their predicaments?  Would you have done the same?
9. Would you like to meet any of the characters?  Which ones?
10. What do you know about the 1930s?
11. What do you know about the years leading up to World War II?
12. Did the narrative in the book bring up information about the past that was new to you?  What?

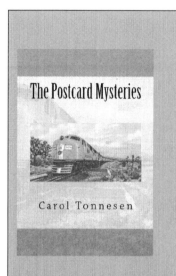

# The Postcard Mysteries

## By Carol Tonnesen

www.postcardmysteries.com

carol.tonnesen@postcardmysteries.com

**Hard Cover**

$9.99

**eBook**

$0.99-$4.99

Availability and Reviews

www.amazon.com

## Would you like to try new mystery series?

The Postcard Mysteries satisfy a reader's craving for mysteries that mix romance and mystery with places and history. Postcards serve as a catalyst that catapults ordinary people into unexpected adventures. Written to appeal to people who believe a person can change their life, these books feature men and women who throw caution to the wind in order to try something different, opening themselves up to mystery, adventure, and finally, love.

*Rumrunner's Reef: A Postcard to a Smuggler.* The sight of a nearly naked man emerging from the waters of Florida Bay provides an interesting start to Lizette's vacation. But, are the Florida Keys really different from Chicago?

*The Fishing Bridge: A Postcard to a Traitor.* British agent Charles Littleton longs to be a cowboy. Trudy is drawn into the dangerous world of secrets by a postcard. Meet Bandit, a talented Border collie with all the answers.

*The Highlands: A Postcard to Deception.* Set against a backdrop of Scotland's Sheep Dog Trials, veterinarian, Iain copes with deceptions and murder that threaten to destroy his veterinary practice. Can Aylee and her unexpected Border collie help him?

*The Zephyr: A Postcard to a Thief.* Follow rancher Charlie Lind on his train ride from Denver to San Francisco on the California Zephyr. Can he prevent the theft of thousands of dollars' worth of jewels?